THE LAW

Massimo Marino

COPYRIGHT 2014 MASSIMO MARINO

No part of this book may be reproduced in any form or by any electronic or mechanical means, including information storage and retrieval systems, without permission in writing from the author. The only exception is by a reviewer, who may quote short excerpts in a review.

Cover Design by Gwen Gades, UK
Edited by Sandra DaBolt-Nguyen

First Printing: September 2016

This is a work of fiction. The names and the characters are fictional. Any resemblance to living or dead individuals is purely coincidental.

ISBN-13 978-1537056081

From the Author of the the Daimones Trilogy.
Vol. 1, Daimones
Vol. 2, Once Humans
Vol. 3, The Rise of the Phoenix

In the name of Justice

About the Author

Massimo Marino has a scientific background. He spent years at CERN, in Switzerland, and at the Lawrence Berkeley Lab, in California, followed by lead positions with Apple, Inc., and the World Economic Forum.

Massimo currently lives in France and crosses the border with Switzerland multiple times daily.

The first volume of the trilogy, "Daimones", is the recipient of the 2012 PRG Award Reviewers' Choice in Science Fiction, and the Seal of Excellence in Quality Writing from the Awesome Indies (awesomeindies.net) and the indiePENdents.org association.

In September 2013 "Daimones" won the Hall of Fame - Best in Science Fiction Award, Quality Reads UK Book Club.

With the release of volume 2, "Once Humans", the books received the 2013 PRG Reviewer's Choice Award Best in Science Fiction Series, and was shortlisted as a Finalist in Science Fiction at the 2014 Readers' Favorite International Book Awards

The second volume, "Once Humans", starts seven years after the events narrated in "Daimones." The Communities led by the Selected are about to thrive and peace and security reigns on Eridu… not for long.

"The Rise of the Phoenix" narrates the events that resulted in the dystopian galactic society ruled by the new transgenic humans.

"The Law" events take place in the galaxy order that emerged from the "Daimones Trilogy."

Massimo also writes short chilling, twisted, horror stories, oftentimes while having breakfast.

If interested in more details about Massimo Marino, please see his full profile on LinkedIn:

http://ch.linkedin.com/in/massimomarino

CONNECT WITH MASSIMO MARINO

Twitter:

https://twitter.com/Massim0Marin0

Facebook:

http://www.facebook.com/massimo.marino.750546
http://www.facebook.com/MassimoMarinoAuthor

Author's website:

http://massimomarinoauthor.com

TABLE OF CONTENTS

Chapter 1 – The Shadows of the Tribunal	9
Chapter 2 – The Under Levels	20
Chapter 3 – Rejected	31
Chapter 4 – The Insurgence	43
Chapter 5 – Where Art Thou	51
Chapter 6 – But Mere Mortals	61
Chapter 7 – In Her Name	71
Chapter 8 – The Underworld	77
Chapter 9 – Revelations	85
Chapter 10 – Reversal	101
Chapter 11 – The Project	113
Chapter 12 – The Law	123
Chapter 13 – Through Closed Eyes	136
Chapter 14 – Hostages	145
Chapter 15 – Pariah	156
Chapter 16 – Trapped	163
Chapter 17 – An Announced Death	169
Chapter 18 – The Fifth Circle	173
Chapter 19 – Damnation or Salvation	183
Chapter 20 – Rebels	191
Chapter 21 – Winds of War	196
Chapter 22 – Reasons of the Heart	202
Chapter 23 – Diktats of the Brain	209
Chapter 24 – Quantum of Hope	222
Appendix – The Pax Humana	230

Chapter 1 – The Shadows of the Tribunal

Law and Order

THAT MORNING, Tancredi donned his tunic and the necklace bearing the Scholars' Insignia: a double helix, twined in a perpetual embrace, opening up at the top to signify endless opportunities. His quarters did not differ from other rooms in the scholars' building: spartan, essential, and devoid of any mundane amenities.

He looked at himself in the mirror. A young man with the first hint of a timid goatee stared back at him. His black eyes burned from an inner flame and reflected the depth of his credo and faith.

Tancredi raised the hood over his head and smiled. The words of his mentor at the Law School still lingered in his mind: "*The Law is exception-less, a necessary regularity among the occurring and observable properties in all planets. The galaxy is mostly a messy place where many forces are simultaneously at play and unobservable entities and processes govern much, if not all, of what happens. Exception-less regularities—as the Law is—are the exception, not the rule. Our duty is to make the exception-less the only meaningful rule.*"

The daily bulletin floated over the dashboard of his desk. Tancredi glanced at it for a long moment, nodded, then ordered the room to reabsorb the sparse furniture, and left.

The scholars' building rose within the green zone guarded by space marines in riot gear. In truth, the Kritas on Ahthaza, their home planet, had a tendency toward rebellion that never abated. The scholars sensed that and reported on every occasion where they perceived possible dangers and threats, and it was more than enough for the Authority and the Governor to justify a military presence in the space sector—and in some of the planets constituting the old Kritas Alliance—as well as an occupation and freedom restrictions in Ahthaza. The military effectively kept the local population in a subjugated condition under strict rules.

The Authority had preserved the broken remnants of the symbols of past power and glory, as a memento to their present vacuity and demise. Around the planet, other signs of power and might dwarfed the old emblems: the always visible human cruisers and battleships hovering above the cities, patrolling the skies, and the constant presence of the space marines, always menacing.

Unguarded old Kritas shipyards constituted the final resting place of spaceship wrecks, the ones that had escaped annihilation in space. Now, only scavengers and looters frequented those cemeteries. The wrecks stood as forlorn monuments to an agonizing past, and as a lure for nostalgists of lost pride. The space marines arrested whomever they found there during their raids and kept the areas under discreet but constant surveillance.

The space sectors once controlled by the Alliance were still under scrutiny, as those who lived within their borders hadn't yet been considered an integral part of the Union. The human leadership hadn't lessened its tight grip over the last few decades after the end of the war. For these reasons, the role of the Tribunals—and of the Scholars—constituted a crucial element in the integration of those planets, which had once been declared enemies.

Tancredi reached the ground level and stood for a moment at the entrance, absorbing the importance of that moment, his first early morning as a Scholar in Ahthaza.

Farther out, beyond the esplanade in front of the scholars' building, a crevice sliced into the earth—so deep that if one peered down, he could see the rocky, tortured walls disappearing into a thick, black emptiness. The military had christened it—unofficially—the *"Scholars' Fault,"* an innuendo blaming them for the ongoing social tensions in the planet.

Low clouds crowded the sky like a solid vault, and shadows had merged into a dull, grey penumbra. On the esplanade, a shuttle waited to take Tancredi to his first day at the Tribunal. A marine lieutenant approached, and saluted. "Good morning, sir."

Students at the Law School had to salute first to all commissioned-rank military personnel, and Tancredi had to repress the instinct to bow his head. "If only, lieutenant," he said, instead. He smiled as he walked past the marine and started toward the shuttle. The lieutenant glanced at the sky but didn't reply. He signalled back to the crew and followed the scholar. The shuttle's portside dilated.

"We have reports of unrests along the route, sir," the lieutenant said. "I took the liberty to add an escort vehicle and change the waypoints."

Tancredi stopped before entering the shuttle. He smiled again at the officer. "Why? On the contrary." He peeked inside the cockpit and addressed the pilot. "I'm interested. Take me there first." He took his seat.

The lieutenant shook his head. Then nodded at the pilot, who raised his shoulders in a shrug.

The vehicles lifted off the pavement and sped toward the border of the green zone. The perimetric wall dilated just before the convoy exited into the daedalic net of streets of Utthana, the capital city.

The city grew above and below the surface, split into levels reflecting the layers of the citizens' social status in the occupied territories. On the ground, the questionable ones, Kritas who were on constant probation. An inquisition by the Tribunal would determine their ascension to higher levels, or their disappearance to the underground ones where the scholars and military exercised more and more scrutiny on each suspected individual. The lower the level, the greater the marines' presence, and the more likely they would resort to force to ensure uproars stopped at once.

Those on the higher levels had often said, only half-jokingly, that the scholars had changed the law of physics: the higher your level above ground, the easier to float to the top; and the faster the descent into doom and oblivion, the more your fate took you to the underground ones.

Humans restricted and monitored all communication between the levels, and the Kritas had to go through checkpoints and scan areas to change levels. No one, though, had ever heard of any Kritas who had resurfaced once he had fallen to the mythical third underground, or 3U as they called it. Only a few lived in the highest levels of Utthana, enjoying almost the same freedom and rights as the humans. It was a taste of what life would be if they became Union citizens.

Earlier that day, the space marines had acted on rumors that some activists among the Zeros—citizens of the ground level—were to meet that day. Individuals among the Unders, for sure, and maybe even complacent ones from the Above levels, who formed dormant cells of troublemakers—nothing serious (up until then) but enough to justify enhanced security measures. Meanwhile, in the past months, the suspicion of a larger conspiracy had received more and more evidence that now troubled the Authority with fear of losing the control they felt they had.

At the old Alliance Square, the marines had already rounded up a number of suspects when a young Kritas, Mekte, daughter of Yutki, arrived in the area. She stopped at the north access and leaned at a corner to watch unseen. She was a Zero, slim and svelte as all Kritas girls were, with a satin feel to her skin and a gender-neutral look; her thin red-gold hair waved at the slightest breeze and movement, so thin as if it was one with the air.

Mekte had the qualities and the intelligence required to rise to the Above levels, if only she had wanted to. Her heart, though, was aimed at satisfying other desires.

She looked around. A large military transporter had landed on the square, its shining hull contrasting with the pitch black of the old stones of the ground. During the last hour, bystanders had grown in numbers. The marines were busy in their usual show of power and determination, and Kritas received the attentions of patrols in full riot gear.

Small but deadly vehicles hovered with their weapons drawn out, singling out groups as soon as they formed. Sharp orders to disperse had Kritas make the good decision not to try the marines' resolve any further. They walked away, but only to gather at other places, in a ballet that would have been amusing to watch if it hadn't had the potential to bring many of them to a deadly end.

Much higher, the perennial flow of vehicles in the Above levels continued undisturbed, not caring of the events taking place below. On the ground, the marines barked orders to back off, and kept their blasters drawn at anyone who dared to get too close.

A Kritas shouted his anger, "Human skunk!" and pushed away the mouth of a blaster a marine had just pointed at his face. "Freeze!" the marine shouted, but the Kritas stepped forward as though the soldier wasn't even there. Restraining beams flashed from the stun guns of the other members of the patrol. The smell of ozone filled the air. The piercing buzz of the beams carried the menace of thousands of angry stinger-flies. The Kritas fell at once, shaking uncontrollably on the ground. The marines grabbed him, and dumped his unconscious body into a military vehicle, to be sent to the Tribunal for further inquisition.

In the middle of the square, the soldiers held other suspects at blaster-point. From their looks, many had to be underage Kritas, and no one in the square wanted to see them in marine custody.

Mekte tightened her fists in rage as she realized the marines were using the mental probes at their maximum invasive power.

One by one, the young Kritas collapsed under the attack of massive, convulsive syncopes. If they passed the threat probing test, marines ignored them and left them unconscious on the ground, the bodies jerking like broken mechanisms. Instead, they cuffed the unlucky ones, waiting only a little for the convulsions to subside a bit before carrying them, dumbfounded, inside the transporter.

Mekte feared she knew some of the prisoners, and worried they'd soon disappear into the spires of the scholars' Inquisitionary. Step by step, swaying through the Kritas in front of her, she got closer to the scene as the crowd to her right opened with a growl to let an incoming intrusion pass. A convoy of three vehicles approached, with the dreadful insignia of the Scholars camped on the trailing one. In the commotion that followed, her eyes met with those of others in the crowd. They nodded as she breathed out a sigh of relief.

*
**

"We're there, sir." The pilot spoke over his shoulder without losing sight of the surroundings. He glanced at the details on the tactical screen. "It looks just like any other police operation, if I may say."

Tancredi made the side of the vehicle transparent and shook his head. "Do all police operations generate the kind of emotional waves I am perceiving?"

The pilot opened his mouth for a second, but didn't say a word. He didn't have the heightened sense of a scholar, nor the training to formulate any meaningful answer to anything that didn't have to do with navigation.

Tancredi smiled. "As I thought. Stop near the transporter."

At the center of the square, a marine sergeant approached the officer who was supervising the probing procedure on the young Kritas. "Sir?"

"What now?" the officer replied without turning.

"We have visitors, sir." The sergeant nodded toward the three vehicles closing in as the crowd split to put as much distance as possible between them and the incoming convoy, then closing again behind the passing vehicles, as tight as the valves of a shell.

The lieutenant peered in the same direction as the sergeant's eyes and sighed. The situation was already tense, and that intrusion could make things worse, breaking a tenuous equilibrium.

The small convoy slowed to a stop as it reached the transporter. Tribunal guards emerged from two of the vehicles, their stun-blasters drawn and ready to fire. At first, nothing happened within the vehicle adorned with the scholars' insignia. Finally, its side dilated and a hooded figure stepped out slowly, as if it was walking behind a procession.

After a few steps, it stopped, as if a hound pausing while chasing a prey, excited to be on track. It seemed to be smelling the air, heavy with ozone and the anger exuding from the multitude of Kritas.

With a poised movement, the figure lowered its hood. Two black eyes scanned the ones standing the closest; they retreated under the pressure of the scholar's mental probe. All chatter and noises vanished, as if covered by a flood wave of silence. The scholar looked around until those eyes found the officer in charge. His gait resumed.

The officer lowered his head when Tancredi reached him. "An unexpected visit, sir. How may I help a scholar today?"

Tancredi smiled. He sensed the mixture of admiration and frustration emanating from the space marine. "A better question would be how a scholar might help a marines' roundup operation." Before the marine could reply, he continued. "News of the unrest has travelled faster than a message on a quantum-entanglement transponder . . ." Tancredi feigned taking the time to recognize the grade. "Lieutenant..."

"We have everything under control, sir. I don't see how—"

"I know you don't see it, lieutenant. Allow me." The scholar moved past the officer, who rolled his eyes to the Above levels and frowned.

The crowd watched with eagerness, as if the scholar were an actor on stage who had just captivated the whole audience. After a few seconds, Tancredi's voice sounded loud in the muted square. "Lieutenant!"

The officer rushed to his side. "Sir?"

"I sense no danger from all these Kritas, only pride and fear, and justified at that. Why are you probing them?"

The officer hissed his words. "For the Tribunal . . . sir!"

"The Tribunal has a duty to deal with criminals. We restore their minds and bring those who have lost their bearing back into the right path." Tancredi was staring at the space marine.

The lieutenant looked back at the crowd, as though he was searching for someone. "Our probes' signals justify the arrests. Besides, we received a tip." He omitted to end his phrase with 'sir.'

Tancredi pretended he hadn't noticed. "A tip?" He glanced around. "Interesting. And how many Kritas have you already taken into custody?"

"Three for now."

Tancredi addressed his own guards. "Take them. I'll examine these subjects at the Tribunal." He gazed and nodded to the ones still shaking on the ground. "Lieutenant, attend to their needs. Release the others."

"Sir?" The lieutenant replied with an irked tone.

Tancredi raised his eyebrows and stared at the officer. "Did I use words difficult to understand?"

Blood rose to the marine's face. He returned the stare for a moment, then lowered his gaze. "No, sir." He filled his lungs to shout to his men. "You've heard the scholar. Move!"

A murmur rose from the crowd. Attentive eyes followed Tancredi as he headed back to his vehicle. This time, the Kritas created aisles for the convoy to leave, and many leaned forward for a better look, but Tancredi had reverted the shuttle hull from transparency to full opacity.

***

In Ahthaza, the Tribunal buildings soared into the sky, spanning all main cities' levels above and under as well, rooted deep into the planet like needles stuck into the arm of a terminal patient. They were pillars of the human domination in the planet.

The Tribunal of Utthana contrasted with the surrounding Kritas architecture; where this last grew dark, sharp, and convoluted, the Tribunal billowed smooth and translucent, like mist rising from warm waters. Around the tower, patches of gardens reproduced the perfect environment for all species of plants native to Ahthaza. From above, the gardens recreated the symbol of the scholars, with the Tribunal blossoming in the middle. An outermost ring made of the tallest trees from Earth gave the impression that the Tribunal's tower surged as a direct emanation from the humans' home planet.

The citizens at the higher levels experienced a more lenient version of the Law. Scholars showed a benevolent and understanding face to the 'high society' of the Above levels, although their mere presence reminded everyone of the existence of their grimmer face. Like Janus, the scholars looked at the past, controlling the future of everyone.

While humans had access to any level, Kritas had the admittance to only one level below their own, except for the 3U level. That particular level meant oblivion, and '3U' was spoken in a whisper, spurring strong emotional empathy for all Kritas who had been sent there and never returned.

The imposed restrictions worked as a reminder that falling and losing grace was always possible, while ascending to higher levels had to be from the recognition of obedience and collaboration.

At the end of the day, Tancredi leaned tired against the transparent wall in his office. Utthana, the capital city, rose proudly before his eyes. Energy barriers secluded each level, shimmering in the view. He enjoyed the long shadows the crepuscule brought in, and never felt the need to reduce the wall's transparency, even during the morning. Shadows—he had always believed in this—protect, provide shelter, and appease all those seeking refuge.

Sometimes he set the wall to dilate, to breathe in the city's breath. He liked that moment in the evening time and the impression that Utthana laid down quietly in the dusk.

The excitement of his first days at the Tribunal had receded, though, leaving in its place only his sense of duty. He had thought his assignment would be seen as just a first anonymous step in his career, but the more he learned, the more he was troubled for his mission. Perhaps shadows just hid the light and brought only obscurity.

A whisper made him turn; a bulb emerged from the floor. The image of the Councilor to the Dean formed in the middle of the room. "Scholar."

The scarlet-red tunic of the Councilor rivalled the colors of the sky Tancredi glimpsed; in a last attempt to catch the Kritas' star, it disappeared below the horizon. "You're requested in the Dean's office."

Tancredi bowed. "I'm here to serve the Dean."

*
**

Mekte reached the nearest Tribunal Enquiry Office for the Zero level. The TEO's cylindrical structures, disseminated through all levels, mimicked the shape of the Tribunal's tower itself. Officially, they stood for a transparent and open policy of the inquisition procedures, but they constituted instead an additional means for probing and scanning citizens, serving more to gather knowledge than to provide the populace with any.

The Kritas understood that well, and scoffed at the offices. They scorned anything related to the Tribunal, though they feared it and its scholars.

In the TEOs, Kritas could search for information on all past and current inquisitions, though they had little control over the accuracy and extent of the details the Tribunal decided to provide.

Mekte looked over her shoulder before she activated the biometric implant and rested her palm on the exterior wall. She waited for the scan to complete and had to resist the tickling sensation the implant always caused her at the back of her skull during such procedures.

The implant hid her identity and identified her now as a relative of one of the young Kritas arrested the day before. The wall dilated and allowed her entry.

The floor greeted her as she stepped in. "Welcome, Karelle, daughter of Vikri. Follow your name to your assigned station." 'Karelle' pulsated at her feet. She advanced, and the name guided her, matching her pace. She didn't have much time, and the tickling at her skull had already started to grow in intensity, reminding her to be quick.

On the floating panel of her station, information stacked up as she flipped over the virtual screens that appeared one by one under her gestures: the time of arrest, the motivations of the arresting officer, the mental probing results, and the subsequent transfer to the Tribunal, First Instance, Zero Level.

Her eyes fell on the sentence and the charges that had been recorded: a misdemeanor, unauthorized gathering, the list of the administrative infractions, and the immediate release. She had to read that a second time: *immediate release*. She searched for the scholar in charge for all those cases: Tancredi Gilmor, from Earth, at his first assignment after the Law School.

She brought one hand to the base of her head. The tickling had grown to more than a nuisance now, and she knew she couldn't stay there much longer.

She wanted to know just a little more, though, and her fingers dashed to find the right access to the right information. Finally, the 3D rendering of Scholar Tancredi Gilmor's head formed in front of her eyes. She glanced at it, her fingers made the face turn, and she bent her head. Her eyes met his virtual ones.

Mekte stared at that human's face for a moment, then blinked as her vision blurred. The burning inside her head filled her eyes with tears. She disconnected her session and ran out of the TEO, back into the maze of the city streets.

At the first corner, she stopped to catch her breath. A thin rain covered her velvet skin with tiny beads; she looked up to capture the droplets with her tongue, then closed her eyes. Did freedom taste that good? She sighed.

At nineteen, she only knew the conditions of the humans' domination, but now, maybe, just maybe, things might change for her and her people.

Chapter 2 – The Under Levels

A Young Hope

AT THE INTER-LEVELS' THRESHOLD, the marine scanned Mekte for authorization and identification. She didn't move a muscle during the whole procedure. The transparent cylinder that had grown around her collected the biometrics. All of Mekte's details, since her birth, filled the floating security screens. A `pass` verdict pulsated on the dashboard. The cylinder spun and was reabsorbed into its lodge.

"What is your business in 1U, Zero?" the guard asked with a monotonic voice.

Mekte frowned. He could read her name, knew everything about her, but to the human she was just a Zero.

"I have friends in 1U," she said.

"Yeah, I can imagine," he raised his gaze and sneered at her. "You should look for better friends in 1A, rather." The guard chuckled. "Anyway, enjoy your stay."

Mekte shrugged and crossed the stun-field barrier that had just dilated. She stepped on the connecting platform that would have taken her into the dark, into 1U.

The short journey down let her eyes adjust to the dimmer light of the Under levels. She stepped off the platform and walked through the walk-in scan area. She glanced at a second guard who crosschecked the authorization sent from the Zero level's post above. The guard was staring at the security panels, but gave her a nod. Mekte walked through the exit that coalesced behind her back.

The muffled noise from the underground 1U level activities, like a perennial, overlapping humming of different tones, greeted her. How it differed from the sounds of life of the levels above…

The *Unders* supported the life style of the *Aboves* in the economy system that had been imposed after the human invasion. Workers crowded the streets, moving through their shifts and taking turns of duty at the city utility services. The cries of merchants, selling goods and food, resonated in the alleys and could be heard from blocks away. They cried louder in the lower levels, as if—this way—they could lull their rage at each call. The air was thick and humid; a thin rain burst down, always at the same times, always at the same spots.

Mekte's skin took a couple of minutes to adjust to the new condition. The glisten of perspiration would have told everyone she had just arrived from above, but she didn't attract more than a few distracted glances; visits from Zeros were not unusual in 1U.

She hid anyway at the first crossing, far from the faint light of street glowing bulbs in the main road, luminescent blobs that struggled in their fight against the shadows. She peeked at the corner to make sure she wasn't followed. Noticing nothing unusual, she sighed. She never felt safe after a visit at the TEOs; at the last one, she waited too long and risked being discovered.

She looked around. A steady flow of people merged in the streets at every corner, never stopping. The Unders weren't allowed to own vehicles. When you heard one approaching, it could only mean one thing, and your only hope was to not be the target of a marines' patrol.

The greatest danger, though, came from those Unders who tried to make their way back to Zero class by all means. They were known as *hush*, a term used both to quiet down a friend when you spotted one of them and to designate all collaborators for what they were: hu-man sh-it.

She waited a bit longer in the shadow before she felt a bit reassured. No hush around, at least she hoped.

Many of the buildings in the underground levels had been abandoned decades before, after the human invasion, and their connections to the higher level had been sealed.

Kritas had died all over the planet in the last battles, often exposed by traitors in exchange for privileges, as she had learned from some of the elders. The Kritas had fought the humans in the open for as long as they could, and when the price in lives became unsustainable, they retreated underground and re-organized in the darkness.

At first, and after a few years, when there were only human soldiers to fight, a successful rebellion seemed within reach. Then, the scholars arrived, and with them, the mind scans; all cells had to become dormant again, retreat underground, and re-discover how to fight at the mind level, too.

In the effort to recover parts of the technology that would have helped the rebels hide and fool the scholars' mental abilities, many had died or gone missing after recovery missions at the shipyards. More years had passed, and the rebels` forces dwindled, but their hope remained young.

Mekte passed both hands through her thin hair; then she pushed it up into a dirty cap. She bent to grab some dirt and rubbed it on her face, hands, and arms to look like a low-skilled worker just out of her turn. She stepped back onto the main street.

She merged with the others and had walked only a few blocks when she glimpsed a marines' patrol approach. She rushed to the stall of a food merchant, pretending to be looking for something to eat. She took a seat and bent her back as though she was broken from a hard day of work.

"What do I serve you, dear?" the merchant lady bent forward trying to get Mekte`s attention. "Hey," she nudged her with her hand, "if you want to sit here, you have to eat."

Mekte glanced at her, then at the food displays. "Your soup. Looks delicious."

The lady nodded, "It *is*," and dipped a large scoop into one of the boiling blobs.

"No meat, please," Mekte urged.

The lady snorted. "Why didn't you say that before?" She plunged her tool into a different blob and retrieved a portion: a waggling jelly sphere. The merchant was about to hand it over, but then she hesitated. "That's three credits. You do have credits, don't you?"

"Of course. I just received my pay," Mekte replied and touched her palm transducer to authorize the payment.

"Which must not be that much." The merchant frowned as she examined the dirt on her face and placed her hand over Mekte's until the credits transferred.

The buzz and the street noises subsided, squelched by the approaching patrol. Mekte took the soup from the merchant, lowered her head, and plunged her tongue into the sphere. She sucked in, trying to look fully absorbed in eating her meal.

The marines closed in, brandishing their blasters and the empath probes to measure stress intensity and detect threat levels. When they reached her height, they stopped. The implant at the back of her head tickled and her muscles contracted, but she withstood the discomfort and kept eating.

The marines resumed their patrol and disappeared behind a corner. Mekte exhaled. She dropped the soup and left.

"Hey, you didn't finish…" the merchant lady yelled at her.

"Delicious!" Mekte cried over her shoulder as she strode down the street. She spat when the merchant cried back at her, "Go fuck a human!"

*
**

Seated in the admittance hall of the Dean's office, Tancredi waited for the wall to dilate. At the reception desk, the assistant kept looking at him through the floating screens of his dashboard. The temptation to explore the assistant's thoughts burned in Tancredi's mind, but scholars didn't probe other scholars, unless done within a constraining, internal protocol. It usually meant trouble for the probed scholar.

Finally, the assistant spoke. "You will be received now." Tancredi stood up and nodded at the assistant. The wall dilated and he entered the Dean's office. The assistant's eyes were still glued to his neck when the wall coalesced behind him.

Tancredi had never met the Dean in person before; a middle-aged woman with piercing eyes and long crow-black hair that was held into a knot so tight that it appeared to be a helmet. The sensations of power, wisdom, and crude determination hit him as he stepped in.

The Dean didn't seem to notice his presence and kept her eyes on the dashboard screens over her desk, so Tancredi had enough time to glance around. Relics of the past covered the walls, from different planets and races. He noticed the many books among them; real ones from a past long gone. One in particular, floating above its own pedestal, attracted his curiosity. He leaned to one side and tried to read the title when a tridimensional rendering of the city of Utthana emerged from the center of the room. He straightened up.

Behind her desk, the Dean continued to seem too busy to even look at him; she kept interacting with panels that blossomed in front of her, only to disappear after a few manipulations from the tip of her fingers.

Tancredi took the time to examine Utthana. Some areas pulsated as if they were a living thing; most of these pulses were located in the Under levels.

"It is getting worse," the Dean said without raising her eyes from the floating panels.

He jolted. He didn't expect to be addressed in that manner. "What is, Ma'am?" He stiffened.

She looked at him and studied his face for a moment. "It didn't take long for you to get noticed, Gilmor."

That wasn't a question, and it didn't sound promising. "I'm here to serve—"

"Cut that nonsense out, Gilmor." The Dean stood up and walked to the city rendering. "I've received complaints coming directly from the marines' headquarters." She paused. "What were you thinking when you showed up at Alliance Square?" Her eyes searched his.

Tancredi swallowed. "I did not abuse my authority with the marines. They were—"

"They were acting based on serious reports. They accuse you of undermining an important ground operation." She pointed at the blinking zones in the Utthana representation. "You see these areas?"

Tancredi nodded.

"These are areas where we registered a growing rate of incidents and where diligent scholars helped track individuals who the Tribunal then confirmed to be deviant. Incidents are becoming more serious now."

"I found no evidence of deviancy in the Kritas I've examined, Ma'am." Tancredi eyes didn't blink once.

The Dean tightened her lips and looked at him as if he himself was an anomaly. "I didn't ask what you found or didn't find, Gilmor."

Tancredi lowered his head. "My apologies."

She gestured at the dashboard and a screen blossomed up, with Tancredi's head rendering rotating slowly inside it, along with his complete past curriculum. "In spite of your credentials and grade, you are now assigned to field operations with marine patrols. Maybe you'll learn something."

With a jerk, he raised his head again. "Ma'am, if I may—"

"You may not!" She lashed out. "Maybe the time spent in the underground levels with the patrols will teach you—again—what we're supposed to be doing here, and why. You're dismissed, Gilmor."

Tancredi bowed. "As the Dean commands."

She looked at him as he took leave and shook her head. When the wall dilated, she called, "Gilmor?"

He stopped at the exit and turned around.

"For as long as you're assigned to the underground patrolling, your quarters have been transferred to 1U," the Dean said.

Tancredi breathed hard, opened his mouth, but suppressed his protests. He had been demoted, an out-of-proportion measure, he reasoned. He nodded because he had to. He left the Dean's office with a bitter taste in his mouth and new questions he needed to find answers to.

The assistant raised his eyebrows without shielding his feelings: a wave of condemnation reached Tancredi.

He paused to stare at the assistant, but his gaze was met with defiance. Tancredi shook his head, his lips curved in a half smile. He left the Dean's quarters with a precise destination in mind, the Tribunal's Archives.

*
**

Mekte resisted the impulse to start running when her objective came into sight: a thrift shop, and not a particularly special one, either. The shop attracted those Kritas in search of the perfect compromise between their needs and their few available credits. It was always crowded.

She stopped on the opposite side of the street and hesitated for a moment in search of familiar faces, or for anything suspicious, but found neither. She nodded to herself, decided to cross, and mingled with those who searched through piles of clothing and other everyday objects. She avoided those Kritas attracted by drugs, various kinds of distillates, and those who flocked around the most recent brain transducers for solitary excitement.

At the back of the store, the second-hand prosthetics counter required customers to part with more of their credits if they wanted to turn a need into a satisfaction, and there were fewer patrons among those aisles. She froze when she noticed one patron who was lurking in a corner. He must have just decided that it wasn't the time yet to acquire new enhancements as, after exchanging one longing look with Mekte, he was directed to the shelves filled with drugs of all sorts, of a short lasting effect, but less expensive.

Mekte put back the noise suppressor rod she had feigned to examine and reached the rear of the shop, at the after-sales service desk. "I need a new hood," she addressed the techie behind the counter.

The guy didn't raise his gaze from the cartilages that flexed and contracted as he manipulated and stimulated the synth-nerves with pointy tools and pincers. A spark raised a plume of smoke and he threw the ruined prosthetic into a bin. "Crap!"

The techie glanced at her for a brief moment and snorted. "You're on the wrong side of the shop, girl. Hoods are that way." He nodded toward the entrance.

"To reveal my new self," Mekte insisted.

The guy froze, stared at her with squinted eyes, then gazed around rapidly. He put down his tools and adopted a serious tone. "Get behind me. Be fast."

Mekte reacted at once and rushed behind the counter. With a single fluid push, the techie sent her against the wall that swallowed the girl as if it was indeed a vertical liquid barrier. The wall rippled briefly before it came to rest again.

After the wall spit her out into a narrow hall, she stumbled to regain her balance. "Welcome back," she heard as she straightened herself up.

She searched for the voice. Her own face camped on a large floating panel, flanked by smaller ones showing the details of her biometrics.

"How come your mother lets you wander all alone in the Unders?" said the voice, followed by a chuckle.

"Shut up, you idiot." A stern voice interrupted the exchange. "You know well her parents died, and *how*." A tall Kritas advanced into the hall and ordered, "Check security, instead."

Mekte didn't move, nor say a word. The voice didn't comment further.

The tall Kritas stopped in front of her. With his right hand, he raised her chin and looked deep into her eyes.

"What's going on? You weren't supposed to be here today, Mekte."

"I know, but something happened." She jerked her head aside.

He sighed and lowered his hand. He nodded. "Something always happens. Follow me."

She kept pace with him through narrow corridors, passing through interconnected rooms. On narrow metal slabs along the walls, Kritas technicians worked on military devices that Mekte recognized at once to be seeker-mines and other explosives.

"We're getting ready, at last," her host said without slowing down or looking back at her.

He led her into a larger, round hall, that was dimly lit. At a wide central stand, Kritas officers interacted with four 3D models of Utthana, highlighting intricate trajectories through blocks and buildings from the Under levels up to the Zero one. Bright red, pulsating dots showed the paths of the marines' patrols.

Around the curved wall, inside virtual shimmering spheres, data analysts were moving and merging symbols together on diagrams and sources of live data flashing in as more panels popped up, floating in front of them.

The tall Kritas stopped and faced her. He crossed his arms. "So," he stared. "What's so urgent?"

Mekte glanced for a moment at the renderings of the city blocks that spun and expanded under the precise gestures of the operators. "The last meeting..."

"What about?" The tall Kritas bent his head.

"Somehow the humans knew about it and proceeded to arrest many bystanders, but then...they have been released without further interrogations."

The Kritas shrugged. "How does that affect us? None of our agents have been arrested."

"That never happened before. There was this scholar... He showed up at the Alliance Square that day. *He* did that." She breathed hard. "Released them, I mean. I searched for him."

"You did what?" The Kritas stepped forward and towered her.

"I searched for him." Mekte took a step back. "I've been careful, it only took a minute at the TEO."

He grabbed her arm and pulled her away to a corner. "Mekte, are you crazy? They've recorded your presence."

She jerked her arm free and stared at him with cold eyes. "I concealed my identity, and if you don't care about those kids, why should the humans?"

"Now I do." He puckered his eyebrows.

"I posed as a relative and left before the implant failed." She caressed her neck as the memory of the pain surfaced in her mind.

Kaulm humphed and walked away from her. "That was stupid." His hand clenched into a fist. He pivoted to face her again. "Stupid! Which TEO?" he hissed between his lips.

"T57, blocks away from the square."

"Distance means nothing." He pushed her to the nearest datalink sphere and interrupted the work of the Kritas inside. "Open the TEOs' network," he commanded.

Mekte opened her mouth and rolled her tongue in excitement. "I didn't know we could do that?"

Kaulm glimpsed at her. "Now you do."

"Link's open, sir," said the operator.

"Mekte, location and time," Kaulm asked.

"T57, time clicks 8345," Mekte replied at once. The operator entered the information on the floating dashboard.

A display blossomed on the sphere and detached from its surface. Kaulm grabbed it with his fingers and dilated it to examine Mekte's recorded visit to the TEO.

"Find all interactions with the records of any arrest event at Alliance Square," Kaulm ordered the operator.

The sphere shimmered as it retrieved the correlations and filled with connections and live links: bioputer computational nodes blossomed on its surface and the operator's hands danced among them and through all the symbols. The data analysis had just started tracing all combinations when one of the links flashed red, then another, and another. The number of links laced to others grew before their eyes, and a net formed and kept expanding on the sphere surface like a corrupting plague. Mekte shivered.

An alarm resonated. "Network intrusion, we're being backtracked," shouted the operator.

"Abort!" Kaulm jumped in the sphere and doubled the operator's efforts to break the connections and collapse the nodes. The more links they interrupted, the more others formed under their hands. Kaulm grabbed his pulse gun and opened fire at the main, central neural node. The sphere collapsed; the bioputer fizzled and died off.

The hall filled with alarmed Kritas, many with their blasters drawn.

"Can they trace us?" Kaulm shouted at the operator who looked back at him with a blank stare. *"Can they trace us?"*

The main display filled with security breaches showing troops gathering and moving toward the thrift shop.

Mekte groaned. "I wasn't followed." Her hands were shaking.

Kaulm's upper lip trembled. "You put us all at risk."

Two Kritas rushed to his side and stood at attention. "Commander, the humans are converging to the area!"

"Initiate the evacuation! Now!" he replied. The evacuation alert resounded throughout the base.

The technicians in the room shut down the sphere, extracting the main nodes, and gathered all that could be transported.

"What am I supposed to do?" asked Mekte.

Kaulm looked at her and shook his head. "You? You may forget your place at Zero, now."

A siren screamed, and the floor trembled. Dust fell off the ceiling. "Seal the base!" Kaulm shouted.

The external monitoring screens showed marines had launched the assault at the thrift store. On the streets, Kritas ran bent forward, trying to duck the flashing bolts the military police fired at them. Sentinel drones converged at the entrance, darted to the rear of the shop, smashing through counters and stands, and blasted through the back wall. The screens blanched with the first flashes of the explosions, and they only heard the blaster-gun shots between the first line of defence of the Kritas and the space marines. For a few seconds, they glimpsed all the colors of death, then the screens went dark at once.

Kaulm's lips contracted.

CHAPTER 3 – REJECTED

THE LAW OF DOUBTS

FOR DAYS AFTER THE INCURSION, bulletins detailed non-stop the news through all networks and info-points across the city stressing the message about security in Utthana and how it could be achieved only with the participation of all citizens. The Authority had promised an undisclosed credit reward and the ascension to higher levels for those law-abiding citizens who helped in the operations, but without providing any offers of protection or anonymity.

That evening, in the common hall of the Presidio-1U, the marines were watching the unamended 3D report of the raid. Scenes showed the fuming debris of the thrift store, then moved to the dark interiors of the Kritas base, zooming in on charred bodies and smashed equipment, treating the former no differently than the latter.

The marines had cordoned off the entire block and had launched a search-and-destroy followup operation. The voice-over described the operation as "a testimony to human determination and the strength of Kritas' collaboration in dismantling a terrorist cell in 1U, the first of many to come. Law-abiding Kritas from 1U and Zero assisted in the prevention of callous and ruthless terrorists attacks and the loss of many lives. Citizens who helped unveil the extreme moral wickedness of the terrorists have been rewarded with a promotion to 2A level, effective immediately."

On a chair, at a far end of the hall, Tancredi frowned when the marines shouted war cries over more images of dead Kritas. He knew many marines had died, but the images instead showed a perfectly executed operation.

"So, scholar... Sir." A marine approached and looked down on him. "It looks like we can find the bad guys even when you're around." He burst into raucous laughter, followed by others, and turned his back to again join his group of friends.

"You think it's a game, don't you?" With a measured movement, Tancredi stood up.

"What did you say?" The marine stopped and looked over his shoulder.

Tancredi snorted. "Hide and seek? An old game. I'll show you what the actual rules are." His black eyes stared at the marine, and his scholar medallion shone.

Sweat beads covered the marine's forehead. A few of the marines chuckled, but waves of tension mixed with fear came pouring from them and crashed on the scholar's empathic mind.

Tancredi stepped up to the motionless soldier. He touched his left temple and the marine's pupils widened. "This is what the first space marine suffered when he rushed into the Kritas' tunnel," Tancredi said with a firm voice. "A blaster jolt hit his flank."

The marine groaned and his body twisted.

"His protective gear burned through his kidney when a second blast struck through."

The soldier fell to his knees; the other marines quit their chattering.

"This is, instead, how a Kritas reacted when she felt her lungs vaporize. You'll notice the pain is quite similar. They're equal in death."

The marine gasped and choked; he rolled to the floor, shaking. His hands clutched his rib cage, then his throat lashed out a scratching sound. Finally, he laid still in the fetal position. His mouth foamed.

Tancredi released the mental grip. "He will recover," he muttered, and turned his gaze around. The marines stared at him without moving; some retreated.

He shook his head, and had the exit wall dilate. Before leaving, he looked over his shoulder. "Death can bring you only more death."

*
**

On the security screen projected by his belt, a military guard at the Presidio's perimetric barrier checked the vehicle's credentials, as well as those of the occupant. He approached, saluted, and glanced back at the screen. "I don't have a patrol unit assigned to you, sir."

Tancredi didn't blink. "That's because I didn't request one."

"Sir?"

"The vehicle's security link is open; patrols will know where I am at all times. I don't plan to venture far."

The guard raised his eyes to meet with his peers in the security post, then silently stared back at Tancredi.

Tancredi smiled. "It's fine, really."

The soldier took a long breath and nodded, interfaced again with the vehicle, and registered the exit time on the screen. "Be safe, sir." He raised his chin in the direction of the security post. The energy barrier dilated.

The vehicle drifted silently out of the deserted green zone, and then into the streets of the 1U level. Emotionless, the aliens moved away to let the vehicle pass. For the most part, Kritas were a resigned race. *They're so much like us*, Tancredi thought.

As he drove, slowly, he searched their faces; some glanced back at him for a moment, but—in general—all turned their eyes away.

Tancredi had studied the history records of the Kritas' initial interactions with the humans. The Tribunal's archives reported events from the years when humans first met with Kritas, when Earth was a planet in turmoil and the humans a race on the brink of self-destruction. He had gone through all the annals, human and alien alike.

He recalled everything, though; he always had the uncanny ability to remember details. Some humans believed the Kritas to be the Heavenly Fathers, even responsible for the origin of life on Earth. They believed in the myth that humans descended from them, so much did the two races resemble each other. The Kritas were one of the most ancient races; however, the myth was nothing but a deception. In the darkness of the cabin, Tancredi grinned. All encounters with aliens had been a deception and an illusion for the race of man. Yet, today's humans were as different from their ancestors and as alien to their pasts as the Kritas had ever been.

He glanced at the vehicle's security reports flashing on the dashboard and at the threat echelons received in real time from the surrounding marines' patrols. Nothing abnormal, a quiet day in the 1U… or night, depending on the labor shifts.

In the distance, he recognized one of the enquiry office's structures. He stopped the vehicle and glanced one last time at the reports, then shut all systems down and got off.

He raised his hood. The air was humid and heavy, and the street dark as a few of the light-blobs had died off, but he decided to walk to the TEO.

Soon, he had the thought to move within a bubble of deprived sensations. Kritas walked away from him, with a blank stare in their eyes. In truth, they always reacted that way in the presence of a scholar. *Another hide-and-seek game*, he thought. He could have broken the thin veil into their minds with ease, but decided not to.

The TEO recognized him, and the wall dilated. No one was inside, but he wasn't surprised. Not that day, and not after the recent events.

He took his place at the first duty station of the TEO and retrieved all data from the marines' assault at the base, data a Kritas could also have had access to. No crude images of kills and violence, the emphasis was firmly on the collaboration between humans and aliens, and on the rewards. He grunted at how different that version of the event was from the truth.

Tancredi sighed and entered his security credentials. "Show me all scholars involved in all military operations over the last month."

The space in front of him filled with the details requested. He examined the various reports and nodded; he was listed among them, together with a list of complaints escalated to the higher hierarchy, both in the military and with the scholars, too, and his subsequent demotion. A bitter smile rose to his lips.

He remembered the lieutenant at the square—and the Dean—had mentioned an informant's tip had triggered the operation... "Show me all correlated Kritas involvements," he ordered in a firm voice.

The system paused, as though it hesitated. "The full extent of information requires 'A' clearance," an impersonal voice declaimed.

Tancredi snorted. "I do have 'A' clearance."

The voice didn't show any hesitation this time. "Scholar Tancredi Gilmor 'A' clearance is suspended." A floating report blossomed in front of him.

He frowned. The ruling carried the signature of the Dean herself. "Select all operations I have full access to."

The floating panels reabsorbed, slowly at first, then faster, and flickered away as if they had never existed. He feared everything would have vanished, but a few persisted and highlighted. "Selection completed," the system announced with a hint of satisfaction.

Tancredi nodded; his access had been restricted only to those events and operations he had direct participation in. He flipped the remaining panels with a finger gesture and found one that showed up the day his problems had started: the Alliance Square operation. He enlarged the panel. "Show me all Kritas interactions with this record."

A TEO access report blossomed in front of his eyes. "Expand," he said.

A display came to life and showed a young female Kritas accessing TEO 57. 'Karelle, daughter of Vikri,' the record stated, plus a note hidden behind a "'A' clearance access only."

Tancredi caressed his chin; his eyes followed the girl's every movement and actions in the TEO. He broadened the extent of his search.

*
**

The automated blast doors had protected each area of the insurgents' base when the marines' assault started, which bought enough time for those in the remote recesses to escape. Casualties ran high, and the Kritas had lost most of their equipment.

At a safe quarter, in a deeper level of Utthana, Kaulm had called for an emergency meeting with the leaders of the rebel cells in the city. Reports and data overlapped on the various panels that showed the evolution of all plausible scenarios in days, weeks, and even months, but all pointed at only one possible conclusion; and it came with a big uncertainty factor.

"We cannot allow for this to slow things down. On the contrary." He stared at the others.

The cell leader next to Kaulm replied, "I agree. We've lost many operatives and we can't just wait for another of these attacks and suffer the consequences." He sighed. "If we do nothing, more will come, soon, and Kritas will lose faith."

The others nodded. Floating over the round table, the bioputers unfolded before them with new simulations and additional scenarios. "We've reached a tipping point," added another of the leaders, pointing at the latest results. "The humans have increased their security threat level, and we'll face even greater risks if we wait any longer."

Kaulm's lips contracted. "Are we all in agreement, then? Are we ready?" he asked.

The leaders looked at each other, searching for signs of doubt or a faltering in their resolve. Their eyes squinted in approval, and their nictitating membranes swept swiftly from side to side.

"Agreed, then." Kaulm nodded. "Tomorrow, at time clicks 4000."

One by one, around the table, the cell leaders' renderings faded and disappeared. Kaulm remained alone. He stood transfixed by new results, which projected a disastrous aftermath. And yet, he felt he had no choice.

The casualties suffered during the assault had exceeded the infirmary's capacity. Doctors had installed additional med units and hadn't paused a moment for days. After the meeting, Kaulm reached the entrance lobby to the med center.

His lips squeezed into a thin line, and his jaws contracted. Through the transparent wall, he looked at the rows of med-units that treated the most critically injured; his people had suffered enough, and it was time to make that stop, whatever the cost.

He rested his hand on the ID panel, and the wall slid open. He stepped into the hall. Walking along the aisles, he searched for familiar faces, the ones who followed him from the beginning and fought at his side for years. He exchanged nods with some, and noticed, with a heavy heart, the absence of many others.

A voice made him stop. "I'm glad you made it."

Kaulm searched for the voice he recognized, tilted his head and stared at a young girl. "I'm glad you made it, too."

Mekte looked down, then back at him. "You don't seem too happy to see me."

He grunted in response.

"I don't blame you...too much. You never heard what I had to say." She sat on the bed. "He's different."

"Who is?"

"The scholar."

"You're crazy. He probably sent the marines after you. All humans are alike."

"Not this one." With a groan, Mekte stood up, pushing away the hand that Kaulm offered her.

Kaulm breathed hard. "I'm telling you, you're crazy. You can't trust humans." He waved his hand, as though to erase her previous words from existence.

She managed to step closer. "We're not all the same, either."

He bent forward, and his face almost touched hers. "What do you really mean, Mekte? What do you want?" Kaulm hissed his words. "You're wounded, they killed many of ours, and you still want to trust a human. A scholar, even!" He straightened up, and his voice was as cold as a night in the rocky deserts and canyons that surrounded Utthana. "Go back to bed and worry about your recovery instead." He left.

Her lower lip trembled. "I'm not crazy," she muttered to herself.

***

The Dean sealed her office. "I don't want to be disturbed."

The scholar assistant's image, projected above her desk, bowed. The image dissolved.

Sometimes, she thought, *being different, being more, can be a curse rather than a blessing.*

A peduncle emerged from the floor, and its bulb flickered. She expected that call. The tall figure that emerged in the rendering spoke first. The voice sounded...ancestral.

"My congratulations on your intuition, Dean."

"It was the only logical conclusion after the tip for the Alliance Square. We were ready."

"A brilliant operation, nonetheless. We hit them hard."

Still seated at her desk, the Dean bowed, but her hands contracted.

"What are your intentions with the young scholar?" the tall figure asked.

The Dean raised her head. "He's special. We've never had anyone like him before. His empathic skills are extraordinary."

"He's beyond control, but we can use that."

"I've already revoked his 'A' credentials, as you requested."

The figure nodded. "Might not be enough. He needs to go rogue."

"Rogue?"

"We need him to infiltrate the insurgence, without realizing he's doing that for us, of course."

The Dean stared at the floor. "It's a dangerous move."

"He's expendable."

"I meant...for us." Her heartbeat accelerated.

"It's a risk we need to accept." The figure approached the desk and towered over the Dean. "Force his hand. Put him under arrest. Don't fail me."

The bulb dimmed, and the peduncle retracted into the floor, leaving the Dean alone in her office.

She took a deep breath and glanced at the ancient book hovering above its own pedestal. *Where does he fall between those lines?* she thought. "The future will justify the past, and the past is deceitful," she recited, and then closed her eyes.

*
**

Up on the Zero level, Tancredi stopped the vehicle in a secondary street, got out, and sealed it. A layer of protection enveloped it, impenetrable to all intrusions, physical or otherwise. He started walking toward the street junction.

Maybe the Dean told the truth. Maybe he misunderstood what he felt, and they all faced a grim future and new, unavoidable confrontations with the Kritas.

Karelle, a fake identity, didn't exist. If the Kritas could fool everyone that way, the scholars would have to step up. He shivered; could violence be the only solution? He was there to find out otherwise.

He reached the main street, shrugged off the bad thoughts, and looked at the entrance of the building where she lived. *Mekte, daughter of Yutki. Who are you?* he thought.

Officially, he wasn't supposed to be there, his brain told him, but he couldn't resist the urge he felt at the TEO.

He looked up toward the Above levels. The highest levels shone brighter. At night, Utthana revealed the class system the humans had imposed on the Kritas' society, but Tancredi knew there was no paradise above waiting for anyone to ascend. In the darkness of the main street, he appreciated instead the shadows of the Zero level.

The entrance dilated, and he stepped inside. He tried to imagine how the main hall would have greeted him in the past, in a different world full of light, life, and expectations for a better future.

A colonnade, with nestled decorations made of stones similar to black alabaster from Earth, rose in the middle; arranged to form a circle, the columns supported two entwined spiraling ramps that led to the upper floors. Ancient symbols—not so different from the hieroglyphs of Earth—covered the perimetric walls and the floor and narrated the story of the Kritas Alliance.

Tancredi didn't sense any Kritas in the vicinity, so he proceeded past the colonnade and into the central circle. Nothing happened. The force field elevator must have been inactive for decades, even before the human invasion. Similar facilities still worked in the Above, he reasoned. He took one of the ramps that also didn't react. *One step at a time,* he thought.

As he climbed, his footsteps resonated. A few door-walls dilated, and Kritas peeked out, only to retreat back inside as soon as they recognized the intruder as a scholar. Tancredi absorbed the sensations that slammed against him: disconcert, fear, apprehension, doubts; in one case even repulsion, but he determined that there were no reasons to worry for his safety.

His presence, for how loathed it was, hadn't prompted direct hostility. On the door-walls, he could seen only numbers: humans identified Kritas by their worker status ID number. Many Kritas had lost their individuality and were considered valuable only because of their contribution to the common facilities and needs.

When he reached Mekte's unit, he read—hand-written in Kritas symbols—'Mekte, daughter of Yutki'. He looked at the scribbling for a moment, then he rested his palm on the entrance panel. The wall recognized him as a scholar and opened at once.

He stepped in and let the wall close behind him. The unit was empty except for a few essential elements of furniture. It looked like Mekte didn't have the time or the means to afford much but the strict necessities for survival.

He checked the sleeping cocoon, but it was cold and the regenerating foam had already lost the body shape memory. The girl must not have used it in days. The cooking area was clean, apart from a couple of sealed blobs, half empty. He dug a finger in one of them and smelled it. It was too rancid for his liking, but Kritas had different tastes.

Tancredi searched around and opened the storage compartments that were aligned into geometrical shapes following a basic symmetrical repetition. The mirroring of those shapes created a sense of harmony Kritas loved so much: a grid of polygons such as equilateral triangles, squares, or hexagons arranged into a regular tessellation. No matter how complex or intricate the design became, every pattern was repeated by the Kritas and infinitely extended to cover all available space. This was symbolic of their expansion into the galaxy, until they were confronted with the new race of man.

A large compartment opened with a huff. Clothing and personal affairs of mediocre quality filled the storage unit; so, the girl still lived here, but her absence seemed to have come unexpectedly.

He activated the neutron spectrometer. He set it to maximum penetration. He didn't know what he was searching for, but if anything was to be found, the device would reveal it, no matter how well concealed.

The device hummed, and the screen showed the molecular details and density of the floor it was pointed at. He started from there, exploring every square foot, but didn't find any suspicious density variations.

He sighed. Then he looked at every wall and surface, ceiling included. He let his gaze wander one last time around the unit.

Where are you, Mekte..., he thought. He put the spectrometer away and prepared to leave, shaking his head. Disappointed, he raised his palm to the panel and his hand stopped before touching its surface. The exit...how could he...

His heartbeat accelerated as he pulled out the neutron device again and switched it back on. He placed it against the exit wall. The device revealed metal, the same metal alloy of Kritas' warships.

The metallic lattice structure showed a subtle but clear change toward the middle. "You cannot fool neutrons," he said.

Tancredi activated the visual rendering and a small rectangular shape appeared within the wall. He rested his hand on the exit that opened...and watched as it carried with it the shape concealed inside. Clever. He let the wall close, and the shape took back its central position.

"Who are you, Mekte?" Tancredi voiced. He didn't have time to waste. He drew his blaster gun, pointed it at the wall, and opened fire. The biochemical bonds of the wall started to disintegrate. He continued until the central area collapsed and revealed what turned out to be a hidden compartment. It contained a bulky object. He took it out and placed the box on the small central table of the room. He examined it briefly.

The box had no visible details, other than a round depression on one of its longer sides. He pushed it, and the box emitted a sucking sound as air penetrated the interior. With a hiss, the side rose and opened in two flaps. Inside... "A book?" Tancredi exclaimed.

Questions filled his mind. Why and how would a young Kritas girl have such a rarity? It would have surely cost a fortune. He glanced at the anonymous back cover, took the book out, and put it on the table. Inside a deeper receptacle, he found a small data cube and a hand-blaster. Tancredi bent his head and smiled.

He took the data cube out, rested it on the table, and switched it on. Large Kritas' symbols blossomed and arranged above the cube. A text appeared. Tancredi's jaw dropped as he read aloud: "*Daimones – Dan Amenta's Chronicles.*"

He glanced back at the book he had laid down with the back cover up. Slowly, he opened it, and read the last words: "Quod Natura Munimento Inviderat Industria Adiecit. — What Nature denied for defense has been provided by the skills of men."

His heart pounded in his chest. He turned the book over and his eyes widened at the title, which claimed, in gold letters, "Our Heavenly Fathers – A Revelation."

He jolted. The swift sound of marine patrol vehicles reached him from street level. He grabbed the data cube and rushed out of the unit.

A few Kritas, too, had become alarmed. They had left their units and now occupied both ramps. "Get back inside!" Tancredi shouted as he ran down the spiral toward the exit. "Move away!"

Befuddled, many Kritas complied, disappearing behind their closing entry-walls. Only a few remained as paralyzed prey, eyes dilated, staring at him as he rushed by with the swiftness of a deadly predator.

The building's exit dilated and he strode out. A powerful white light blinded him and made him stop. An amplified voice ordered, "Scholar Gilmor. Don't move. You're under arrest."

CHAPTER 4 – THE INSURGENCE

BLOOD FOR BLOOD

MULTIPLE EXPLOSIONS ROCKED Utthana's Zero level during the early morning hours. Fires shed a colored light that painted the dark buildings with livid reflections. From the shadows and the dust, Kritas emerged, shocked.

Early workers and commuters lay wounded, calling for help. Throughout the city, patrol vehicles were on fire surrounded by soldiers' corpses, charred beyond recognition. Military checkpoints had also been the target of the attacks. Sirens screamed in all districts, and shady plumes of smoke cut through the sky from the smoldering ruins. The dawn fought against the darkness that morning, and lost.

Both emergency units and space marines swarmed the areas where the detonations occurred, and blocked all immediate access. It is then that the worst occurred. First witness accounts reported Kritas who walked—with a blank stare—toward the emergency units. Some, witnesses said, smiled just before the deflagration disintegrated their bodies and many of the nearby soldiers.

Casualties among the marines numbered in the hundreds. However, the news bulletins gave little details of the casualties suffered by the military, instead choosing to report a much higher number in the loss of Kritas' lives.

The smell of burned flesh hung in the air for hours. Thousands of military vessels traced the sky above and between Utthana's towering buildings, rising to over a mile above the ground. Armored units crowded the streets. Anti-riot fighters hovered, or drifted along all Zero's streets. Loudspeakers ordered Kritas to stay inside, warning that those caught wandering outside faced summary execution.

***

Tancredi woke up. He jumped off the resting shell with a sucking sound, before the nutritional, tissue-regenerating foam had finished retreating from his body. He looked around the unfamiliar room.

His clothing and tunic had been folded with care and lay on a bench. "News," he said; the dim radiance of a floating screen lit up the room.

The screen showed images of destruction, one after the other on the newscast. The headline stated: "Massive explosions rocked Utthana today. Stay tuned for an update in the next bulletin." He watched the scenes of death and destruction in silence for a few moments.

To his left, he noticed a live wall. He walked to it and let it dilate. A bathroom. Preceded by the floating screen, he walked toward the opening. A fluid sphere shimmered in the middle. Without a second thought, he took a breathing jelly that molded to his face and entered into the sphere. The screen adjusted to balance the visual distortions when it crossed the fluid barrier.

Tancredi floated motionless, his eyes riveted to the graphic scenes of the attack. His mind relived the last memories of his arrest the night before and wondered whether the two events had any correlation between them.

The image of an anchorwoman emerged. She pointed at the scenes on the screen, and captured his attention. "The first deflagrations shocked the peaceful Zero level this morning at time clicks 4000, or 3 a.m. Earth equivalent time. Overnight, flames colored the sky over the city with an oppressive orange curtain, and—by daybreak—heavy clouds of dust hovered over the entire level. Thick columns of black smoke rose from burning TEOs that appear to be among the main targets of the terrorists…"

The commentator's voice cracked when she reported the second wave of explosions. "Lt. Col. Michael Lerner, a spokesman for the marines, did not comment on the suicide attacks at the checkpoints, but he did say that the marines will increase patrols, and the response will be swift and decisive: 'We are determined to strike this organization and relieve all of us, humans and Kritas alike, of this murderous threat,' Lerner said."

The 3D rendering zoomed to the journalist reporting from the blast areas. "The extent of the destruction in Utthana became apparent during the first hours after daybreak. More than eight hundred Kritas have been killed and more than twenty-five hundred wounded in today's blasts, according to Roderick Norris, an Utthana health official. Authorities have estimated that the vast majority of those killed are civilians. The military reports only 'limited numbers' in the casualties suffered during the attacks."

Further scenes showed ground and air units swarming through Utthana from every marine station. "Law and order will be re-established immediately," the voice of Col. Lerner concluded.

Tancredi gestured the screens off, but ripples of scenes of mayhem and devastation lingered in his mind. The Authority will profit from this and squash the insurgence no matter the cost in lives, he reasoned.

He stepped off the fluid blob; the layer barrier removed all traces of humidity from his skin as he left the sphere. He went for his clothes.

"External view," he said, and a wall giving a view to the outside reduced its opacity. He looked out. He sighed, and shook his head; he had been brought back to the scholar's building, only not his private quarters. He strode toward the dashboard console and called the Dean's office.

The assistant answered. He recognized him. "Scholar Gilmor," he smiled in the hologram. "How may I help you this time?"

"I need to confer with the Dean."

At his words, a broader smile rose to the assistant's lips. "I'm afraid the Dean cannot be disturbed. I'm sure you're aware of the recent, unfortunate events…"

"Unfortunate? Interesting choice of words... I've been taken to this unit without any explanation. I don't know what I'm accused of, and—"

"I'm sure your curiosity will be satisfied soon. Good day, scholar Gilmor." The hologram faded back into the dashboard.

Tancredi sagged into a stool protruding off the floor. He breathed hard and checked in detail the rest of the dashboard communication links: all external nodes and connections to the Tribunal failed. 'Access Denied,' the floating words blinked mockingly at him; the residence unit had been sealed off. Apparently, the Dean's office was the only external connection he could get, and the official news channels of the Authority, of course, the only thing he could watch. He dressed then sat, again, staring at the void...

※

The insurgence had coordinated the attacks with precision and efficiency. Leadership had spread out to different underground bases to minimize the risk of ever being found—or killed—together. They expected harsh reactions from the humans, and the humans' response came, indeed, with no delay.

In the control room, in front of the main operational dashboard, Kaulm was examining the reports from his section leaders. One by one, they confirmed the success of their part of the operation.

"We have more targets," he smiled, detailing the objectives still remaining. "It is now or never."

In the holograms, the section leaders bowed in agreement, then faded away.

"So, it's decided..." Mekte walked to his side.

Kaulm faced her. "It is."

"We might have another option."

"It's too late, Mekte. Forget about that human." Kaulm devoted his attention to the operation dashboard. A few screens raised. "Units are getting in place for phase two, now." He didn't turn to look at her. "If I'm not mistaken, you're squad's ready, too. Go do your job."

Mekte's jaw tightened, but she nodded and left the control room.

*
**

Nighttime. The deserted roads conferred on Utthana an aura of menace that Mekte never had felt before in all her life. The humans had declared a strict curfew and stated with no uncertain terms that any violation would mean immediate capital punishment for any offenders. Kritas risked their life just being on the streets.

Mekte and her squad deployed swiftly for the ambush site and waited for the patrol to approach. They counted on their biometric implants to hide them from the marines' probes long enough to be able to carry out the surprise attack.

They had mined the road with a new passive technology—intended to be undetectable—that had never been tested in the field before. Manual activation required the presence and proximity of an operator; risky, but the squad knew the dangers and accepted them. Besides, their mission required conducting an all-out assault, leaving no survivors.

The shadows, and the rundown conditions of the Under level industrial suburbs helped conceal their presence.

The ground under Mekte transmitted the rhythmic vibrations from the armoured vehicles of the marines' patrol. The tremor had a strange effect on her, a sensuous one, even; the voluptuous attractiveness of death that only comes from a chasmic despair. She breathed hard and closed her eyes. She was about to flirt with a murderous lover.

Her fingers clutched on the sten-blaster. She held it close to her breast as if it meant salvation rather than perdition.

The humans' vehicles shed a brutal, blinding light all around; the rays of their scanners cut through the dusty air as sharp as scalpels.

The Kritas had chosen an area where the small, single-pilot fighters had trouble venturing, and the humans had to execute a door-to-door search of the factories and the utility buildings supported only by armored ground units. The marines advanced yard by yard, deadly as lava scorching a plain.

At each building, small spider-drones dashed inside, in search of a biological target. When they returned from their tasks, having mapped the entire zone during their search, the marines rushed in for a further, meticulous scan. The resounding "Clear!" cries meant they had slain no lives and that the curfew held.

The Kritas exchanged worried looks. The humans proceeded too slowly and were too cautious. They still had time to discover the mines and spoil the Kritas mission. Every click was a click too many, but Mekte signaled that the plan continued. She eyed the first armored vehicle, and her hand reached for the detonator. Yet a few more time clicks, and one more building, then the column of vehicles would enter the blast area.

The vibrations faded away as the vehicles halted and released the drones. One more building, one more "Clear!"

Her hand trembled on the detonator, and she had to stare at it to stop the shaking. She risked peeking at the marines one more time, then she lay down for better cover.

***

Tancredi jumped to his feet when the eidolon of the Dean formed in the middle of the room. The lack of any shadow was the only telltale sign that she wasn't there, in person, with him.

"Tancredi."

She never had called him by his name before. He'd always been 'Gilmor' or 'scholar'. His eyebrows rose for a brief instant, and he tried to hide it, exerting himself into a profound bow.

"You've been of great help," the Dean said. "Are you aware of the importance of what you've discovered?"

Tancredi straightened up. "The books?"

The Dean nodded.

"How could a Kritas have such a possession?" He frowned.

"How could an insurgent Kritas not, rather?" She stared at him. "But our worries grow with each of your actions."

Tancredi glared. "I would have reported my findings."

"Would you have indeed?" She paused, and her lips contracted. "You acted alone, hid your plans from fellow scholars, and didn't alert the marines." She breathed out. "You even hurt one."

Tancredi opened his mouth, but the Dean raised one hand to silence him. "The Marine High Command requested a formal investigation, and the Governor authorized an extensive probing of your mind to seek for your real motivations."

"I'm a loyal servant of the Law; my intents are honest and—"

"I came to forewarn you," she stopped him. "But I cannot make exceptions. Tomorrow morning, the military command will transfer you to the marines' security ward for interrogation. You've been brought here only temporarily." She stared at him for a long moment. "It's all I've been able to do."

The words of Tancredi's old master at the law school resonated in his mind: *"Our duty is to make the exceptionless the only meaningful rule."* He stared back and pronounced unimaginable words for a scholar. "Maybe we need exceptions when faced with the brutality of the rules."

The Dean goggled at him, and Tancredi's lips contracted as he realized the enormity of what he had just said, but withstood her gaze.

She sighed and puckered her eyebrows. "Maybe the marines aren't wrong for requesting a thorough probing of you." She shook her head. "I leave you with that thought, scholar."

The Dean's image froze, became opaque, and disappeared. Tancredi stumbled and fell back on the stool.

In her office, the Dean sealed the room and opened the quantum link. "I sensed trouble, surprise, but his determination is very strong. I believe he will act tonight."

The tall figure nodded.

*
**

Mekte's hand contracted on the detonator; her pupils widened. She shivered and exchanged a frantic look with the other squad members. "It doesn't work," she hissed in the squad channel. "For Kritas' sake. They're almost upon us!"

Mekte glanced toward a utility bunker next to the mined area. She squeezed the detonator one more time. "It's dead." She turned over. "Abort, abort!"

"No!" a Kritas shouted. The first succession of blaster shots screeched as he scrambled out of his cover, firing at the marines. Mekte gasped in horror.

The first line of humans fell, as the surprise had given the Kritas a few instants of advantage. He kept running, strafing when the marines reacted and opened fire in return.

The armored vehicles guns aimed and acquired the target. From the bunker, a deluge of fire erupted. Blinding bolts hit their turrets, while the exposed Kritas dashed forward and blasted shots aimed at the ground, missing the vehicles and the marines who took cover behind them.

Mekte understood what he was trying to accomplish and her heart sunk. "Fire. Fire!" she yelled.

Targeted from multiple locations, the marines regrouped behind the vehicles and concentrated their shots in an attempt to pin the enemy.

A cry of rage and pain covered the screeching noises of the blasters. The Kritas fighter twisted mid-air, and fumes rose where the protections had melted after a blow hit his right leg. He rolled to the ground and screamed with a long, guttural holler that reminded Mekte of the wild reptiles of the desert.

The turrets opened fire, and massive explosions shook the ground and the surrounding buildings. The hits crumbled the walls, and a cascade of debris covered the area. The smell of ozone added to the acrid taste of dirt down her throat. She was about to die, she thought. Blinded by the thick dust, she kept firing at the marines scattering her shots, not caring anymore about her cover and her safety.

In the middle of the street, the wounded Kritas rose on his knees and screamed with a high pitch when his leg separated in slow motion from his hip. He fell to the side, but pushed on the ground with his elbow and fired one last full energy bolt.

A huge ball of fire erupted. The blast-wave lifted Mekte mid-air with a roaring rumble and sent her flying down the street, in the open. Screams of pain and agony, both Kritas and humans, reached her buzzing ears. She didn't know where or who she was, and the warm air felt thick and viscous like oil, blocking her attempts to move.

Two hands grabbed and dragged her away. Then, a loud sound of thunder invaded her ears, and all was silent and dark.

Chapter 5 – Where Art Thou

I Was Afraid, Because I Was Naked

THAT NIGHT, TANCREDI STOOD SILENT in his house arrest scholar's unit. He thought about the Dean's words. He couldn't allow the military to proceed with the probing. He hadn't considered this eventuality, but the current situation had forced his decision.

His medallion shone in the darkness as he extended his senses and projected his essence, like tentacles tapping around in search for the fuzzy twister of sensations and images he could capture from other minds.

He walked to the exit wall and placed his hand on it. Breaching the wall security hadn't required much effort, to his surprise, and the wall dilated without delay. For a moment, he waited at the threshold, motionless, and listened with all his senses. He waited for the stomping sound of troopers' boots running down the corridor, for the shouts and the many hands to grab and slam his body on the floor. He waited. Nothing happened.

He leaned forward, only to meet a deserted passage. He hesitated, still. A faithful scholar would have waited until dawn and faced, even welcomed, the opportunity to demonstrate he had no faults, that no cracks had tarnished his faith. His heartbeat rose, where was his faith? But he had a certainty that went beyond faith in the Law and the Scholars.

He stepped outside and the wall coalesced behind him. He sharpened further his empathic skills and used them as a light in the darkness, to ensure his path was clear.

Before he reached the end of the corridor, he froze. His heart pounded in his chest, when a wave of rage and alarm hit his mind. Images of a violent fight with a young man, a scholar, apparently, flooded his induced spatial visualization.

He exhaled hard when he realized he had picked up a nightmare from a scholar asleep in her cell down the corridor.

He reached the entrance hall and the exit without further incidents. Once outside, he looked back at the scholars' building. Maybe that was his last chance to reach his residential unit again, but undoubtedly all his belongings had been confiscated for examination. He raised his shoulders; no one in Ahthaza had the means to extract any information or collect evidence against him. The loss, though, was not a recoverable one either. He took a deep breath.

His mind recalled the images of the young Kritas female—an impostor, a member of the insurgence, perhaps—and of her books; in his mind, he could see her fingers following his traits in the rendering at the TEO, he could almost feel her touch. He looked around and left everything behind, firmly decided to find answers.

*
**

A blade of light cut through the darkness. The implant in Mekte`s brain activated at once and a burning sensation spread through the back of her neck. She woke up. A tremor from the floor rose through her spine, and a low thrumming resonated around her.

One strong hand clasped around her mouth and muffled her mounting groan. "Shhhh," a whisper blew into her ear.

Her eyes widened and she tried to rise, but someone forced her back down using the full weight of his body. "Don't move, or we're dead," said the raucous whisperer.

She didn't dare budge, and kept watching the light blade sweep through cracks on a collapsed wall to her right until it disappeared. The tremor faded away.

An acrid stench reached her nostrils, and she tried to turn her head away. The hand contracted and held her firm, then it relaxed a bit. "Promise me to be quiet. We should be safe, for now," the voice rustled.

She attempted a nod.

Her unknown companion lifted his hand and sat upright.

She pushed herself on one elbow and whispered, "Where am I?"

A ruffling sound and the floating screen of a security device blossomed with a soft humming and provided some light.

"You scared me," the voice spoke with a normal tone, this time.

She squinted toward the faint glow, but couldn't see his face. "Khulel? Is that you?"

"Still alive." The Kritas smiled. "We're the only survivors, for all I know."

She brought one hand to her face. "I remember an explosion close to my position; nothing else. Did you bring me here? Thank you."

"Of course," he said. "Three days ago."

"What?" She tried to sit up, but the whole world spun and a black curtain fell over her eyes.

"Take it easy!" Khulel wrapped an arm around her shoulders and lowered her down with care. "I feared I'd lost you. You vomited blood, and I had nothing to stop internal bleeding. I thought I would have to watch you die. Then, it stopped."

A diffused pain enveloped her body like a shroud; she took a deep lungful of air. "Why're we still here?"

Khulel grunted. "All around buzzes with humans, and we have no means to communicate with base."

"So, no rescue's coming…"

"Afraid not."

Mekte nodded. "What happened?"

"After the blast?" Khulel gave a nod, too. "I thought you were dead and was leaving, but you jerked. I managed to carry you away. Found this place. Our implants hid our presence. As you saw, they keep looking." He waved the floating screen to shed light around. "We're inside a maintenance waterway, half obstructed by debris. I added some more after I got you here." He nodded at the broken wall. "Are you thirsty?"

Mekte shook her head. "My throat is a knot."

"You need to drink some." Khulel plunged a piece of fabric into a broken pipe and brought it to her lips. "Don't worry about the taste. It's bitter but it's safe."

Her nictitating membranes blinked back the moisture in her eyes. "Thank you." She smiled.

"Human troops are everywhere and shout warnings that it's too dangerous for Kritas to stay," Khulel said. "The humans are deporting everybody, and Zero has become a buffer zone." He paused and sighed. "Those who come out in the open are crammed inside military vehicles and taken away. There's a curfew enforced every night."

Mekte looked at him sideways.

"What?" Khulel wrinkled his brow. "How do I know all this? I didn't just sit here watching you for three days."

Mekte searched his eyes. "What do we do now?"

"We stay alive, and we try to find our way out of this mess." Khulel stood up. "Ah, one more thing." He stared back at her. "Who's Tancredi?"

Mekte stared back at him, eyes wide open and mouth agape. She frowned.

"You talked through your hallucinations," he muttered.

*
**

Tancredi spent the rest of the night hiding, and only his training as a scholar saved him from being spotted by patrolling units. The military couldn't have improvised such a deployment so soon, he reasoned; someone had to have planned it ahead of time.

From his hiding place, he observed the operation that had started before the first light of day and continued since, uninterrupted.

Marines escorted Kritas out of buildings, block by block. Over the course of a few hours, he witnessed Kritas aligned by the hundreds waiting for their turn to be examined by mental probe devices before boarding military transporters that landed and took off from the nearby large avenue.

A marine thrust the mouth of his blaster into the chest of a Kritas who collapsed to the ground, out of breath. "Take this one out." Two soldiers rushed to carry the Kritas away.

Loudspeakers repeated the same message at regular intervals. "Stay within the lines. Your security is our primary concern. Stay calm and cooperate. Stay within the lines."

Other cries and groans marked further marines interventions when some Kritas, apparently, couldn't manage to 'stay calm and cooperate.'

Once at full capacity, the transporters lifted off with their load of prisoners for unknown destinations, all while more landed, taking the spot left vacant. Singled out Kritas ended up into military ground vehicles that came and went, too, unrelenting.

Battleships had shown up above Utthana's sky, and Tancredi wondered whether that was maybe the Kritas' ultimate destination.

Past mid-day, the deportation had to involve many thousands, at least. Meanwhile, marines in riot gear poured into the intra-levels checkpoint gates, and the Under levels were exactly where Tancredi believed he needed to return to as soon as possible.

Before the fall of the night, military authorities ordered all 'law-abiding' Kritas still at the Zero level to return to their residence units and to respect the curfew. "Violators will face summary execution," a flat, monotonic voice repeated the menace at short intervals.

Tancredi left his hideout and mingled with the late Kritas who rushed to leave the streets under the watch of marine patrols. He reached a checkpoint gate. The "Humans Only - Life Danger" signal shone with impudence and shed light across the intersection in an otherwise left-in-the-dark area. The military had locked down all access points with the same force field that protected humans-only zones. Harmless for a human body, and usually distressful for a Kritas, the military had turned it into a lethal trap. The act of crossing the barrier recombined the molecular bonds in the synapse-like connections of a Kritas' brain, making them fall unconscious in seconds. Now death occurred instead.

Patrols swept the Zero level's deserted streets with an increased rate, but the time lapse was large enough for Tancredi to enter the threshold, unseen.

*
**

In the feeble light of the floating panel, Khulel stared at Mekte. "Are you serious?"

"What do we have to lose? Or I…"

"I don't know." Khulel shook his head. "Even if you're right, we're talking about a scholar, not just any human."

"That's exactly why it's so important."

"I'd suggest you keep this to yourself, for the time being." Khulel checked the area outside the waterway, beyond the debris. "Right now, our goal is to get out of here safely, and make contact with the others."

With an effort, Mekte stood up; the inquisitive eyes of her companion analyzed each of her movements. She winced. "How do you feel?" Khulel asked.

"I couldn't assault another humans' patrol, but I can walk." She attempted a forced smile.

"Ok." He nodded. "Curfew will be enforced again soon. We'll move then."

The streets and the neighboring area emptied in advance of the official nightfall time for the Under levels. Khulel and Mekte checked the surroundings once more, and exchanged a mute look. Without a word, they climbed over the debris and made their way to the waterway's opening.

They advanced through an eerie 1U, darker than Mekte could ever recall. An unnatural silence morphed their steps into a noisy disturbance. With its tickling sensation, the biometric implant embedded within their brain warned them of incoming patrols and helped them steer away from their paths.

As they advanced, a sudden and sinister screeching sound of marines' blasters broke the silence, probably marking the end of more Kritas' lives.

"We can't go on like this." Mekte pulled Khulel's vest.

Khulel pushed her into the dark shadows of an underpass. "Are you okay?" He examined her quickly.

Mekte's lips trembled and her eyes' membranes fought to get rid of the tears that blocked her vision. She pushed him away. "We'll all die."

"Shut up." He slammed her against the wall. "Just shut up!"

Mekte sobbed. "How many more lives, Khulel?" She lowered her head. "You need to help me. Please."

He sighed, guessing her goal. "The human?"

"I need to find him."

A flash blinded them for an instant, followed by the thunder of the explosion. They cowered. Slabs in the pavement popped out, and dust covered the whole area after the shock wave rolling above hit them. Sirens echoed down in the streets, followed by the piercing, loud howls of military vehicles. The humans converged toward the blast area. Mekte and Khulel ran in the opposite direction.

***

The evacuation the military had enacted allowed him to find shelter in abandoned residences of 1U. From a distance, he now looked like all other Kritas workers, and he pursued his quest, having decided to find the one person who could bring some light into what seemed a black hole of violence.

During day time, when the military allowed workers in 1U streets, Tancredi was careful to avoid attracting any attention, limiting to follow the flow of commuters and probing with the lightest of touch. At the law school, during the interrogation tutorials, he perfected non-intrusive mind exploration methods that left the target unaware of the probing, although the information thus obtained lacked complex details.

He searched for the strong reactions the presence and behavior of the marines' patrols provoked in nearby Kritas; he searched for determination, for anything different than fear, resignation, and frustration. Anger and resolve would have given him a clue, like a beacon, someone to follow and probe with more determination, or even question directly.

Insurgents, for how submissive and obedient they might have acted, he was sure would have revealed cold and analytical minds.

No fear, but hate; no frustration, rather indignation; no resignation, but eagerness, and marines' troops would be seen just as targets to an insurgent's mind.

He spent the first two days near the areas affected by recent attacks, where the feelings might have been the strongest. He kept a safe distance from the patrols and the checkpoints.

In the first days, he gambled with his life also during the nights, when—he reasoned—the insurgents might be more active, giving him a chance to find them, but he only got to witness marines shooting Kritas during the curfew without a warning, in cold blood, and with a cold spirit. He gasped each time for air when the execution happened, and when the anguish of the dying Kritas reached him. There were no scholars around to warn the marines that those Kritas constituted no threat, and he had to resist the urge to make them stop the killing.

Many need to see and fear what we've become, he thought. On the last execution, he waited for the marines to leave the area, reached and knelt next to the dead Kritas. *"We need to climb out, out of this pit of destruction,"* he thought.

He grabbed the body by the shoulders, and made it turn. It felt light in his hands. He closed his eyes in pain, and shed tears. A Kritas girl, the back of her skull obliterated by the blaster; on her face, a sweet smile harbored as if she finally had been liberated. He thanked the heavens she wasn't the one he was looking for. In the desolated streets, no one heard him crying.

On a few occasions, Kritas had recognized him as a human, and Tancredi feared they'd betray him to the marines. To his surprise, they never did. They exchanged a mute look, with surprise at first, and then with a begging in their Kritas' eyes, as if they felt he wasn't just another human...for only a moment, though, before a veil fell over their inner light and all connection vanished.

The violence escalated with a pace that shocked him. There hadn't been a day without an attack, without a Kritas walking up to a patrol or approaching a checkpoint and causing a massacre. An act of desperation, of rebellion, and of defiance.

For every Kritas who committed suicide, tens of marines caused more deaths. The marines reacted with more brutality and were now shooting on sight in the face of any suspicious activity. As a word, 'humanity' had lost its meaning. Tancredi suffered the pain from every killing.

The area he was probing that day had seen one of the most brutal attacks of the previous days: a coordinated assault on a marines' convoy that had left many bodies on the ground, Kritas and humans alike.

The official news at the public info-pole screens scattered all over Utthana reported a great victory for the Authority's troops, and the scenes showed—for the most—the dead bodies of many Kritas assailants. Buildings had crumbled, and debris had tumbled down through structures still standing like shattered trees of a maimed petrified forest.

The main blast had left a large, oblong crater that reached both edges of the avenue. Nobody had removed the rubble or cared to. For days, the news flooded the bulletins with the blind violence of the extremist terrorists and how they succeeded only in being killed, leaving no survivors, and destroying properties, hurting all population.

Many Kritas continued to pass by the site, slowing down, and even stopping for a moment under the glare of the marines, and accepting with passivity to be probed and scanned while doing so. Tancredi only sensed sorrow and sadness, souls broken from the loss of all hope. For some, a desire of revenge clutched their heart for a moment, with an intensity that stopped the breathing, but it was soon repressed.

He needed to risk more, Tancredi reasoned, maybe even follow some of the most reactive. He tried to identify his target.

A Kritas bumped into him and didn't stop to excuse himself. Tancredi startled and turned to watch him disappear around a corner.

"Don't turn!" A voice at his back froze him. "Who are you?"

He sensed a Kritas behind him.

"What are you doing here?" The Kritas grunted. "Dressed like a worker, but you work nowhere. You lurked for days. What do you want?"

"I intend no harm." Tancredi whispered and extended his mind to appease and relax.

The Kritas snorted. "Ah. A scholar, even. I should kill you right now." A jet of saliva syphoned out from the Kritas mouth and landed on Tancredi's boot.

Tancredi retreated his mental touch. "Wait! I'm looking for someone."

The Kritas didn't reply.

"A girl. She looked for me at a TEO."

Tancredi sensed hesitation and doubt.

"You didn't say *a Kritas*. You said a girl..." The voice paused. "What do you want from her?"

"I want to give her what she wants from me."

Silence. Tancredi tilted his head. "Is she with the insurgence?" He risked.

The Kritas breathed hard. "First, stop probing Kritas around. Second, I might contact you again."

"Where will I find you?"

"You won't."

The rustle of receding steps faded in the distance; the Kritas had left. Tancredi turned around, but none of the bystanders seemed to have noticed anything. He avoided making contact with anyone's eyes.

A marine patrol approached, and Tancredi joined the flow of people leaving the area.

Chapter 6 - But Mere Mortals

That Thou Art Mindful of Them

MEKTE SAT ON A SMOOTH, concave metallic pillar in the middle of a small, empty room, and waited. The sharp light from the walls blinded her. She knew other eyes observed her. Probes captured all her mental and biometric parameters: the implant tickled in her head without pause, but its masking properties had been overruled.

She had already told the truth and every detail she remembered about the mission. For sure, Khulel had done the same. She shifted her weight on the stool and stared at the metal door. She breathed with long, slow breaths.

"Who is Tancredi Gilmor?" A loud voice resonated in the room.

Mekte jolted, and then hesitated for a short moment to find the right words, how to explain, make them understand, but she changed her mind at the last moment. "A scholar," she sighed.

Silence. Then, the same voice asked her in an urgent tone, "Have you met with him before?"

Mekte kept staring at the door. "No, not in person at least. I searched for his records at a TEO, and —."

The voice interrupted. "Does he know anything about you?"

"No! How could he?" Mekte protested, but then her stare blanked. "I don't know. Why are you asking?"

The door slid into the wall and a figure camped in the middle. She squinted her eyes, but the light was too strong to see anything more than a dark silhouette.

"Because he searched your residence unit, and he's looking for you."

Mekte turned her gaze away, her mouth opened. She had recognized the voice. She looked back. "Kaulm, I'm no traitor. I never met with him."

Kaulm stepped forward, and the light's intensity dimmed back to normal. The door slid and closed with a huff. A metal stool emerged from the floor. He took seat. "I wonder, Mekte. I wonder whether your actions betrayed us all already."

She stiffened. "Am I on the wanted list?"

"No, and that's surprising. There's no mention of your name anywhere."

She tilted her head, and then leaned forward. "What do you mean by 'he's looking for me'?"

Kaulm stared at her. "Because your Tancredi Gilmor wanders through the whole 1U seeking a girl. And that girl is you."

Mekte's eyes widened. "Let me meet with him!"

Kaulm stood up, and the stool receded into the floor. He walked to the exit.

"Let me do it." Mekte pleaded and stood up as well.

The door opened. Kaulm talked over his shoulder. "We'll see. They'll take you to the infirmary now."

Two guards entered and glared at her. Kaulm left.

"Kaulm." Mekte limped forward, but the guards blocked her way. "Kaulm!"

***

In her office, the Dean checked the newest reports on the main dashboard. On one side, a floating screen showed the official bulletin bearing the AHA crest of the 'Ahthaza Human Authority,' while on the other side, an anchorwoman resumed the latest events, "The recent escalation of the insurgency's violence has caused the loss of hundreds of innocent civilian lives. The Authority's fast intervention has restored, though, the order in the Zero level.

"Lt. Col. Michael Lerner, here, agreed to comment on the situation with us: 'We are appalled by the cruelty that is manifest in the extremists' actions. It is obvious their goal is to spread terror among the population. Their absolute lack of respect for Kritas' lives have prompted the Authority to proceed with an emergency evacuation of all areas at risk in order to protect lives. Zero level is now patrolled by sentinel drones and the situation is totally under control.'"

The scene changed to show images of the drones patrolling the streets, swiveling at corners as they balanced on their six legs.

The anchorwoman's face appeared again and she continued. "Thank you, Colonel Lerner. Today marks one week since the first attacks to Zero's infrastructures, perpetrated by violent extremists, shocked Utthana. Targeted civilian transportation—"

The Dean gestured at the screen and it faded away.

The private, direct quantum link to her office activated. She looked at the tall figure that formed in front of her desk, and bowed. "Tancredi has just been contacted."

"Good. Does he suspect anything?"

The Dean shook her head. "No, we've been very careful."

"Excellent. Keep monitoring, and keep me posted." The rendering faded and the link interrupted.

"As you wish, Governor." The Dean sighed, alone, in her office. A frown crinkled her forehead and she stared at the empty space where the Governor had stood. The book floating above a relucent pedestal attracted her gaze.

***

Trapped between two clashing worlds, now Tancredi was also trapped in the Under levels, too; although risky, he had attempted to go back to Mekte's residence, but the Authority had declared an exclusion zone for the entire Zero level. No Kritas, no humans, no one but military and scholars could access the area. He surely was a scholar, but not one welcomed there anymore; he scoffed at the thought.

The day the military shut down the facilities, he had approached a transition gate; marines guarded the access non-stop, flanked by a sentinel drone. If the "Trespassers will be shot" warning signs weren't dissuasive enough, the sight of glaring soldiers and their drawn out sten-blasters were, for sure. He could not trust his luck this time and renounced.

With the increased security measures, the suicide attacks petered out, and 1U lived through a pause in the violent episodes, but tension veiled everything like a shroud wherever he went.

He didn't want to ruin his chances to find the Kritas girl, so he refrained—as he had been asked—to probe anyone but the marines, and these last only for his own protection.

To his satisfaction, his empathic skills told him of a new factor: Kritas now followed him. Oh, they were careful, never the same one, and never for too long, but their minds' focus lingered around his person, and he sensed the mental transition when one 'handed him over' to the next: the release from one mind, and the embrace into another ran over his skin like a shiver that grabs you when a cloud briefly hides the sun, until the warmth caresses you again a moment later.

He played their game, mingled with the workers when their shifts ended and they filled the streets to rejoin their dormitories, and kept wandering with the others who left theirs, heading to a new shift.

He kept walking when someone muttered behind him, "Tomorrow, and the days that follow." A hand pressed a small object into his. "Keep it with you at all times. Use your imagination, scholar."

Tancredi clinched his fist around it, then, after waiting for the Kritas to walk away, he opened it to glance at a data cube glaring in his palm.

He smiled; he had taken the first step, though he had no idea where the stairs would lead him.

He reached the dark halls of the abandoned building he used as a hideout. His mind extended: he was alone. He activated the data cube and heard a voice, *her* voice. He wouldn't need to be a scholar to also feel the depth of her soul, too.

*
**

Mekte remembered Kaulm words: "For this operation, you will be on your own," but she wasn't worried. It could have been a trap, a tricky human's way to creep into her mind and attack the insurgence at its core. She had agreed with Kaulm, she had to do it by herself and with her own resources.

At the base, she had recorded a message for 'her scholar', as Khulel called him. He had listened to her words as she prepared the data cube. "Are you sure?" he frowned.

"No," she sighed. "But he's different."

"Well, he behaved," he donned, "and refrained from using his skills on me."

Mekte looked at him and blinked. "Thanks for helping me with Kaulm."

Khulel laughed. "Back at the waterway, your feverish gibbering was crazy enough to be believable." He leaned closer and touched her nose. "But tell me," he grinned. "Could it be that you like him?"

She punched him on his chest. "He's a human!"

"Well, they're not that different from us. Some of their females are attractive, actually." He chuckled. "They seem to be aroused all the time."

Mekte gasped. "Khulel!"

They both laughed. How she longed for that laughter together.

"So, when will you meet him?"

"Soon, I hope."

***

Three days. Three days had passed. Tancredi feared he had misunderstood the message. She had said, *'Our paths will cross underneath where you felt despair while everybody else saw threats...'* and *'when your path diverged to meet with mine.'*

He believed she'd given him a location and a time, but now he wasn't as certain as when he heard those words the first time.

He spent mornings roaming the 1U district right under the Alliance Square, above on the Zero level. He remembered that gloomy day and the thick clouds. The only threat he perceived came from the marines and their hostility. Doubts marred his unyielding resolve to apply the law. His path had diverged, and he became estranged from his own people.

Under the increased security measures, the 1U had become a huge prison camp. Sentinels crisscrossed the city and probed Kritas. The drones couldn't do the same with a scholar's mind; nonetheless he kept away, each time, the tremor in the soil warning him of their approach.

Kritas observed him, he didn't really need to use his skills to feel their 'eyes' following his every movement, but that reassured him, rather; it meant he could be contacted again, soon.

To spend the nights, he had chosen the most remote 1U suburbs, thinking they might have given him more protection, but that early morning, when everything was still engulfed in the darkness of the curfew, he woke up to the shouts of soldiers.

The screeching sound of the restraining beams tore the pervasive silence that enveloped the blocks every night. Muffled screams and cries came from the street level.

He scrambled out of his hideout in the rubble of a building the marines had flattened only the day before as retaliation against a suspected insurgent who had lived there. He took cover and peeked.

The marines had unfinished business in the area. A group of Kritas knelt in front of a platoon equipped in heavy riot gears. The docking bay of a military shuttle lurked like a gigantic red eye, and sentinel drones blocked both ends of the streets. Their lights flooded the scene.

A soldier bent and shouted inches away from the face of one of the prisoners. "Lower your eyes, scum." He hit his temple with the blaster. The Kritas collapsed to the ground.

Someone cried, a Kritas female, kneeling down with her children. "I don't know where my son is," she screamed to the soldier who was questioning her. Tancredi touched her mind and tears came to his eyes. A dreadful sensation of hopelessness and mortality twisted his guts; the ghastly feeling of being worthless and impotent before injustice.

A mental impact like a gust of wind coming his way startled him; he recognized the scanning probe of a nearby scholar.

He shut his mind, and, undetected, retreated deeper into the rubble until he found a niche below the street level. The 'wind' scanned the area, bending and twisting, searching with an invisible, subtle touch.

At the law school, Tancredi excelled at that game, a hide-and-seek played at a mental level. He never thought one day he'd have to resort to that skill against another scholar to save his own life. He wrapped his consciousness into a veil of voidness.

The wind approached, found the niche, and lingered on. It twirled as if it had gotten trapped for a moment, and settled before it moved along the walls, tapping hesitantly in its search. Then, it breezed out.

On the street, the scholar shouted his orders. "The area's clear. Take these ones to the Tribunal."

"Aye aye, sir."

Tancredi cringed at the scratching sound of bodies being dragged away on the pavement; the Kritas' cries vanished when the marines locked them inside the shuttle. The swooshing sound of the vehicle lifting off made him breathe with relief mixed with anger.

Blades of light flashed through the debris as the Sentinels once more checked the surroundings. After a few minutes, all was dark, yet again; the soil transmitted the fading vibrations of the drones leaving the area. He closed his eyes. He was ready to cross a chasm his soul had yet to recognize.

*
**

Mekte woke up soaked to the skin with her sweat. Tiny beads gave her perlaceous reflections. She dreamed about him, but it had been more a vision than a dream. His eyes, black and burning like coal, penetrated her, and fire erupted from his orbits and consumed her, transformed her, transfigured her purest inner essence.

They became two pulsating blobs of energy, attracted to one another. Filaments protruded in the space between them and interlaced. Then, they accelerated, pulled toward each other and a huge, silent flash burst when they collided; the vision imploded, and she awoke.

She shivered and sat on the edge of her cot. She let her legs dangle and scratched her feet together. Stretching, she felt the solid reassurance of the ground with the tip of her toes.

She checked the time; just past 5000 clicks, but she was in no mood to try to catch more rest. She stood up and glanced at her cot; the humid stain matched her body shape. She shook her head.

That was the day. That was the time when her hopes and her dreams would meet reality. She undressed and rubbed her skin to help it reabsorb the humidity. The unmistakable fragrance of her excitement hit her nostrils; the vision had enraptured her.

She reached the bath and took a deep breath to spend a few minutes in the balm cocoon; the only luxury they had at that base. She preferred holding her breath over using a respiratory membrane. She thought of her vision again and, floating, embraced her legs.

When she stepped out, her breasts were turgid and her skin released again the flavours of her excitation. She damned Khulel for having put ideas into her young mind.

She cleared her mind of all thoughts and waited for her mammary glands to shrink to normal shape before putting her clothes on. The door signaled the presence of a visitor.

She caressed the entry visor and examined for a moment the person who waited outside her unit. She sighed, and then activated the audio-only interface. She waited.

"You're awake. I passed by to wish you good luck."

"Yes, I'm awake. Thank you," she said.

"May I come in?"

She glanced to the floor. Her hand moved. The entrance opened.

Mekte smiled. "Good morning, Kaulm."

He raised his hand to show two fluid blobs. "I brought some treat. It's at the perfect degree of fermentation."

Mekte's eyes widened. "Where did you find those?"

"Some of us have connections in the Above levels." He smiled.

"It's been ages since I have tasted the last one." Mekte reached out with one hand, but Kaulm raised his even more. "There's a catch."

"Always with you." She tilted her head. "What do you want from me?"

"Nothing. Just you to have this." He opened the other hand to reveal a shiny, tiny oblong cell. "The treat is to make the pain more tolerable."

She frowned. "I see. I'm really on my own on this."

Kaulm lips tightened. "I'm sure you'll do the right thing in case you've fallen into a trap." He paused. "I'm sorry, but—"

"I know." Mekte's eyes stared at the explosive device and drew her hand out.

He nodded. "A drink, first. To life."

"To hope!" Mekte took one of the blobs and plunged her tongue in, followed by Kaulm. The taste brought her memories she thought long gone, when her parents were still alive. Her eye membranes chased the tears away.

Kaulm lips tightened. He took her hand and placed the cell on her palm. He activated it, and Mekte repressed a scream. The cell penetrated into her flesh and released a tissue regenerating drug that burned like a blaster jolt.

"It's programmed to sense the pressure of your fingers and—"

"I know how it works," Mekte cut him short. "One impulse to activate it, two within one click to detonate it."

"If you're captured, you'll take down many with you."

"Thanks for these reassuring words." Her half-smile mocked him. "You're right, though," she dropped the now-empty blob. "It was at the perfect degree of fermentation."

***

In the insurgents' main base in 2U, the surveillance screens shone bright in the dimmed light of the crypt hosting the control room.

Kaulm's voice sounded cold and deprived of all emotions. "What's the status?" He stared at the agent bent over at the main station.

"The nanobots she ingested have reached their destinations and are all functional. Biometrics are normal, for the situation." The agent raised his gaze to meet Kaulm's. "If it's a trap, we'll leave no one standing. The bomb is active now."

A long moment of silence followed, broken only by the humming of the bioputers that powered the duty stations aligned along the rocky walls in the crypt.

"Right." Kaulm looked away. "Anyway, we have to avoid her capture at all costs." He nodded. "The risk's too great," he muttered to himself, firmly convinced that no single Kritas life was more important than the whole.

The agent reacted at the last remark, as if Kaulm had spoken to him. "Risk is contained. Our agents are nearby and the marines' deployment hasn't changed in these last days. Although their number would be enough to swipe the market clear with little effort, the explosion will obliterate the whole area. We'd suffer ourselves very few casualties."

Kaulm glanced at the floating screens that showed the position of the insurgent agents. "Good. Even if nothing happens, keep monitoring her every movement."

"Understood."

He turned toward a Kritas who had stood a step behind him during the conversation. "Khulel, keep an eye on her. Let's not rush to conclusions too soon."

Khulel nodded; then continued to survey the operation.

CHAPTER 7 – IN HER NAME

REASONS OF THE HEART

IT NEVER REALLY RAINED in the underground levels, but the humidity charged the air as if the whole 1U had become a dank crypt. The damp clothes weighed heavy on his shoulders.

City services had degraded; the heightened security measures impacted the efficiency of the Kritas work force; meanwhile, deportations counted already in the tens of thousands.

It dribbled a dusty mizzle from the high vaults and the ceilings, and rubble littered the streets. There wasn't a block without a destroyed or abandoned building. Fierce urban conflicts had defaced the under levels.

Tancredi neared the expected meeting place with the Kritas girl. The memories and the feelings of the previous night still haunted him. Misery and desolation were like heavy rain in a cold, strong wind; they clouded the vision, made you gasp for air, and stole your warmth until all that remained was despair, and the only desire left was for anything that might give you shelter.

What are we doing? He thought.

He searched in his heart and in his brain, but no answer came to lessen his trouble. Yet, he had only certainties when he left the law school heading for his assignment and mission at the Utthana Tribunal. Waves of frustration seeped into the hearts of many, but despite all the misery, he had witnessed some sweet moments shining in the darkness like feeble flames. Despite all the hardships, Kritas' resilience had made them return to the streets.

Tancredi glanced around. For a time, in between work shifts, the streets had regained the characteristic noisy presence of bargain shoppers. He directed his steps into the maze of the open market.

The sentinel drones maintained their positions at the margins of the area, their flexible body structures bent like a U, both tail and head guns pointed at the market stalls. He sensed their intrusive scans on the population.

In the past days, he had noticed how marine patrols avoided the crowd. Fearing its violent potential, they had delegated the close surveillance to the drones. Near the many checkpoints, only a few Kritas dared to venture; the marines enjoyed oases of tranquillity marred by their fully-charged blasters, their mouthpieces blinked with menace at any nearby walker.

Tancredi stopped, and closed his eyes. He extended his senses and observed the reflections of thoughts and minds around him, but that day the mental fabric differed. That day he was alone; his Kritas surveillance constant had abandoned him. He nodded to himself, and waited.

*
**

Mekte was thirteen the day her parents died. Bio-technologists, they helped the insurgency. Kaulm had taken her into the ranks, but never revealed to her the truth about what had happened to them. 'They fought to give you and all Kritas a better future,' he once told her, but Mekte's mom's words were carved onto her heart: *'Violence and hatred cannot build a future; they're but ripples of a broken past. Kritas and humans need to look in the same direction, and stop glaring at each other.'*

She checked the tracking of her data cube one more time and smiled with trepidation. Her eye-membranes blinked in unison as her gaze went from the virtual screen of the tracker to the thrift market stalls and tents and back. Her traits showed resolve and determination; her lips had turned into a firm, steady, thin line, but inside she trembled. She put away the tracking device and walked toward the market maze and the first stalls. She mingled with other bargain seekers.

She saw him. Her heart jumped in her chest.

Tancredi felt the change in the crowd; he turned around and their eyes met.

They say time stops in those moments; the two young souls looked at each other, afraid to move and thus curse the magic.

Mekte smiled, then regretted it, and the smile vanished at once. He frowned for a second, but bent his head and smiled in turn. A full, warm smile. His eyes widened and forced Mekte to smile again.

Tancredi glanced around, then tried the first, timid steps. His black eyes fixed on hers, clear like pristine water and blinking as if ripples went through them. Light reflected from her hair, which glowed like flames. He thought she looked younger than he had judged from the records at the TEO. She was smiling at him, and he thought she was beautiful.

"It's you," Mekte said when he stopped an arm away from her.

All Kritas had unique modulations in their voices, but hers marveled Tancredi, as if she had sung those words.

He stared at her for a moment. "Yes, and it is you."

She drove her gaze away. Perturbed, she took a deep breath. "My name's Mekte." She looked at him again for a moment. "Mekte, daughter of Yutki." Her eyes dazed around.

"I know your name." He nodded. "Are you afraid of me?"

Her eyes widened, then lowered. "I've never been this close to a scholar."

The word resonated in his mind. *Scholar!*

Standing in front of the young Kritas, the world had disappeared for Tancredi, but now his logic yelled at him; he could be in front of one of the terrorists, maybe she was responsible for the death of hundreds of innocent people. Yes, he was a scholar, an enforcer of the law. "And yet," he said, "I believe you risk every day to face one in the Tribunal."

She jolted as if he had just slapped her face. "I try hard to avoid that; besides, I'll probably be dead before that happens." She caressed the palm of her right hand; inside, a tickling reassured her that the device was ready.

Tancredi grabbed her arm, pulled her away from the alley, and took her inside the nearest bazaar's tent. Mekte's hand contracted, and a vibration inside her palm cut her breath short.

Shielded by the presence of other patrons, Tancredi released her and peeked outside. "Are you alone?" he said over his shoulder.

"Is the scholar afraid?" Mekte said to his back. She glanced around as well. Kritas patrons crowded the bazaar tent. Her hand relaxed.

Tancredi faced her. He wondered whether he had to probe her mind right there with all the strength he was capable of. "How can you fool the TEO scanners the way you did?"

Mekte shook her head. "I made a mistake." She stepped away from him. "I shouldn't be here with you."

"I could extort that information from you right now." Tancredi stepped forward. His eyes narrowed.

She frowned as a tingling sensation grabbed the back of her skull. "I thought you were different. You're all the same." She turned and made to walk out of the tent, but Tancredi blocked her path.

"Wait, wait!" He stopped his probing. "I'm sorry. I'm now a pariah to my own people, and I'm not accustomed to making friends." He curled his lips. "Can we start all over again?" He offered his hand. "Tancredi. Tancredi Gilmor."

Hesitant, Mekte breathed hard. She raised her arm straight and opened her palm. Tancredi nodded and placed his on hers.

She shivered, her mind was set. "Blessed be, Tancredi Gilmor." She grabbed his hand. "Come. There's not much time."

***

Mekte took him to a food parlor. The owner nodded briefly at her when they entered. "He's with me," she added when she noticed the cold stare the owner gave the human.

The Kritas glanced outside at the street, then took her aside. They exchanged a few words, then she gestured at Tancredi. "Over here."

She led him to a table the farthest away from the entrance. A waiter brought two blobs with a glimmering fluid inside and put them on the table. He stared at Mekte while tightening his lips. He avoided meeting the human's eyes.

Tancredi waited for the waiter to leave, then bent forward. "Where are we?" he uttered.

She feigned surprise and glanced around. "It's a food parlor."
He snorted. "Who are you?"

"Someone who's betting her life on you." Mekte caressed her right hand and took one of the blobs. She stuck her tongue into it. Her eyes studied him. She took a sip and savoured it. She nodded. "You freed those boys the very same day."

It took a few seconds for Tancredi to realize whom she was referring to. "I sensed no danger in them."

"Do you feel you're in danger now?"

He shook his head. "I went to your apartment."

"I've been told."

"Our Dean says you're with the rebels."

Mekte looked into his eyes for a long moment. "You've not tasted it." She pointed at the blob.

"I can't drink from it as you do."

Mekte's eyes searched for the owner, who had kept staring at them the whole time. She pointed at the table. The owner shook his head and gave a nod to one of the waiters. After a while, a Kritas brought a bowl and slammed it in front of Tancredi. "Don't make a mess," he said before leaving.

Mekte chuckled and took the other blob. "May I?"

Tancredi didn't reply. Mekte stared at him and bit the blob, then poured its content into the bowl. Her eyes glittered. "Try it."

He glanced at the liquid, bent his head and sniffed. The smell wasn't bad. He brought the bowl to his lips while studying the girl's face.

Mekte smiled. "We need to trust each other, yes?"

His eyes contracted. He took a sip, then a second. "It's... different."

"We are different, but I hope you'll discover we are the same as well. I hope you like the taste." She plunged her tongue into her blob.

"I found a book in your apartment. A real book." Tancredi put down the bowl.

Mekte sighed and looked away. "My mother's legacy..." She raised her gaze again. "I suppose you found the other one as well, the one in the cube."

"I got arrested. I don't have them with me if that's what you're asking," he paused. "Legacy? I'm sorry."

"I was thirteen when she died. My mother used to say that violence is rooted in the ignorance of others." Her eyes glistened with hope. "I want to know you, and show you who we really are."
Tancredi curled his lips. "Those books testify to the cruelty our race suffered."
"Those were complicated times."
"Times always are. What's your goal?"
"To have you give voice to our suffering. Start a change."
He grunted. "I'm no one. *You're* no one."
She smiled and shook her head. "We are the most important of all, instead. We can be the first." Her hand touched his across the table. "Can you trust me?"
Tancredi looked at her hand. "As things are, I don't think I have a choice."
Mekte nodded, then signaled with a twitch of her head. Two Kritas approached. "I need you to wear this." She placed a dark, sensorial deprivation strap on the table.
Tancredi glanced. "I thought you said we had to trust each other."
"I don't...yet. Have you ever been to 3U?"
"3U?" He tilted his head and frowned. "Is this where these gentlemen here will take me?"
Mekte's gaze didn't change and she didn't reply.
"Okay." He took the strap and placed it over his eyes. It molded to his face and adhered, then it extended to cover his ears, too.
Tancredi expanded his senses to probe around him. He could 'see' the aura of the Kritas in the parlor and feel their sensations.
Mekte took his hand in hers. He jolted when the strap transmitted her voice; it sounded softly in his ears. "Don't do that, please. Don't worry; I'll be with you at all times. I trust you, others don't."
Perplexed, Tancredi stiffened but retreated his mind. Blind and deaf, he let Mekte guide him.

CHAPTER 8 - THE UNDERWORLD

REASONS OF THE HEART

THEY WALKED FOR A LONG TIME. In his mind, Tancredi counted steps into the thousands. He tried once more to use his empathic skills, but Mekte had squeezed his hand. "Please...." How could she feel his probing?

He smelled mold and decay, and they walked through areas covered with debris. At times they climbed down flights of stairs, and he touched stony walls in narrow passages.

"We're almost there," Mekte's voice sounded reassuring inside his ears. The floor descended, slowly at first, then with ever-steeper slope along a tortuous path.

Tancredi frowned. If this was part of the insurgency's infrastructure, they had more resources than the military ever believed.

They came to a stop, then walked again for a short distance on a smooth surface. The strap transmitted again Mekte's voice, "Lean on me." She grabbed his arm. Tancredi nodded, but didn't reply.

The floor moved under his feet, but he regained his balance at once, thanks to Mekte's support. He was at her mercy, but somehow he didn't worry for his safety.

After a short time, Mekte spoke again, "Let's go." She pulled him and guided his steps again.

Under his boots, he suddenly felt an irregular surface, as though they walked over a primeval rock-bed.

Mekte's hand pressed on his chest and he froze, then her hands touched his temples and the strap receded. "Welcome to 3U."

Tancredi blinked at the cold blue light of twirling jellies gripped at the rocky vault of a gallery. Bulges on the vault cast shadows that created the impression of being inside the rib cage of a primordial beast. A murmur rose, and the rustling of dragging feet made him turn. His eyes finally focused. Tens of Kritas stared at him. Fear, surprise, and marvel struck him in waves.

He gazed at those nearest to him. Some wore old, ragged clothes. Those were the fortunate ones. Others, he realized, didn't even stare at him; inner demons and ghosts had captured their eyes and caring hands guided their gaits.

A little hand touched his right leg, and then soon retreated. He looked down at a little boy, dressed with only a blanket draped around his shoulders.

When Tancredi held out his hand, the child ran back to a girl who had the boy's same hair and hid his face in her tattered tunic. She looked too young to be a mother, and was too skinny; her lips trembled, and her face showed the signs of many sleepless nights.

Older Kritas stood farther away, in the back, and tried to keep straight with the remnants of their past strength. Their eyes showed no expression but that of long-gone hopes.

He searched for Mekte and found her a step behind him.

She studied his face to guess his thoughts. "Welcome to my world." A sad smile rose to her lips, and her eyes filled with tears. Her voice cracked. "Welcome to the forgotten people." She made him turn and face them again; without realizing it, Tancredi took a step back. His eyes and his mind widened in that moment.

*
**

When alone with Mekte, later that day, Tancredi had only one question, "How's that possible?"

The cell they shared had been excavated in the same veins of rock that anchored the foundations of Utthana. "These units had been dug out well before the human invasion, as a final refuge.

They're old. Very old." Mekte paused and smiled. "Much older than I am, anyway."

There was little comfort provided to the Kritas hidden in the facilities' underground cells. Refugees, salvaged people, renegades, didn't need much, but they had lost everything. He looked around; a communication pod, a bioputer, and only the essential furniture.

Mekte anticipated his question. "We do provide them with food, medicines, clothing, for what is possible. Some of those you call terrorists only care for these people." She took out a glittering band that she adjusted around her arm. "We all wear this. We are their only hope. Maybe, because we are the ones who still believe in a better future."

She took him to sit together on one of the wooden benches covered with piles of shredded fabrics sewn together. Later on, they would become the mattress upon which they would spend the night.

"How come it has never been found?"

"By humans? Do you think they care? 3U is a people dumpster."

"What?" He bent forward.

"The Authority maintains just one access point to this level, and it's a one-way only. All others have been shut down during the years. There are other places like this one, all connected underground. More even deeper than this level."

"I don't understand…"

Mekte took his hand. "Here there's only grief. Others believe the only solution is to fight the humans and hope to win our freedom by force one day. I don't. Not anymore at least." She looked into his eyes. "Do you?"

Tancredi stood up and passed both hands through his hair, shaking his head. He walked toward the curtain that functioned as a door and lifted one side.

The dim light of a multitude of other cells littered the walls of what Mekte called a 'residence unit.' A silo with a high rocky vault ceiling resembling one of those oldest Kritas buildings, a spiral with hundreds of units like the one he and Mekte occupied. And it wasn't the only 'residence' either, if he had to believe Mekte.

Large halls connected to each residence via galleries, like the one he had arrived in earlier that same day, with points of collections to gather food, and medicines to be distributed, and emergencies carried out. Survival engineering.

He peered back inside. "Some of those people are ill, others are maimed, or seemed to have lost their minds, even. What happened to them?"

Mekte sighed and stood up slowly and it seemed she bore a heavy weight on her shoulders. She joined him at the entrance, raised her chin, and curled her lips. "There's one thing the humans keep functional in 3U." She stared at him. "The Tribunal."

Tancredi gasped when he guessed what was coming next.

"The mindless ones? Those are the ones expelled from its walls," she said. "The others have suffered incidents at work or have been condemned to 3U."

Tancredi brought one hand to his face and closed his eyes. She nudged him. "Don't feel too bad. The marines dictate the rules down here, more than the scholars. Some of the Kritas who end up here show up after months of absence with no news, not even for their families. The TEOs claim they've been released. We think the military further detains them for who knows what reasons."

He shook his head. "I cannot believe it."

Mekte lifted the curtain and pointed outside. "Just look. It's in front of your eyes."

That night, Tancredi couldn't rest his mind. Mekte slept on the other bench. Her breathing, regular and deep, marked the passing of time.

He twisted and sat on his bench. In the dimmed light of the cell, he searched with his eyes for the girl still asleep. She hadn't lied to him, he had tasted the sorrow and the pain in her words. In his mind, he hunted, in vain, for a clause in the law, a teaching from his training, anything that would justify the corruption, explain what he had seen in 3U, something that could allow him to reply, to give answers, to rationalize . . .to sleep.

He projected his mind, gently, and caressed hers with soft mental fingertips. In her sleep, Mekte moaned.

Her anguish and regrets, her sorrow vibrated under his touch with low humming tunes and shone in his mind with dark colors.

He had to catch his breath and his heartbeat accelerated. How could she live with that grave weight burying her heart?

Mekte groaned. He made his 'touch' even softer, but a hollow emptiness made him gasp for air, then the first images reached him: his convoy reaching the Alliance Square and the marvels and the doubts that rose in Mekte's heart and mind when she, somehow, believed he had taken her side. He felt how her fingers trembled when she caressed the contour of his face in the Tribunal Enquiry Office, and he saw a glimpse of hope raising bright as if a new sun had casted a warm light on a cold plain. The veil of sorrow fought against that beam, and her voice pronounced his name, sung in a melodious chord. With a convulsive spasm, his lungs filled with air.

Mekte rolled over and rose to one elbow. *"What are you doing?"* She sat upright and reached for the cover as she felt naked and vulnerable all of a sudden.

Tancredi retreated, mentally and physically. Speechless, he was still prey to the undertow of her emotions and feelings. He opened his mouth to reply, but no words came out, and he was too slow to dodge the blow. Mekte's hand left a burning sensation on his face, but it took him out of his torpor.

"I'm sorry," they said at the same time.

"Sorry, sorry, Tancredi." She caressed him with the same hand that had been so harsh an instant before.

He grabbed her hand, kept it on his face, and closed his eyes, unable to keep her gaze. "Don't say that. Don't say that..." He opened his eyes. "Did you feel me?"

Mekte lowered her eyes. "You woke me up."

"How could you...?"

She stood up, their hands still laced together. "There's something I want you to see, first...and understand."

Tancredi looked up. "What's happening to us?"

Mekte smiled. "Come with me."

*
**

They left the residential unit through a large gallery. Mekte led him into a labyrinth of connected tunnels until they ended up at a dead-end. She stopped and placed her hand on a small depression. After a few moments, the wall receded and slid open into a narrow tunnel; an oblong, small gliding shuttle slowed down to a stop in front of them. The entry bay opened.

Mekte answered his unspoken question. "We came down through one of these. I'm sure you remember." They stepped in. "All your questions will be answered, but I want to share something with you; something special to me." The shuttle sealed and drifted away.

They looked into each other's eyes, their minds and hearts raptured with a growing wonder. When the shuttle stopped, its door opened to a suspended ramp. They followed it, higher up onto a platform. A glittering crystal column stood in its middle. The outer ring of the platform glowed in the twilight, and a draft of crisp air came from the depths below and played with Mekte's hair.

"I come here when my courage falters and I risk losing faith." She touched the column with her fingertips, gently, as though she had feared she could break it.

Around, above, and below them, sparkling dots crowded the surface of a vast dome and twinkled like the countless stars at the center of the galaxy. "Here are the memories of all Kritas who lived and died in Ahthaza." Mekte let her gaze wander. "It's our most precious relic of a past long gone."

She gestured with symbols that had blossomed atop the column and glanced at him, then pointed to their right: the light of two dots grew brighter and projected two glistening globes. When they reached the platform, they formed the life-like images of two Kritas standing next to each other and in front of them. They were both smiling. Her voice broke. "My mother and father."

Tancredi touched her hand.

She looked at him with tearful eyes. "Their loss has not been in vain. It changed my heart." Her lips trembled. "I come here every time we are again tempted to respond to violence with violence. I come here to think of new ways."

She took a deep breath. "Eventually, we will all change. One person at a time, until we all learn." She raised her chin. "I believe, Tancredi. I need to believe that one day . . ."

She couldn't finish the phrase. In silence, he pulled her into his arms and held her tight.

She lay and clung to him. Shivering, she tucked her face in his chest with a flush of embarrassment. "I'm sorry, I don't know anymore why I'm showing you all this," she managed to whisper.

He bent forward, wiped off her tears and closed her eyes with a gentle kiss. She shuddered. Her anguish slapped his mind like a shockwave and he held his breath.

Her eyes widened. "No!"

"Don't fight it..." He kissed her again between the eyes, and everything faded as if a dark light coalesced around them. It was hard to breathe; each breath violated his lungs like a burning fluid, hurting and clutching them. A longing void took the place of his heart, and a knot clamped his throat.

He struggled, but didn't battle the darkness, he absorbed it, instead, processed it, and made it his.

Mekte moaned and her hands clasped his arms. Then, the dark veil receded, tore apart, and Tancredi's eyes widened. He trembled. He sensed her, close and familiar, even closer than her body now glued to his.

Mekte stared at him. "Tancredi..." Her hands crept over his sides, pressing softly into the contours of his body.

His blood flushed up. He hadn't words to describe the vortex that tortured his emotions; he sensed nothing but her, nothing but her soul, nothing but her heart. When she pressed against him, his breast was one great ache. Their eyes met, her lips opened, and he couldn't resist the call.

That night, they searched for each other. Their eyes didn't stop at what made them different, and their hands trembled at the touch of the other. They breathed the same air, and their hearts jumped in their chests at the same time. He thrilled beneath her mouth. She swooned under his lips in a bliss that made her feel released, liberated, free. They became one flesh, one body without a mind. Their hearts pumped a burning and sentient blood, beating in unison. Then, they remained perfectly still, locked onto each other, conscious of everything, afraid of nothing. That night they discovered how similar they were.

She rested her head on his chest; his searching hand caressed the velvet skin of her back. "You are my first."

She drew back from him and rolled over to look into his eyes. "How is it with human girls?"

"Human girls?" He frowned. "Well, they are...well...human." She smiled. "Was I your..."

Tancredi blushed. "Yes, you are my first, too."

She curled against his body and hugged him with all the strength she had.

"I didn't know that happened with you," he said. "I mean, your breasts became fuller while we..."

"I didn't know it happened to you, too...down there. It's so small, now." She giggled.

"Is that funny?" He stiffened.

"Oh, no, no." She hugged him.

"I was just kidding." He smiled.

She shook her head. "I was thinking of Khulel."

"Oh." He stiffened even more.

She rose on her elbows. "Idiot. It's not what you think. Something he said." She smiled at him again. "He told me he believed human women were always aroused." She winked.

His eyes widened and he gave a chuckle. He frowned and looked into her eyes, to get lost in those clear waters, and caressed the curves of her face. "Are you?"

Her pupils dilated.

He glanced at her breast.

She started to breathe hard, and her hand reached down below. The human boy and the Kritas girl collapsed into each other's arms.

They caught their breath again. She caressed the hand he rested on her hip and followed its contour with her fingertips. "What if this is our first and last time?"

"It won't be." He kissed her and held her close to his heart, hoping time could just stop.

CHAPTER 9 - REVELATIONS

DIKTATS OF THE BRAIN

ACCESS TO THE IRC, the Inquisition Research Center of the Tribunal, required the highest clearance levels. Secured by the Marines and managed by the Scholars, its activities were known only to those who worked there, those who had a need to know, and those unlucky enough to be prosecuted there.

With the increased rate of arrivals of suitable 'hosts,' scientists at the IRC lacked no specimens to try breaking Kritas' secrets. Scientists promised the Dean and the governing authority a breakthrough for years, but nothing had proven to be successful thus far.

The laboratory's activity never stopped; technicians and scientists interacted and rotated at multiple duty stations without interruption, each presenting with a detailed live rendering of all brain activities of each probed prisoner.

Beyond the transparent wall, the Dean observed the rows of med-units where the Kritas terrorists suffered IRC invasive procedures. The Governor believed in security via repression, and applied his methods on all planets of the sector under his rule. In Ahthaza, though, he believed he had to be particularly ruthless, especially under the new circumstances. Results had proved him right, during the past years, and he wanted to resolve the unstable situation in Utthana in a swift way.

'*We need to make an example out of these terrorists,*' he had told her during their last meeting. She knew he implied '*whatever the price in lives,*' too. She shook her head.

The lead scientist approached. "Ma'am?"

She peeked at him and judged his face; she noticed his lips were too tight to be bringing any good news. "Progress?" she asked anyway. "The Governor wants results," she added.

The scientist nodded. "We've learned a lot in the recent weeks, but the implant still eludes our attempts at neutralizing it before it wipes out subjects' minds."

The Dean stiffened and narrowed her eyes. "That's not enough."

"I can show you."

"I don't need to know how it works or doesn't work." With a quick tilt of her head, she pointed at the rows of med-units behind them. "I need you to break that implant without destroying their minds."

The scientist nodded again, but his eyes showed no conviction. In the med-units, the sedated Kritas lay motionless, but a war rampaged in their minds, and it always ended in one way.

"What will I need to tell the Governor about your lack of progress?"

The scientist raised his chin, and his voice betrayed his pride. "It's not something you can simply remove. It fuses with the brain. It becomes part of their brains." He rolled his eyes. "We're inching toward a solution. It's only a matter of time."

"Time!" The Dean scoffed and her lips curled down. "I'm afraid time's what we lack the most."

The transponder at her belt pinged and demanded her attention. She stared at the scientist, who lowered his head and left her. She accepted the incoming call.

The face of her Councilor appeared on the floating visor, blossoming in front of her eyes. "We lost him."

She interrupted the link at once and glared back at the prisoners.

*
* *

Mekte removed the strap. Tancredi blinked and looked around; his eyes questioned hers: in a gallery burrowed in the rock, similar to the one of the day of his arrival, a Kritas stared at them.

He wasn't one of the wretched people he had seen so far in his first days in 3U. Ruggedly built, with the physical aplomb of a trained soldier.

Mekte signaled the stranger to approach. "This is Khulel."

The Kritas walked up to him. His gaze pierced Tancredi's eyes with the intensity of a sniper in search of a hit point, waiting for the right moment.

"Khulel," Tancredi nodded. "I'm—"

"I know who you are, scholar," the Kritas said. "Mekte's not the only one to believe you might be of some use, I'm afraid." He turned to the girl. "Do you still trust him?"

She smiled at Tancredi. "I do."

Khulel hesitated for a moment, then looked back at him. "If you let her down, I promise I'll kill you. No second thoughts." He stared at him for a moment to let the message sink in, then reached for the rocky surface of the gallery's wall. With his hand, he pressed on a bump; a section animated, the rocks retreated and separated from each other, then they rearranged, chasing each other and overlapping to form an opening. A flood of light invaded the gallery.

Surprised, Tancredi raised his hand to shield his eyes.

"Be nice," Mekte uttered to Khulel.

Khulel raised one eyebrow. "Follow me," he said, and walked across the opening.

Their steps resonated within the metallic structure of a narrow tunnel until they stopped in front of a massive bulkhead. A bulb emerged from the top, and a vibrant blade of blue light brushed their bodies multiple times.

"Stand still," Khulel said without turning.

The light vanished as the bulb retreated, and the bulkhead opened with a huff. A long corridor with transparent side walls opened in front of them.

Two Kritas drew out their blasters and glared at them. Khulel nodded and paced forward. Mekte took Tancredi's hand and dispelled the reticence that had grabbed him. As they passed by, the two Kritas guards followed them, walking a few steps behind.

"In case you're wondering, scholar," said Khulel over his shoulder, "this is not a military facility. We cure people here, the ones humans send to 3U to die."

Tancredi glanced at the facilities beyond the walls. "Only them?"

Khulel stopped and faced him. "I don't share any others' hopes which come from having you here," he glanced at Mekte, "nor do I approve of the care that you've received so far. You're not here to ask questions, human, or question our motives."

Mekte stepped between them and put her hand on Tancredi's heart.

He took a breath, lowered his sight and nodded at her. "It's okay."

Her eyes glued into his. "We risk more than losing a war we've already lost."

He tilted his head.

"Let us show you. I need your help." She sent an oblique look to Khulel. "*We* need your help."

***

The Dean sealed her room as soon as the Councilor walked in. "Who knows about it?" she asked without wasting time in preambles.

The Councilor frowned. "The surveillance team, me, and you... for now."

"How did that happen? We need to collect more intel." Her lips tightened into a thin slit. "I can't just tell the Governor we've lost him."

"I've already taken measures."

"Meaning?"

The Councilor pointed at the dashboard on her desk. "May I?"

The Dean nodded, then faced the middle of her office when a rendering of the Under levels of Utthana appeared and expanded. She watched at the areas that highlighted as the Councilor explained.

"These are Gilmor's whereabouts after he was allowed to escape from house arrest. Exact locations and views." The Councilor raised more symbols from the dashboard and connected them together. "He interacted with no one until the moment of the first contact."

The Dean stared at the floating screens that rose from a blinking location; in the scene, a Kritas approached Tancredi from behind.

"As you can see, he was given a data cube." The scene zoomed to the moment of the handout.

"How do we know it's the insurgents?"

In the screen, the Councilor highlighted the face of the Kritas on a separate screen, then the same face showed up into multiple other screens; same Kritas, different personal data, different origins and backgrounds, different times and places. "For how unheard of it sounds, the actual identity of the subject is uncertain."

She looked at him with a muted question.

"That's their implant at work."

The Dean heaved a sigh. "Go on."

"We monitored the situation from afar. He wandered for a few days in 1U, chose different hiding spots in these precise locations," further areas highlighted in the under levels' rendering, "and was careful to avoid any close contact with marine patrols."

"When did we actually lose him?" The Dean squinted, her face contracted in a worried grimace.

"Soon after the second contact."

"A second contact?" She glanced at her Councilor.

"He met with a young Kritas." Two more screens blossomed and revealed a Kritas girl's face and details. "Gilmor was searching her place when we arrested him." The image of a Kritas residence unit came into view. "She goes with at least two names: Mekte, daughter of Yutki; and Karelle, daughter of Vikri. We don't know whether any of those is real."

"She must have the implant."

The Councilor nodded. "I'd say so."

"What do we know about her?"

"Not much, I'm afraid. Nothing suspicious...low profile until her visit to a TEO. That's where we got evidence of her second identity."

The Dean waved her hand at him. "Continue."

A large screen showed a 1U street, then the scene zoomed to the entrance of a food parlor. Mekte and Tancredi walked in.

The Councilor voice lowered. "This is the last precise location and intel we have him. From there, the trace fades. They left the premises through a rear exit, then we lost contact."

The Dean stared at the screen, then gestured on it to bring up the planimetric map. A model of the parlor appeared, rotating slowly in front of her. She enlarged it and examined the layout for a moment.

"We searched it already, of course," the Councilor continued. "We got in with the excuse of a regular administrative check. We found nothing."

"Who's the owner?"

"A merchant, regularly registered. No criminal records." The merchant's data appeared on an additional floating screen. "We didn't want to raise suspicions. Anyway, we put the parlor under surveillance, nothing visible or intrusive, though."

"What about the patrons?"

"Mostly regulars. Kritas."

"We must assume that Tancredi Gilmor is now with those radicals."

"Yes."

"You mentioned you took measures…"

"I ordered a thorough search with sniffers." A screen showed a rotating, tiny rod, and its schematics. "We sent tens at first." The rods' acquired data showed up, overlying the under levels map. "At first we didn't find anything abnormal," further zones in the city rendering highlighted, "then, we discovered uncharted areas."

"How's that possible?"

"And this is not the most surprising discovery, either, I'm afraid," the Councilor said. "The rod stopped transmitting, thus we sent more. That's how we found it."

The Dean opened her mouth as further details came into view. On the 3D map of the city, where the rods stopped relaying, the borders of the overlapped data formed an empty zone that extended into 3U.

"Don't worry," the Councilor added. "We left no traces. The sniffers self-destroy after they lose contact."

*
**

Under the rocky vault of a vast hall, the humming of the med-units played together in a modulated rhythm whose pattern followed the blinking of the panels and controls. Nurses checked the vitals' diagrams floating above the units.

Mekte, Tancredi, and Khulel advanced through rows of med-units and bunks surrounded by medical equipments. Kritas of all ages lay there unconscious. Tancredi noticed how nurses whispered to each other, as if they were in a sort of a temple.

Mekte stopped at a med-unit caring for a child patient. "There weren't as many at first." Her hand rested on the crystal canopy. "And never children." Her head tilted and a sad smile curved her lips.

Tancredi approached and looked inside the unit. A young boy looked asleep. He glanced at the brain activity; not exactly flat, the wave flickered at times as ripples of thoughts and sensations came to the surface, but they receded at times.

"This is our best facility, and we're stretched thin now." Khulel pointed at the center where a large, opaque hemisphere rose from the ground. "Critical cases are treated at the intensive care center."

Tancredi nodded and glanced around. "What do they suffer from, exactly?"

Mekte and Khulel exchanged a look.

"We don't know for sure." Khulel frowned. "Physically, they don't present substantial harm, though they certainly have suffered a physical stress, but their minds don't work anymore."

Mekte touched his arm and made Tancredi turn to look at her. "When they arrive at 3U, they're only able to act on instinct. Their bodies work, but they're not there."

Tancredi started to understand. "So you want me to find them."

"Right," said Khulel. "Your empathic skills might reveal what really brought them into such a catatonic state."

Tancredi drew a deep breath. "I might not be able to restore their minds . . . "

Mekte took his hand; he held it and caressed it with his thumb.

Khulel noticed and looked away. "Some become extremely aggressive, but it's only during flashes of consciousness. We've never seen anything like that before."

"We should start with those cases then," Tancredi said.

Mekte smiled at Khulel, but he didn't share her faith. "I'll have the doctors get some patients ready for you tomorrow," he said.

Tancredi nodded. "Will your doctors share their diagnoses with me? Freely, I mean."

Khulel stared at him, but Tancredi didn't blink. "Fine, scholar. I'll instruct them." Then he addressed Mekte. "You'll both stay here at the center for tonight. I arranged for two units."

Still holding Tancredi's hand, Mekte smiled. "There's no need to stretch resources. One's enough."

"I see," said Khulel. He signaled the two guards. "Take them to their quarters." Then to Mekte, "I'll see you both tomorrow at 6500 clicks." He walked away.

Tancredi waited for him to leave. "He doesn't seem too happy about it."

She squeezed his hand. "He's worried and cares for me."

"As I do." He sensed a glowing warmth grow inside her.

They followed the guards.

***

That night Tancredi, sleepless, kept staring at the ceiling. He knew she was awake, too, so he broke the silence. "What will I discover tomorrow?"

Mekte hesitated before replying, and took a long breath. "During the war, all military personnel received a brain implant to protect and hide their minds. The implant changes the synapses as needed, and hides itself and them from probings. The resistance was formed when it became clear our military was going to lose the war. The last resources had been used to extend the underground facilities years before the invasion, your invasion, with the hope to continue the fight one day. New recruits received the implant as well, and our scientists made it even harder to detect."

"You have one too!" Tancredi exclaimed. "That's how you fooled the TEO and can feel me."

She nodded. "But it's not just those with the implant who are sent to 3U with shattered minds."

Tancredi remained silent. She stretched one leg over his, then tilted her head. "What are you thinking?"

"I'm thinking about the connectome."

Mekte sat upright. "The *what*?"

"The connectome." Tancredi rose on his elbow. "It's what we call the network of the multiple patterns in the billions of connections in the brain. It encodes your identity, your memories, the way you think even." He paused and turned his gaze away. "It's far-fetched, but the only explanation I could think of is a failed attempt at rewiring the connectome." His heartbeat accelerated. "Mind, I'm just speculating."

"And you guess this, how?"

"We learn to see it, and in some cases we're able to influence it. Temporarily, though," he added. "This is what your implant must be doing as well. Or, maybe, it just masks the underlying true connectome, allowing you to project a different identity, for example." He winked. "I can't say more without a deep probing, but I understand why the Authority would want to acquire its technology."

Mekte stood up. "We need to tell Khulel."

***

The communication room was dimly lit. Glowing reflections at its far end were broken by the shadow cast on the black stone floor. In front of the gleaming floating screens, a figure raised virtual symbols off the main dashboard and connected them. A warning flashes its blinking words: 'Communication Established. Hard Encryption Level Established.' A visor lit up and a face appeared.

"Good day, Kaulm." Khulel frowned. "The scholar will start today. I would've briefed you right after."

"We need to step up the operations. Time's of the essence, now. The humans must have made some progress."

"How so?"

"Marines have launched massive search-and-arrest operations. They target all Kritas with a connection to our operatives. I fear they must have hacked the implant somehow." Kaulm breathed deeply. "We're sending more people down to 3U; get ready to provide shelter."

"I can't believe it." Khulel shook his head. "There must be another explanation." His eyes widened.

"I'll let you judge. This has just come in." A scene blossomed in front of Khulel.

Kaulm continued in a monotonic voice. "We haven't been able to reach them in time, but we're now rescuing as many as we can in various locations."

Khulel's hand started to shake. He recognized the place. The night scene showed a district in 1U. Silent and calm at first, then he heard the swooshing sounds of fast and deadly marines' small fighters as they surrounded an entire block. A snarling sound grew in the distance just before sentinel drones came stomping into view. Transporter vehicles converged into the area, stopped, and opened their docking bay; marines in heavy gear swarmed out.

Khulel stared at the scene. Kaulm's voice resounded as if it came from the depths of a pit. "This is happening all over 1U and 2U now."

Residents in the buildings awoke and some had started to get out in the streets. Flashing restraining bolts crisscrossed the area and enveloped them tightly, like a spider trapping its prey. They fell to the ground with a suffocated scream trapped between their lips. The drones drew out their blasters, flooded the area with their blinding lights, and initiated their scanning probes. Marines shouted orders and cordoned off the entire block, storming all buildings at the same time.

The first screams hurt Khulel like blades to his stomach. He struggled for breath when the marines taunted Kritas with their blasters, pushed them to the streets and took them prisoner into military shuttles waiting with their sides open, glowing reddish against a dark interior.

Marines pressed the detainees inside as though they were sacks of rubbish. Families with children, old and young people alike, girls, boys, no one escaped the swiftness and brutality of the operation.

"They've arrested everyone in the targeted residences," Kaulm continued, "but some were singled out; the ones with a connection to one of our agents captured during the last weeks of operations."

A guttural scream rose when a marine grabbed a female and started to search her. A Kritas rushed to attack the soldier with his bare hands. He slammed against the soldier's back with the full weight of his body. They fell to the ground, rolling and screaming, glaring at each other, an intricate struggle of limbs, struggling to snatch the blaster out of each other's hands. Other marines pointed their guns in search of a clean shot.

The Kritas woman begged. "No, no, please, don't."

It lasted only a few seconds, a soldier slammed the butt of his blaster to the Kritas' forehead; a thud and the cracking sound of smashed bones created an eery, frozen moment of silence. The Kritas woman screamed, fell to her knees, and covered her face with both hands.

Two marines rushed to pull their comrade back to his feet. His face contorted in hatred; before anyone could react, he took aim and fired. Blood splattered when the blaster's jolt sizzled through the torso of the Kritas and cracked it open. The fumes of the Kritas' dissolving flesh lingered over his motionless body, unwilling to disperse and be forgotten.

The female rushed to the body and knelt. A shriek pierced the air; she screamed at an invisible sky and indifferent gods, keening for her dead; her hands and arms covered with blood and organic fluids as she tried to recompose the maimed body.

Her cries made him shiver. Khulel fought to keep his voice steady. "Where's my sister? And her family?"

"They've been taken away with the others. We don't have more information. I'm sorry."

He nodded and joined his hands together in front of his puckered lips, as if he was praying, but gods had always been deaf to prayers.

***

Mekte messaged Khulel that she and Tancredi had reached the medical center ahead of time. "Tancredi thinks he may know why our people's brains have been damaged. Humans must be messing with the implant, but there's more. He will explain it all when we arrive. He needs a neuro-enhancer drug. We'll bring a data cube with the formula."

When they arrived at the laboratory, Khulel confronted Tancredi. "If what you think is true... The doctors here are ready to satisfy all your requests. Patients have been prepared."

Tancredi didn't reply and addressed the medical team. "Can you prepare this compound?" He inserted the data cube on a bioputer, which showed a rotating 3D representation of the molecular structure.

The doctors examined the complexity of the drug and conferred for a few seconds. One of them turned his head slowly and gave an oblique look at Tancredi. "We can."

"How long?"

The doctor stood tall. "It's a clever composition of heptanoic acid, phosphatidylserine, and cyclohexyl-bishphenol connected by nitrogen bridges. Potentially toxic, I have to say."

Tancredi raised his hand. "It'll help if patients are administered the molecule while I attempt synaptic recombinations."

The other doctors fell into a thick and agitated confabulation. "Can you actually do that?" The lead doctor frowned.

Khulel stepped forward and faced the doctor. "Do it."

Tancredi waited for the entrance to grant him access to a special care unit where he would meet with the first Kritas patient.

In the lab, the medical crew monitored the signals received from the med-unit. Mekte and Khulel observed via the floating master dashboard that collected all diagrams and received visuals from all angles.

The entry door opened with a sigh. Tancredi stepped in and tilted his head. "Why the restraints?" Glittering energy bands held the Kritas in place, blocking his head, torso, and his limbs. "He's unconscious, right?"

Khulel voice resounded. "Not for long. We have interrupted the sedatives."

"Why?"

"Do your job, scholar," Khulel ignored his question. "Impress me."

Tancredi raised his chin toward the source of the voice. "Is the drug ready?"

"Whenever you want it administered."

He nodded, stepping toward the cocoon that sheltered the Kritas and activated the retreat mechanism for the protective canopy. A young male, physically trained, he noticed. A quick examination revealed old wounds and scars. *'A soldier,'* Tancredi thought. He checked the med-unit panels. The Kritas was being treated for fractures, second-degree burns, and a skull fracture with tissue laceration.

"What are you doing?" Khulel asked.

"Learning from his body before probing his mind. This Kritas has taken part in the fights of the past weeks." His wasn't a question, and he received no reply.

"From the med-unit data, the majority of the injuries are recent. Actually, all from the same event, I'd say." He raised his sight and observed the surveillance bulb on the right wall. "I suppose he has the implant."

In the lab, Khulel muted the communication from his side and gave a cold look at Mekte. "How much did you reveal to him?"

"He needed to know. Besides, he would have found it anyway. I shared no details."

Tancredi's voice broke the tension. "Can you deactivate it?"

Khulel reestablished the link. "No."

On the screens, Tancredi's image nodded from all angles. "All right. I'll start an exploratory probing now." He breathed hard and tilted his head. "I sense the implant." He touched the Kritas' temple regions and closed his eyes. "It's...strange."

Mekte got closer to the floating images. Khulel touched her arm and muted the link again. She nodded.

The sensation of multiple, recombining knots greeted Tancredi in his developing vision as he obtained the empathic connection with the Kritas' mind. Dark spires surrounded a color-changing spherical region. He knew he would have needed to force them in order to penetrate that mind. The spires tightened where he attempted a 'touch', and relaxed afterwards.

After the colors, he started to hear sounds, whispers, bursts of images, all uncorrelated and without a definable pattern. Chaos and multiple forces at play left him undecided for a moment on the best approach.

He retreated and opened his eyes. "It's like multiple personalities are conflicting to gain control," he said. "The dissonance is unusual, as if a rational consciousness is no more." He raised his gaze. "Can you inject the drug now?"

Khulel glanced at the med crew, but they had already initiated the procedure. In the rendering above their dashboards, the drug started to penetrate the brain, and the internal flow triggered spikes in the brainwave's diagrams. "It's flowing," a doctor said.

In the cell, the Kritas groaned. His eyes rotated and his translucent nictitating membrane blinked multiple times. His eyes flipped backward and he now growled like a hunting predator. With a jerk, his back bowed and pulled on the restraining bands, then he collapsed back with his eyes shut tightly. Drool gushed from the left side of his mouth. His eyes opened at once, injected with blood, and his sight dashed around for a few moments before they fixed on the scholar.

Tancredi bent forward. "Do you understand me?" he said, but the Kritas' eyes, again, darted everywhere.

Tancredi nodded. "Probing." He touched the patient's temples; at once, the Kritas' eyes dashed back at him, glaring. The last thing Tancredi heard was Mekte screaming his name.

The med-team rushed out of the lab.

※

The small intensive care unit didn't allow for much room. Khulel walked up to Mekte and rested his hand on her shoulder. "Let the doctors examine him."

"He's waking up." Mekte held Tancredi's hand in hers. She stood up and followed Khulel to the exit.

"Don't worry. He'll recover. The docs say there's no permanent damage."

She nodded and peeked into the room to watch the doctors around Tancredi.

"I wonder…" Khulel muttered.

"What?"

"He suffered from a sort of concussion. If we acquired that capability against scholars…"

"He's not here for this."

"I know." He raised his hand. "Was just a thought."

Mekte faced him. "I want to change things, Khulel."

"Of course." He raised one hand and turned his gaze away.

The doctors came out. "He's awake now. You can question him, but we advise moderation. He needs to rest."

"Sure," said Khulel. He entered the room, followed by Mekte, who rushed to Tancredi's side.

"How are you?"

He smiled. "I'm fine. What happened?"

"Well, that's something we'd like to hear from you, scholar." Khulel stood at the foot of the med-unit.

Mekte took Tancredi's hand. "You groaned, then you fell to the floor. When we reached you…if he hadn't been restrained…"

Khulel finished the phrase for her. "Our patient would've attacked us all."

Tancredi tried to pull himself up but fell back with a moan.

Mekte caressed his face. "Take it easy."

He sighed. "It all makes sense now."

"What does?" Khulel grabbed the borders of the med-unit.

Tancredi looked at Mekte first, then his gaze fixed on Khulel's. The Kritas bent forward. "What, scholar?"

"When I probed his mind the second time," Tancredi breathed out, "the spires I saw surrounding his thoughts swayed. The first time, they had prevented me from penetrating deeper. The drug interfered with them; it's a nootropic molecule and it enhances all cerebral functioning."

Khulel pupils contracted. "Get to the point."

Tancredi nodded. "Clearly, someone has modified his connectome."

Khulel's fists contracted and he snorted.

Mekte reached out and touched his arm. "It's the complete coding of an individual through the patterns created by the connections in his brain, neurons, and synapses. If you control the connectome, you'd control that person at the same time."

Tancredi nodded.

"What have you seen, really, scholar?"

"After I reached deeper through the spires, his mental activity was chaotic and overwhelmed me. I wasn't prepared."

"And this is because of your drug?"

"No, can't be. The drug enhanced it, but couldn't create anything which wasn't there in the first place. Something else, more powerful, reacted against my intrusion, in a sort of self-defense." Tancredi paused and his gaze went from Khulel to Mekte. "Before I lost my senses, I glimpsed images and traces of subliminal commands." He paused. "Someone had implanted orders for him to kill . . . Kritas."

The two Kritas jolted and stared at him. "*What?*"

Tancredi reached for Mekte's hand and pulled himself up. "We can't waste time now."

Khulel and Mekte's transponders emitted an insisting humming sound. They looked at each other, then toward the entrance as two Kritas guards rushed in and saluted Khulel. "The humans are mobilizing, sir. We are here to escort you to the headquarters."

Khulel eyes thinned into a slit. He glared at Tancredi. He drew out his gun blaster. At once, the guards did the same.

"Khulel!" Mekte raised her hand in a vain effort to stop him. Her eyes widened in fear.

He stared at her for a moment, then he flipped the gun in his hand and offered it to Tancredi. "You might need this, scholar." He took a blaster from one of the guards and handed it over to Mekte. "Be safe, Mekte."

Mekte breathed out.

"Let's go," he told the guards.

Mekte's hand found Tancredi's and held it tight to stop her own from trembling.

Chapter 10 - Reversal

Seize the Moment

AT THE MARINES' BASE, the ground trembled under the rhythmic pacing of troops marching in tight formation. Officers shouted orders as marines in heavy gear boarded the vehicles that lined up on the tarmac. Sentinel drones had left their hangars to constitute the first line of the planned assault, moving out like a swarm of ants. Excitement and trepidation impregnated the sensations received by the embedded scholars' units ready to participate in the operations. The directives couldn't have been more clear: use of maximum lethal force at first signs of resistance and on sight of the insurgents.

Special cryogenic units assembled their devices to be ready to hibernate insurgent bodies and capture their brain patterns before death would have rendered the task impossible; images, memories, and any other information would be extracted in the labs, even better than if the specimen was still alive. They only needed enough time to prepare the body before a full cerebral death.

From her office in the Tribunal tower, the Dean followed the preparations on her dashboard. The floating screens showed the entire base, the details of the scholar units, and the live messages of the operatives on the field.

The locations of the initial strikes had been monitored in the past days, and active and passive sensors had been deployed, ready to spread into the stealth area where the bulk of the insurgent forces were believed to be hiding.

She nodded as the information accumulated and represented the situation on the field with increasing details. She sighed; she was obeying orders, but she'd have liked to give her scholars more time, and probably avoid a blood bath at the same time. But in cases such as these, involving military operations, the Governor and the Authority had the higher hand.

The wall announced the arrival of her Councilor. She acknowledged and let it dilate.

"Good day, Ma'am." The Councilor bowed.

"This is going to be everything but a good day." She stood up.

"Ma'am?"

She ignored that. "Still no sign of Gilmor? Never mind, I would have been the first to know, right?"

"Is the Dean worried about anything specific?"

"We are alone, and the office is sealed." She shook her head. "The quantum link with the Governor's battleship is not yet open. Let's skip formalities."

"As you wish." He bowed again.

"C'mon. You've been with me since the beginning. It's what? Thirty years now?"

"About so, yes." He smiled at some of their shared memories. "And you've not changed since."

She smiled back. "But time flows anyway." The Dean went to the transparent wall and observed the traffic of vehicles at the marines' base and that had kept landing since the early hours of the day. "Doesn't it surprise you?" She paused. "The Governor's decision, I mean."

The Councilor hesitated. "May I speak freely?"

She turned and narrowed her eyes. "We still have some time before the connection."

"The Governor seemed hard-pressed when we reported the lost signal from Gilmor."

She nodded. "I had the same impression. The news accelerated whatever plan he had in mind. Maybe made him change plans, even."

"What do you think?"

"Something's not right. I believe he's not sharing everything with us."

The quantum link activated and the Dean raised her hand, urging for silence.

The Governor's commanding deck in the orbiting flag battleship formed within the virtual rendering. A tall figure gave them his back as he was addressing officers on deck. "I want this to be a decisive blow, and one that will break their spine." He clenched his fist.

The officers gave a brisk nod of acknowledgment.

"I want real-time updates from now on." He turned. "Are your scholars ready?" he asked them in a stern voice.

The Dean and her Councilor bowed. "Governor," said the Dean, "our units are ready to intervene and support the marines."

"This time the marines will need little support from scholars," the Governor stepped forward. "I want you people to sift through everything the marines unveil and detect anyone with the implant, dead or alive. You will work in tandem with the cryogenic units."

"Tancredi Gilmor's still there."

"We'll re-acquire the signal soon. Who knows what he's been sharing with those fanatics."

A gush of blood rose to her face. Her voice trembled, and she stiffened. "Scholars don't betray, Governor!"

"Convictions and beliefs are shattered every day, Dean Merril. A man can find any kind of motivation to justify his acts. Gilmor's capture is of the highest priority, as is that of the Kritas girl." His eyes fixed on the Dean's. "I can relieve of your command if that's your desire," he warned.

The tone of his voice sent a cold shiver down her backbone, but she withstood his stare. "That won't be necessary, Governor."

***

Khulel stepped into the Command and Control room. Around a circular dashboard, Kaulm and other high-ranked insurgents were assessing the situation and the latest intel. The bioputers' spheres churned in the effort to come out with reasonable answers to their strategic questions and discover all possible correlations hidden by the overabundance of data. Thousands of units were being alerted all over Utthana, and reports confirmed the alert state had been raised to the highest level. The operation involved marines and scholars together. All questions boiled down to essentially two: 'Can we survive?' and 'What is their target?' and—so far—neither had been answered.

Kaulm noticed the movement. "Khulel. How's Mekte and her host?"

"They're safe. I don't think the medical center's a target."

"Have you been briefed already?"

"I have. What do you think triggered this kind of deployment?"

"We can't tell yet, but things precipitated pretty fast. The projections on the humans' first deployments indicate an all-out assault on all fronts. The main target is undefined, yet, but it's obvious it's in the Under levels. It might be they're after a vast sweep-and-destroy operation, but I fear the worst. I trust my guts better than those spheres." He nodded at the bioputers.

Khulel pondered over the projected troops movements. "Aye. They're strategizing in order to succeed."

"They won't. We need to buy ourselves time while we determine their objective. Sentinel drones have been sent hunting already." He raised and enlarged the floating screens from the bioputers' latest analysis. "You'll lead one of the missions."

Khulel walked up to the central board where the insurgency team leaders struggled to fully define the best counter-operation.

"You'll lead team F here," Kaulm enlarged a model of the concerned area, "and stop the drones together with the support from teams S and T. They're on your orders."

Khulel nodded as he recognized the locations that appeared above the board.

"If we cut the access to these levels' thresholds we might stop them long enough to counter-attack the marines' units from behind. It's our city; let's use it to our advantage." Kaulm paused. "Unless they plan to annihilate the under levels with anti-matter devices, we will be able to relocate the bulk of our forces away from the theater while causing massive damage."

"Where are you going?"

Kaulm snorted. "Where would I go? Someone needs to coordinate the efforts." He glanced around at the people in the control room who lowered their heads at him. "Your team is ready to deploy. The intel's uploading now." He placed his hand on Khulel's left shoulder. "Good luck."

Khulel did the same. "See you later."

They both smiled and exchanged a farewell look.

※

In the medical center, Mekte helped Tancredi get dressed. One of the doctors showed up soon after the med-unit stopped relaying his vitals. "You shouldn't leave." He looked at Mekte. "He needs more rest and time in the med-unit."

"I'm afraid time is what we don't have." Tancredi secured the gun blaster to his belt.

The doctor looked at the gun. "We have security in place, and you're definitely safer here than anywhere else in 3U."

"How do you know that?" Tancredi asked without stopping getting dressed.

Mekte approached the doctor and put one hand on his chest. "Thank you for your concerns, but we need to go."

The doctor stared at her for a moment, then he sidestepped. "As you wish." He cleared the exit.

Tancredi waited until they had left the center, then he grabbed Mekte by her arm. "What was he trying to say?"

Her lips curled. "This area, where we care for everyone we've been able to rescue. . .it's concealed."

"Concealed?"

"Stealth technology."

"This isn't surprising and might explain… Mekte, we should evacuate."

"What?"

"Think of it. Why this large mobilization? You've been discovered."

"It can't be. How?"

"I've no idea, but are you willing to take the risk?"

Mekte stared at him.

"We need to move fast," he said. "Can we take everyone out of here quickly?"

"Yes, there are other safe areas. We need to warn the people at the medical center." She pulled on his grip.

He held her firmly. "Wait. They have security in place here, right? I meant we need to move the people at the residential unit. Those able to walk at least." He caressed her and his lips tightened. "We don't have time for the others."

She looked back at the center for a moment, then nodded. "We need to run."

At the residential unit, Mekte headed first to the cell they had occupied before.

Tancredi ran behind her. "What are we doing here?"

She frowned, surprised. "Do you want to call people out one by one?" She activated the bioputer and a virtual dashboard appeared. Her hands darted on the symbols that rose from it; outside the cell, a loud alarm resounded.

"What have you done?"

She adjusted the strap of the blaster. "You called for an evacuation, right? I just gave you one."

People had already started to gather outside of their cells, and the information poles projected the evacuation orders.

Tancredi noticed other Kritas with pulsating arm-bands among the crowd urging others to get going with gentle but firm directives. Mekte followed his sight. "Those are the caretakers; people rely on them."

Many pressed the caretakers, asking for confirmations, seeking for reassurances and details. Mekte reached the nearest group that moved toward the exit galleries. A caretaker recognized and approached her. "What's going on? Why the evacuation?"

"The humans are launching an attack. We're not safe here anymore."

He stopped her. "We've been told, but we received instructions to stay put and wait for further instructions. They'll never find us here."

Resolute, Mekte raised her chin. "These are your further instructions. Evacuate. Now help all these people out."

The caretaker hesitated.

"Now!" Mekte raised her voice. That did it.

A low rumbling marked her last word. Dust and debris fell from the top of the vault. People screamed and rushed toward the main exit gallery.

"Mekte!" Tancredi jolted, jumped forward and pushed her away to the ground an instant before a boulder and a rain of rocks crashed and raised a thick cloud of dust. Coughing, he cleaned her face. "Are you ok?"

Mekte nodded and looked at the boulder. At its foot, a contorted pulsating band lit the swirls of dust for a brief moment before it died off.

Tancredi pulled her onto her feet, and together they joined the others who were rushing out of the residential silo.

*
**

The large avenue bent into a narrower passage between massive, dark buildings that had been evacuated five days before; therefore, the insurgents didn't expect casualties among civilians.

The complexity of their structure and its edges made them resemble concretion of gigantic crystals grown through the millennia. In the passage, the incoming drones would have been closer to each other, and within the range of the planned blast.

The insurgents waited. The drones kept advancing, probing the area all around. Their blaster cannons and the mine launchers looked for possible targets.

Khulel's implant started to tickle. "Team leader here. Get ready." He glanced at its scanning device. "No humans yet. Matters not. Let's destroy those sentinels."

The slabs of stone vibrated under his body as his eyes stared at the area where the blast would have reduced the drones into shattered metal, if they were lucky. If they weren't . . . well, the drones would have been able to shatter the insurgents instead.

Through the visor of his helmet, Khulel checked one more time for his and the other teams' positions.

He thought of Mekte, but repressed that image away. This wasn't the time to indulge in those kind of reveries. His implant disturbed him even more now, and he brought his hand to scratch the back of his neck in an instinctive attempt to reduce the discomfort, only to find it covered by the protective pad. He rubbed his neck, jerking the pad.

The first drone appeared at the turn, followed by another, and another, and still more kept coming. Blades of coherent-light browsed around as the drones probed the area. The swirling sound of the guns spiraling their aims at probable targets seemed almost joyful in their expectation to deliver death.

The ground shook and the stones groaned. *Even our soil hates them*, Khulel thought. The scanner released an alarm in his visor, and multiple dots appeared at the edge of the maximum range scan. "Marines units," he said into the transponder. Then he grunted, "Fucking humans. They're too far away from the drones."

The transponder transmitted a reply in his ear. "No worries. They'll get closer."

"For sure." He sighed. "Blasters at maximum power. No one retreats without orders." He checked the scanning results once more. "S and T, stay hid until after the humans have engaged."

He received visual confirmation from those teams on the visor and smiled. *At least Mekte and the others will have had more time to escape.*

The closest sentinel drone slowed down and stopped. Its body bent into a U shape, and it scanned the area with both head and tail sensors as if it had detected a new, unexpected threat. The other drones gathered behind, stopped, and targeted the whole area around them.

"Crap! Something's raised their threat levels," Khulel voiced in the transponder. He glanced over and took a quick decision. "Forget the humans. Detonate the charges as soon as the last drone enters within range."

He set his blaster to explosive bolts. "I'll make them move!" He rushed into the open, then started firing at the first drone.

The drone cowered under the assault, and its sensors fought to acquire a target through the blaster hits. The rest of the group of drones jolted; their pods scratched the ancient stones of the pavement as they rushed into a wedge formation, then shot a barrage of counter fire. They charged.

The whole road section rose under their pods, then it fractured. A massive flash of light erupted from the cracks. The shock wave hit Khulel and sent him flying with the debris as if he had no weight.

He landed hard on his back and rolled over. He curled while rocks, dirt, rubbles, and drones' parts fell all around. The subsequent negative-blast wind sucked the dust back in toward the center, and a mushroom cloud rushed high from the central crater.

His heart pounded in his chest and ears. The ozone made his nostrils contract as the air ignited under the deluge of blaster explosions that his team sent into the area right after the deflagration.

Three drones farther away from the blast's center, though maimed and jerking their broken pods in the air, responded to the fire. The explosions rumbled, and the buildings waved and crumbled under the hits.

"Khulel. Khulel!" The voice reached his ears but not his brain. He tried to rise to his knees but fell over twice before he managed to stand up. He stumbled and looked around, lost. "Get down. Get down, dammit!" the voice insisted.

Blasters tracing shots lit up the area with bursts of color and lights. By instinct, he hustled into cover behind larger rubble. He breathed hard and took off his helmet. He was hit but couldn't tell where: he felt nothing.

"Teams S and T engaging," he overheard on the transponder. His outfit's life support system shot him up with adrenaline and pain killers. His eyes widened, he put his helmet back on and checked his vitals. It wasn't yet the moment to die.

"I'm all right, for now," he muttered, shook his head and tried to focus at the battle scene. His eyes dashed in all directions.

"Heavy fire. Hold positions. Marines engaged," a scratchy voice grasped him back to reality.

Khulel tried to understand where he was with respect to his team, but his sight was blurred. He fired up the visor scan but nothing came through. "I lost tracking."

"F leader," a voice from the transponder replied, "you're half block away down the main road. Follow the explosions. We're right in the middle," the voice cracked.

"Understood." He looked up, and then stumbled in the ankle-deep dust and debris.

***

The ground trembled under Mekte and Tancredi's feet. Kritas ran through spirals of dirt. The walls wobbled and the whole gallery groaned as if they were alive and in pain. Light blobs flickered and died off. The entry bays into the gliding shuttle tunnel opened along the walls, and wedges of light cut through the darkness.

The gallery crammed with people screaming for help, and caretakers shouting to line everyone up and speed them into the incoming vehicles.

"This is taking too long!" Tancredi pulled Mekte away.

"What are you doing?" she resisted. "This is the fastest way out!"

"I can shield you from the scanning. Can't do it here."

Mekte glanced at the crowd.

"C'mon, Mekte." Tancredi took her hand. "There must be another way."

Mekte nodded. "There is. Follow me!" She ran down the gallery, and he scrambled behind her.

They stopped at the sight of incoming transporters entering the area. Armed Kritas rushed out of the opening bays and surrounded them. "Mekte of Yutki," a Kritas faced her; a bright spot blinked on his tracking device. "We have orders to escort you to safety."

The guards drew out their blasters and aimed them at Tancredi.

"You alone."

"*What?*" She pushed the soldier away. "I'm not leaving without him." She backed off, reaching for Tancredi.

A rumble made them all turn toward the head of the gallery. Fumes escaped from cracks opening along the vault, glowing with a dark-yellow light. Vapor hissed with anger as rocks from the ceiling fell to the ground and on the Kritas crowd waiting to board the shuttles.

Tancredi shouted, "Marines!" The far wall crumbled, and airborne seekers' mine packs swerved through. Blasters screeched from the breach and drew scintillating rays of ionized dust particles in the thick air as the first explosions covered the screams of the wounded civilian Kritas.

"Get down!" Tancredi shouted and rushed Mekte behind the nearest Kritas vehicles to take cover. The gallery resounded with the whooshing noise of the seeker mines, chasing the Kritas and exploding at contact. The smell of burned flesh and ozone blended together in a pungent mixture.

"We need to go!" Tancredi glanced over at the battle, but Mekte didn't budge.

She stared at the floor. "I can't."

"What?"

Her eyes locked on his.

In assault gear, the marines advanced behind sentinel drones. Cries of pain echoed in the gallery as her people fell one after the other. The Kritas guards and caretakers attempted a desperate resistance, but the drones had them pinned down. Their number dwindled under the concentrated blasters fire they endured.

"I can't leave them," her voice cracked.

"Mekte. We'll die!"

She smiled. At once, she embraced her blaster, leaned to the side, and opened fire.

It is in moments when everything collapses and all hopes are lost that one either succumbs or rebuilds, renounces or reinvents, and finds the strength to search for that iota of uniqueness that makes you yell, 'I'm not finished.'

Tancredi rose to his feet and closed his eyes. His sight vanished but his *view* expanded.

Muffled, Mekte's voice died out, "Tancredi . . . "

His *touch* reached the Kritas guards but didn't stop there. It grew and enveloped the first seekers' mines that searched with growing fury their next target. Their processes and directives scintillated as an aura grew, surrounding each but fusing them all together. He split them, grabbed them, and quenched them. The mines slowed down and rested. Their sensors fired incoherent signals that left the artificial intelligence disoriented, unable to decide what next step to take.

The battle's momentum hung, undecided. The Kritas militia took the mines in their focused fire, and the first explosions shook the already-violated ground.

Tancredi's mind stretched out and sensed the nearby marines: cold and resolute. He stopped breathing for a moment. The soldiers had only one main target in their mind: him!

He opened his eyes and searched for Mekte. He shivered. She was so beautiful, so different and, yet, so hurtingly familiar. Everything separated them, so why couldn't he fathom now his life without her? His eyes caressed her traits, and his mind enfolded hers as a coffer protects a jewel.

He couldn't allow this any longer and risk losing her. He raised his hands and started to walk.

"Tancredi!" Mekte screamed.

The Kritas stopped firing. On his visor, the marines' commander saw the highlighted silhouette of his objective advance. A deadly silence enveloped the gallery as the marines ceased fire as well. The drones advanced and passed beyond Tancredi.

Overwhelmed, the Kritas dropped their guns. The marines surrounded them and the cryogenic teams entered through the breach.

A marine officer walked up to Tancredi. They stared at each other. From the back, two marines carried Mekte and pushed her to the ground, at their feet.

The officer touched his belt and a floating screen blossomed. "Main target acquired. Secondary target acquired."

On the screen, the Governor smiled. "Proceed with the next phase."

"Aye, aye, sir." The screen faded away.

With a stern voice, the officer activated his transponder. "Terminate the wounded and hibernate the brain implant carriers. Capture the others."

Chapter 11 - The Project

In Deadly Spires

THE SKY SHONE BRIGHTER by one additional star when the flag battleship established a geostationary orbit above Utthana. The spaceport had been evacuated and patrolled by marines for the imminent landing of the Governor's shuttle.

The Governor had summoned the Dean, her council members, and the Governing Board of the Authority to the Inquisition Research Center and mentioned his desire for no ceremonial welcoming at the spaceport.

From her office in the Tribunal tower, the Dean waited for his arrival. She stretched her tunic, and controlled over and over the latest updates on the dashboard.

So far, the marines had suffered heavy casualties, but so did the insurgents. The military still conducted a thorough search of the stealth area uncovered in the Under levels, and the Authority touted the resounding success of the operation with a hourly broadcast across the planet.

Her hands clutched together as she read again the internal communication: the prisoners had been sent directly to the research center, bypassing all Tribunal's authority and overruling her previous directives and her prerogatives, too. She went back to the transparent wall and stared in the distance. Nothing really justified the Governor's order of the large gathering in the capital, certainly not Tancredi and the Kritas girl's capture, nor the success of the operation, no matter how important it might have appeared in the Governor's eyes.

She adjusted the medallion on her necklace. She'd been denied access to her scholar. It mattered not what he did or didn't do, Tancredi Gilmor was still a scholar and under her authority.

She shook her head. The marines had adduced planetary security exceptional measures. The orders had been signed by the Governor himself; the marines' base commander smiled when he answered her formal request in those terms. And now the unscheduled meeting at the IRC without sharing with her any agenda.

The wall announced her assistant. She let him in.

He bowed. "The council members have all arrived."

"Let the Lead Councilor in," she said and took place at her desk. The dashboard floating screens showed the Governor's shuttle entering the atmosphere and descending toward the spaceport.

The assistant bowed and retreated. The wall coalesced to dilate again a few moments later.

"You wanted to see me."

The Dean nodded; then she sealed the room.

*
**

An energy dome rose around the IRC facility, and a large deployment of marine units and sentinel drones guarded the whole infrastructure.

The scholars' transporter landed on the authorized pad; military vehicles waited on the ground to take the scholars to the access points. The Dean and her Council entered a buffer zone and waited for the credential checks.

After the third exhaustive control on a council member, the Dean's Councilor took a deep breath. "Who authorized these new measures?" he asked the officer performing the checks. "Direct orders from the Governor, sir." The marine replied without taking his sight off the dashboard. "You'll be escorted to your destination shortly."

The Dean took the Councilor aside. "Stay calm, we'll know soon what's going on and the reason for all this. It's a demonstration of power and can only mean one thing. Whatever the Governor had in mind, he's ready now to show it off."

"I agree, but this is outrageous." He grunted.

The Dean didn't reply.

After the formalities, the group of scholars followed a marine squad into the compound.

At the IRC main entrance, other military personnel took over and led the scholars to a further military checkpoint prior to reaching the underground laboratories.

The Dean frowned.

The Councilor stepped forward. "Since when are the laboratories a restricted area to scholars?"

"Sir, stay with the group." The officer at the check point stopped him. He pointed to the scanning pad placed before the entrance. "Please," he said with a stern voice.

The Dean lowered her head, and the scholars complied. The marine at the security dashboard nodded.

After the scanning, the entrance dilated into a large, bare hall. In its center, the Authority representatives had already arrived. They lowered their heads and greeted the council members.

A colonel of the Governor's Guards approached and smiled. "Welcome, Madame Dean of Utthana. Council members." He greeted them with a brief nod. "This is a momentous day. The Governor will join us shortly."

The council members murmured, but the Dean raised her hand. "We're eager to meet with the Governor."

The wall dilated. The Governor entered, followed by the commander of the base, a Colonel, and his staff officers.

"Thank you for having accepted my invitation." The Governor smiled. "Today marks a milestone in scientific research and in our fight against the rebellion." His gaze found and paused on the Dean first, then moved to all her council members. "I don't have your mental abilities," he looked at the Dean again, "but I know you all have questions. Rest assured, they'll receive proper answers." He signaled the colonel, who stepped forward.

"I'm sure," he said, "you all noticed the enhanced security measures at your arrival. As of this morning, the Inquisition Research Center is under full military jurisdiction and in heightened alert. All communications to and from Ahthaza are monitored and censored accordingly to COMSEC, the communication security military code. An authentication system protects all transmissions against the acceptance of fraudulent—"

"What does that really mean?" the Dean interrupted.

The Governor tilted his head and took a long look at the Dean. "It means no communications to and from the planet will be possible without approval. We are at war, and IRC scientists have just given us the means to win it." He grinned.

The lights went down and a spotlight pointed at the Governor. The wall to his left became transparent and revealed scientists and technicians working in a large laboratory. At the far end, multiple floating screens filled an otherwise bare wall, with only a thin margin between each of them.

Scientific personnel worked at many brain renderings and followed the results of their activities on virtual diagrams that changed accordingly in a seeming festival of lights and shapes. Brain areas sparked and highlighted on those renderings.

Nearer to the transparent wall, in the middle of an otherwise empty, lit area, an unconscious Kritas lay inside a med-unit inclined toward the hall for the hosts to see. To his right side, an expanded rendering of his tri-lobed brain rotated at a snail's pace. In the back, from an opaque area of the brain convolution, darker filaments created a feathered net that pulsated and flickered.

From the rear of the lab, one of the scientists moved to the front and stopped next to the right side of the med-unit.

"You all surely recognize our lead scientist, Dr. Clark Grubeck," said the Governor. "Doctor Grubeck is the newly appointed director of the *Kreate* project: the Kritas Education and Training Exploitation programme." He smiled, filled his lung, and raised his chin. "Doctor Grubeck, please. We all can see you, now."

Grubeck lowered his head and glanced at the Governor.

The Dean tilted her head toward the Councilor. "I don't like this," she murmured. He nodded.

"Thank you, Governor." Grubeck placed his hands on the floating panel in front of him and stopped the brain rendering from turning. He cleared his throat. "We worked for years to understand the brain implants we found on Kritas' military personnel as we collected evidence of its existence during the last several years of the war."

He made the large, floating brain twist, tilted it and expanded the view of the back cortex for all to see the area from which filaments extended over the entire surface of the brain convolutions. The filaments pulsated where they penetrated inside the tissues. He touched the opaque area, which highlighted.

The med-unit dashboard raised, and Grubeck issued a few commands. The Kritas in the med-unit jerked and arched his back, then relaxed again.

"As you can see, we can now interact with it. We worked on the assumption that the implant masked or hid existing neural connections of its host in a passive way. We were looking for abnormalities and inhibitions in brain functions and structures." He paused.

"We were wrong." He paused again and his gaze wandered over the audience for a brief moment as if he searched for a reaction but couldn't find it. "What we discovered, instead, was a much increased brain connectivity in the orbit-frontal and rear cortices, extending into the deeper para-central lobules." He touched the brain model and highlighted the different zones.

He turned around. In the hall, all eyes stared at him.

"What's unique about the implant," he continued, "is that it enhances the subjects' structural and functional connectivities with unparalleled efficiency and with a short reaction time. The increased structural wiring replaces its natural counterpart, but it declines with time as soon as the stimuli stop. An implant's prolonged activity destroys the original wiring patterns, the artificially induced ones fade away, and the subject is reduced to, well, to a mindless idiot."

He stepped forward. "Finally, we now understand how to trigger specific rewiring and induce behavioral changes." His lips curled in a half smile. "At least temporarily, and with minimal damage. But also for this side-effect, we're close to eliminating a few of the current issues we still have."

The noise of chattering rose in the hall. The members of the Authority nodded to each other and gesticulated toward the lab and the large floating brain.

An even broader smile spread across the Governor's face. "Please, I know what you're thinking. Hold your excitement for a little longer. It will be clearer soon." The chatter subdued as the Governor captured everyone's attention. "Doctor Grubeck," he said. "I believe we are convened here today for a little demonstration..."

"Absolutely." He lowered his head at the Governor. His lips tightened. He signaled the personnel in the laboratory. "We'll proceed right away."

The back-end wall of the hall where the hosts were gathered brightened up. Everyone turned to the source of light. Two contiguous cells seemed to open directly into the hall. A cylindrical, transparent barrier restrained one male Kritas in the middle of the cell on the left. His hands were tied behind his back. On the second cell, a female Kritas, unrestrained. She paced the cell, her eyes lost in the void.

The scholars stood still, while the Authority members stepped back.

"Worry not," said the Governor. "Those two terrorists are in their detention cells, far from here, and don't present any danger to you." He stepped forward and touched the wall. "They're not really there. What you will see happening is live, but in a remote place. They cannot hear nor see you."

The Kritas female reached the front wall of cell, just a step away from the Governor, who grinned.

The Authority members retreated even more.

She stood in front of the Governor, a blank stare on her face, then resumed her maniacal gait.

A metallic bar appeared on the floor, but the Kritas female didn't seem to notice it.

The Governor let the scene sink in for a few moments, then he turned. "Doctor Grubeck," he said, "would you briefly describe the setup of the experiment for the benefit of our guests?"

The scientist lowered again his head. "The two subjects," he said, "carry the Kritas brain implant. On your left, the male was captured yesterday during a military operation. He was part of a terrorist group that would surely have performed more criminal acts today if our forces hadn't confronted them."

Some of the spectators nodded and glared at the prisoner. The Dean kept looking at Grubeck, but from the corner of her eye she noticed that the Governor, instead, stared at her. She glanced at him and forced herself to smile.

"The female, instead…" Grubeck paused. "This particular terrorist is one of our first successful subjects. As you might have guessed, we're still in the preliminary phases, so she doesn't look perfectly right in her mind." He paused.

"Well, she'd be noticed if she walked down the street." The Governor chuckled, followed by most of those present among the civil servants.

Grubeck waited for the laughter to settle, then resumed. "Her brain is fighting our modified implant, which explains her behavior, and the rewiring we engineered conflicts deeply with the natural attitudes of the subject, of course. Without the proper stimuli, her mind falls back into a…let's say a confused state."

"That's a minor detail for now," the Governor interrupted and waved his hand. "One thing you all need to know…" he waited for everyone to look at him. "One thing you all need to know is that thanks to the brilliant work of Doctor Grubeck and his team, a Kritas subject, a carrier of our modified implant, can detect and react to carriers of the unmodified Kritas implant." He stared at Grubeck. "Please continue, doctor."

Grubeck blinked and hesitated for a moment. His jaw tightened.

The Dean glanced at the Governor. His eyes were fixed on Grubeck's.

"Of course, Governor," the doctor finally said. He took a deep breath. "As the Governor said," he paused, "the second specimen has been instructed to perceive a lethal, imminent threat when confronted by another Kritas who is also an implant carrier. The perception induces a strong survival reaction within the subject. We've remodelled the fight-or-flight reaction to only one possible solution for the subject: eliminate the threat."

The Dean sighed and stared at the cells, then she closed her eyes.

"As you will all be able to witness now, the results of our research will allow us to proceed more expeditiously against the terrorists," Grubeck continued.

With a huff, the wall separating the two cells descended into the floor. The female Kritas stopped her gait and twisted around. She opened her mouth into a terrified screaming when she saw the other prisoner, but there was no audio to reach the hall, and the audience stared at the scene unfolding in an eerie silence.

She stepped back and her foot stumbled on the metal bar on the floor. Her eyes didn't leave the other Kritas. She bent, with measured movements, still looking at the other prisoner. Her hand tapped around and searched until she grabbed the bar. She jolted, and ran into the other cell and hit the cylindrical barrier with the bar. Over and over again, her face transfixed with fury into a muted shout. Her eyes betrayed a rage and a hatred which was proper only to altered minds.

In that surreal silence, everyone watched as if they had entered a state of trance, unable to resist the morbid fascination of violence and death.

The Governor filled his lungs and exhaled. A satisfied grimace altered his face, but his eyes didn't leave the Dean's neck.

The male Kritas slammed his back against the cylindrical barrier, away from the madness that was assaulting him; his eyes widened in a terror that grew as each blow was delivered with a hypnotic regularity.

After a brief hesitation and muted exclamations, the audience erupted into applause. The scholars didn't participate in the enthusiasm.

The Governor nodded and smiled as if he was at his re-election speech. He raised his arms. "Yes! Kritas terrorists will become their own, fatal threat." He waved his arms, encouraging the spectators' excitement. "Countless human and marines' lives will be saved through this enduring struggle." He looked at the scholars. "As should have been already the case for so long by now. But we did it, at last!"

The Dean turned her head, slowly, and glared at him for a split second, then smiled and lowered her head.

The Governor frowned, then nodded, "*We* did it!" he boasted again, enjoying a thunder of applause.

After the event, members of the IRC facility took the authority members and the scholars on a guided tour of the new laboratory infrastructures. When alone with his personal guards, the Governor called out. "Doctor Grubeck!"

The wall dilated and the scientist entered the hall.

"I believe you understand that shortcomings are not to be shared with anyone, only their resolutions."

Grubeck lowered his head. "Governor, we can't yet do what you have said to those people. A rewired Kritas will be aggressive toward any Kritas in range, and the rewiring is still highly unstable."

"It doesn't matter. They're all terrorists. You're working toward solving this problem, right?"

Grubeck nodded. "Certainly, but—"

The Governor raised his hand. "There's no *but*. We have already something we can work with. And that's what we have achieved so brilliantly. Thanks to you, of course." He added. "Be proud for what you've done for your race."

The Governor walked toward the exit wall, followed by his guards, waited for it to dilate, and left Grubeck alone.

A virtual dashboard activated and rose in front of the backend wall. Remotely, a series of commands blinked on the panels and, this time, the audio from the cells filled the hall. The female Kritas shrieked still her fury, cadenced with each swing against the cylinder that protected the other prisoner.

The cylinder lowered. The male Kritas yelled, "Stop it! What are you doing?" and tried to stop the cylinder's downward movement, pushing against it with his back and feet. With a last shove, the metal bar, this time, reached and cracked his head. He looked stunned and his pupils dilated.

The female hit again and again. The cylinder disappeared into its socket, and the body collapsed to the floor marred with blood and cerebral matter. The female prisoner kept hitting; blood spurted and traced the floor with colored strikes. The Kritas' torso and head turned into a wobbling mass that trembled under the brunt of each new impact.

The fury stopped. The arm that held the bar stiffened, and a quiver descended from the female's head until her whole body shook in the throes of convulsions. She bawled incoherent words at first, then her guttural moans resounded in the hall.

A final gasp. Her body warped and she fell to the floor. Her eyes rolled over, and blood seeped from her ears. She froze at last.

Grubeck paled.

CHAPTER 12 – THE LAW

AND THE EXCEPTIONS

WHEN HE WOKE UP, Tancredi was cold, and his feet were numb. He was thirsty; his mouth was dry and his tongue detected a taste of dust and metal. His muscles ached, and he had tried to ignore their cramps until the pain numbed and his body muted.

He had lost count of the hours, or were they instead days? He searched for Mekte's presence, her mind and her thoughts, but found nothing. She wasn't there. Then, he noticed nothing and no one else was there, either. An isolation ward.

They had a similar facility in the Tribunal, but there, *there* the isolation reached a level he wasn't aware was possible, yet, at the Tribunal; at least not for anyone without his training. In detention, isolation enhanced the effectiveness of a mental inquisitive process; no interferences, no disturbances, but this wasn't the Tribunal, he reasoned. *"They cannot scare me with their empty spaces,"* he muttered the words of ancient poetry, *"I have my own deserts."*

He couldn't distinguish the cell's boundary: the cylindrical barrier that constrained him blurred the vision, both physical and mental. He could stand straight, or bend his knees against the barrier to rest the muscles of his back, but that hurt after a while.

Stretching his mind served him no purpose. Around, he only perceived emptiness. Oh, they'd tried to probe him, a few times, even, but he had repelled all of their attempts. So far, he hadn't needed to exert himself that much.

When he surrendered to the marines, he expected interrogations, coercions, even physical hardship, but this had surprised him. He received a shot as soon as they brought him inside a military vehicle, and lost his consciousness, only to wake up inside the cylinder.

After he had first regained consciousness, his knees hurt when he stood up, and it had required a considerable effort. How long had he been in that cramped position?

No one had replied to his initial calls and shouts, then the mental probings had started and increased in intensity at each new attempt, testing him, trying his capacities. He could resist them; they just didn't know how much and for how long.

In his mind, he relived the past events. He recalled the memories, vivid as if he was still there, witnessing the last days, again, and savoring each moment.

How did the marines find him? They must have traced him, for sure. But if they could trace his position, then he didn't really escape the first time, did he?

How stupid. He had been a pawn in a game played at a higher level, but by whom? The Dean? The military? The Authority?

His mind went back to when and where it all started, as Mekte told him in her first message in the data cube. That day . . . did the lieutenant at the compound trick him? Made him eager to change the route that day and go instead to the Alliance Square?

The memories at the square added to one another and enhanced the mental images he recreated. He reviewed the scene and analyzed the sensations of the bystanders.

In his mind, he saw himself at the moment when he stepped out of his shuttle. The crowd had reacted with mixed flows of fear, anger, surprise, interest, annoyance. Then questions and doubts, and . . . was there a pinch of hope, too?

He tried to isolate each sensation, crawling back to their source. The marines exuded surprise, anger, annoyance; fear and anger from the Kritas, too, in whirls that in his mind glowed with different colors, and his brain translated into different fragrances and sounds.

Then he saw *her*. Mekte was there, too, surrounded by the sweetness of hope. The golden glow of expectation for the future shone around her. Her eyes had followed him as he left the shuttle, and she focused on each of his movements and actions.

He hesitated. Shouldn't he collaborate with his own people? Reveal what he saw, what he learned from them, the Kritas? Not much, yet—he admitted with himself—but enough to better understand what to do next, how to avoid a path of death and destructions. Understanding . . . someone would call it betrayal.

Plans. What plans did the Kritas have? Mekte planned to survive, to help others survive, to break the cycle of violence and hatred. He had seen the derelicts, the pariahs, the maimed ones, those wounded in their bodies and in their minds, and he didn't perceive a threat from them, he didn't taste the bitter flavour of hatred.

Could he betray her? Could he understand her fully? Is this our plan? He mulled over and over. What's the ultimate goal of the Law if not to achieve integration, protect everyone from brutality, hostility, and cruelty? Sure, they dealt with the inevitable violent ones, but their goal was to recover them, remove the hatred; not by force, but by breaking the mental knots and barriers that fueled their loathe. Break the chains.

He believed *that* was his ultimate mission when he had been assigned to the Tribunal in Utthana, and that it was indeed the mission of every scholar. How different he found the planet, instead. Oppressors and oppressed, mistrust and fear from both sides. Who was chained to whom? A binary vision, black and white. Where were all the colours that flourish in life?

Was the Dean part of it? Maybe, but part of what, and why? A conspiracy to revamp military operations starting from Ahthaza? Decimate the Kritas, cull their race as the humans had once been culled? Could this be the goal?

Sure, Mekte's doubts proved that also among the Kritas a violent solution had its staunch followers. It's always the easiest path: brandish a gun, blast away to fight for your own perceived rights, obliterate all others, see them just as mere obstacles. Peace and understanding is difficult. War is easy.

He recalled the two books he had found in Mekte's residence, the *Daimones* and the *Heavenly Fathers*. Each a kind of bible for their respective races, the humans and the Kritas. Bibles, but whose foundations laid at the heart of what had doomed the human race hundred of years before.

Was someone trying to re-enact—in a disguised way—what had happened on Earth? The same atrocity endured by the race of men as they discovered they weren't alone in the Universe? Was this just a link in a chain of a vengeful history repeating?

He breathed out. Now, nothing mattered anymore. He had surrendered; he had lost. All was lost. He had betrayed everything he believed in. His studies, the Law, the brotherhood of the scholars, and more. Even his own race. Nothing mattered anymore. His chin dropped and he closed his eyes.

Mekte. From a remote recess of his mind, he recalled her voice, her taste, her smell. His heart changed rhythm, and his mind sharpened. He straightened up.

Mekte. Where did they take her? What were they doing to her?

He didn't know how, but he had to get out of there—wherever that was—and find her.

Mekte, Mekte, Mekte. Her name resounded in his mind, persistent, incessant. He filled his lungs. He needed to play them, trick them, and be the one finding answers and discovering things.

A new mental probe arrived, throbbing, pushing at the boundary of his mind; he faked the barriers he had erected. He let them bend and falter under the newly increased pressure.

*
**

A relucent dome covered the tip of the Tribunal's tower. Five landing pads formed a pentagram around it, protruding from the sides of the tower, giving the impression from above that one was looking down at a blossoming and welcoming flower.

The shuttles, with the Deans of the five regions that shared the main areas of influence in the planet Ahthaza, rested like bees stretching their legs on petals and absorbed the warmth of the rising sun.

In the first moments of dawn, when looked at from the landing pads, the dome shone golden. From the heights of the Tribunal, one could enjoy a glorious view of Utthana. No one in the Council Room, however, paid attention to anything but the reports, the intelligence notes, and the assessments of the latest events coming from scholars embedded in field operations who were active through the main cities in Ahthaza and from privileged connections within the space marines corps.

Inside, the center of the Council Room glowed from the many screens, diagrams, and renderings that floated and revolved in the middle of the Circle, where the council members had their seats.

The Dean of Utthana occupied the 'Protector of the Law' chair, a larger seat with the Scholars' symbol carved on its backrest.

The Dean stood up and looked at every person present in the council that day. "All of this points to a coordinated operation to justify, throughout the whole planet, the same measures that have been adopted here in Utthana."

The lead Councilor raised his chin; his scarlet toga glimmered. "I'm afraid the information our colleagues have gathered is unmistakable."

The members nodded. The Northern Area's Dean stood up to voice his concerns. His white hair, tightened in a knot, contrasted with the deep darkness of his eyes. "This amounts to sabotage and treason." He gestured at the symbols of the dashboard floating in front of his seat. A series of diagrams took life. "The marines act on reports and threat levels that have been tampered with, there can't be any doubt now. And this fraudulent manipulation is spreading to all regions." He sat back shaking his head.

"That we can agree upon. But who is, or who are the perpetrators?" The Protector of the Law, the Dean of Utthana, replied. "The Governor? The military? I don't think the Authority would have any internal leverage to pull this off. And we can't levy accusations without flawless proof." She stepped off the Circle and stood in the middle; the screens and renderings flickered and disappeared. "The military holds prisoners Tancredi Gilmor and the Kritas girl identified as Mekte, daughter of Yutki. They're in isolation. Gilmor is a scholar, and the military has refused any details regarding his detention."

The lead Councilor nodded, pensive. "In other circumstances . . . " he had started, "but there are no other circumstances. This could mean one thing."

All members fixed their eyes at him.

"They know, Gilmor and the Kritas girl, something the military needs to keep secret."

The Dean lowered her head. "I believe the same. Can we risk this council to do the right thing, then?"

"We don't know who's pulling the levers, from how high, and in what hierarchy," the Councilor said.

"If a martial law were to be declared, scholars would be replaced by military personnel in all key positions. We don't have much time." She turned to operate her dashboard. The rendering of the model of the Interrogation Facility filled the space within the Circle. "We need to act before it's too late."

*
**

The fight continued in the underground levels. Marines and drones swarmed through the city but encountered a fierce resistance that had slowed down their penetration. In the Space Marine HQ Command and Control, the 3D Utthana model presented pouches of uncharted and contested areas.

"How could the scholars miss that, and how could you?" the Governor snapped.

The Marines' Commander in Chief, a veteran general from the times of the war against the Kritas Alliance, ruled over all troops stationed in Ahthaza and wasn't used to be confronted that way. He clenched his jaws before replying, and continued to stare at the image of the Governor. It contrasted brightly with the dimmed luminosity of the CC room; the marine squinted his eyes and spoke through his teeth. "Scholars' methods are soft, Governor, and—frankly—they held us back."

The Governor stared back. "For how long has this been out of control?"

"It's hard to say, sir. We're still evaluating data from the sniffers, but from the terrorists' response I'd say their preparation must have begun years ago, at the very least."

"Years!" His eyes widened up. "Under our nose?"

"Afraid so, sir." The marine raised his chin.

The Governor sent a cold stare toward the general. "And yet, all past reports state that only sparse pouches of the old resistance remained, weakened, and faded in their resolve and capabilities."

The marine nodded. "If I may, sir, I think the scholars have grossly underestimated them."

He searched for a sign of hesitation in the marine's steady gaze. "It's hard to digest, General, that it is *just* because of the scholars. Even for me."

The marine puffed out his chest. "Governor, the military was right in pushing for certain programs to be kept secret."

He stared at the general and took a long breath before replying. "At the moment, I can't think of any political solution to these… uncertainties. I'd like to have more time."

"We don't have much time, Governor."

The Governor caressed his chin and took a long look at the soldier. "Where are we with the rewiring?"

"Now that scholars are less of a factor, I've pulled resources from other programs, sir," the general stepped forward, "and we're concentrating all efforts on the operation at our main base."

"What's the ETA?"

"Within the week, we will be able to deploy the first units."

"I'm sticking my neck out for this, General. It has to end swiftly."

"We will be swift, Governor." He grinned.

"You'd better be, General." He paused. "I'm not the one who will take the blame." His eyes pierced the general's.

"I understand, sir." The general stiffened.

"I'm sure you do." The Governor's image froze, and then faded away.

The general faced the base commander, who had stayed in retreat and in silence during the whole exchange. "And the same goes for you," he said in a stern voice. "You'd better give me the results we need."

*
**

The marines' security ward complex featured a circular floor plan. The complex rose beyond the Utthana city limits, on a flat area surveyed by sentinel drones around the clock. An energy vault protected the overall structure. Four buildings were arranged in concentric rings and surrounded a fifth cylindrical one: the central detention area. The buildings connected to each other through five radial gateways so that from above, the structure resembled a gigantic bullseye.

The external ring presented a smooth surface all around, with no section breaks nor structural details. It absorbed most of the light spectrum and appeared to the naked eye as an anomaly in the tridimensional space, as if it was the threshold into a dark void.

A scholar shuttle, in full stealth mode, travelled the plains at low speed toward the facility. On the onboard navigation dashboard, a detailed rendering of the building showed the emplacement of its surveillance systems.

Without taking his eyes off the flight's instrumentation in the cockpit, the Councilor breathed out hard.

The Dean tilted her head. "Now what?"

He shook his head. "Nothing."

"Nothing and no one can hear, see, or intercept our chat. Even the flight recording is disabled. So, again, now what?"

"You're a brave woman."

She smiled in the dimmed light of the cockpit. "Am I? What makes you say so?"

"You face a grave risk."

She huffed. "I couldn't expose the Tribunal institution, or the scholars. If anything goes wrong, it will be just the crazy design of a delusional lady who felt her influence and power were in jeopardy."

"Nevertheless . . . "

"You're here, too." She winked.

"Where should I be when a delusional lady takes on a crazy design?" He glanced at her and smiled.

She harbored only a half smile. "I should've acted before. The signs were there…"

"Let's hope we're not too late."

The Councilor kept gliding the shuttle down the five degree slope to the planned landing spot. "We'll touch ground shortly."

She glanced at him and nodded.

The shuttle descended, fending the air without creating turbulence. It was invisible and inaudible unless one knew what to look for and when and created only a slight variation of the air refractive index. Its passage looked like a billowy shimmering in the air, which faded away almost instantaneously.

"What time is it?" the Dean asked.

"We're in time for the rendezvous." He glanced at the navigation instruments and pointed to a blip on the terrain rendering. "Our contact is waiting." He averted the Dean's question, adding, "I've known him for many years. Don't worry."

The shuttle landed at the foot of a low hill. The security scan on the dashboard showed the presence of one target to their north, identified by the onboard probes as a friendly military vehicle.

"The area's clear," said the Councilor as he imported the contact location on the perimeter scanner and tagged it.

She nodded. "Let's go then."

They left the shuttle and its cloaking envelope from the dilated port side. The reddish light of the cabin severed the outside night darkness. Behind them, the opening coalesced, and only an attentive eye could detect the slight slant that distorted the dim scenery where the invisible shuttle had landed. They glanced farther down the plain at the huge security complex that rose high in the distance.

The military vehicle approached. It stopped next to them, and the rear entry bay opened. They boarded. The entry closed, followed by a sucking sound.

An intense white flash warmed their faces like a sudden gust of a desert wind and left them blinded for a moment.

The Councilor's hand rushed for his blaster but he froze when a stern and altered voice resounded in the bare cabin. "Don't try stupid things, Councilor."

His hand floated inches above the gun's handle, hesitating, then desisted and relaxed along his side.

"You're being scanned, now. Don't move."

Despite their still-impaired vision, they distinguished a silhouette in front of them and the mouth of an assault rifle blaster ready to fire.

"You've got quite an arsenal with you, for two peaceful scholars." The voice sounded amused, and this time it wasn't distorted. "Maybe I shouldn't worry too much, then."

The Councilor breathed out. "For a moment I thought we'd been double-crossed. Why all the precaution, Maj—"

"No grades, no names, Councilor. We should be safe in here, but I prefer it this way." The marine stepped forward into the slight illumination.

The vehicle seemed to be destined to transport and cargo roles. Storage units and cargo conveyors occupied much of the space. Standing personnel harnesses dangled off the bulkhead for when flight roughness might require it. The soldier wore an anonymous fatigue uniform, and still aimed the blaster at them.

The vehicle hummed louder and lifted off the ground, sending a brief vibration through the metallic floor.

He finally lowered the gun, and then activated a navigation panel. "We'll be at destination shortly."

The Dean tilted her head. "Who's piloting?"

The marine snorted. "Let's say that I'm not the only one in the corps to be concerned about the events of the last year."

"A whole year?" the Councilor asked.

He paused, and stared at him, then nodded slowly. "So it's true; scholars aren't involved, or you would know." He gave a snort. "Here." He handed them two sealed flexible bags. "Wear these, they'll adjust to your size."

They looked at him.

He grinned. "You don't want to venture into the base with your scholar outfits, do you?"

They opened the bags, and frowned when they took out two worn-out and dirty maintenance-workers' uniforms.

"Yes, they do smell," he smiled. "No one has clean, brand-new gear where you're going, nor do they shower daily."

The Dean glanced at him and bent her head, but then undressed and donned the tattered uniform. "You just said we scholars are not involved. In what?"

The marine's traits stiffened. "It's not honorable for the Corps. That's not the way we fight . . . and win." He took out a data-cube. "Load this to your tracking devices. There's the location of the cell you're looking for and a few other things we believe might interest you."

"You're not answering," she said.

"As I said, I like it better this way. You'll discover everything by yourself." He stared at her. "These are dangerous times."

The Councilor adjusted a cap on his head. "So, where are you taking us to, exactly?"

A wicked smile rose to the marine's lips. "Just to the main hangar for the training of the sentinel drones securing the complex."

"What?" the Councilor frowned.

"If you go through there, you'll be able to get straight into the maintenance tunnels, travel fast, and mingle with the workers. It's all in the data-cube."

The Dean reached for his arm. "Tell me. Why are you doing this?"

He looked at her hand first, then his eyes met hers. "I believe in principles, Ma'am, and in their guidance. When they're shattered, I get upset and try to change things."

He took out two small cards from inside his jacket. "These are your workers' IDs. Put them in the front pocket of your vests." He waited for the scholars to comply. "If you get in serious trouble, flash them to a security post terminal. One of us is on duty today and knows about your presence today."

"*Us?*" the Councilor asked.

He curled his lips. "Remember, only if you get in serious trouble."

"We won't abuse." The Dean nodded. "After this is over, though, we should share more . . . us scholars and you all, whoever you are."

The marine tilted his head. "One step at the time. For now, you have more urgent tasks to attend; and things to learn."

The Dean knitted her brows.

"Get ready, we're almost there." He glanced at the navigation panel.

A pinging sound preceded the announcement from the cockpit, "We are cleared to enter the docking area. Landing in two."

The three exchanged an intense look. The marine broke the moment of silence. "Stick to the route on your tracker and you should be fine. Use your scholars' tricks, but I don't need to remind you about those, right?"

The Dean walked up to him and placed her hand on his arm. "I hope I'll see you soon in other circumstances, Major." She smiled. "And I know your name, too. I can see it in your mind."

The marine opened his mouth, but then he sighed and shook his head. "Tricks. Be safe, Ma'am. I'm sure we'll meet again." He grinned. "You too, Councilor."

The Councilor lowered his head.

A faint thud and a sudden, gentle jerk told them they'd just landed. With a hissing sound, the docking bay bulkhead bulged forward and twirled open. From the hangar, metal banging against metal, echoing noises from workers and tools, and the regular thumping from marching sentinel drones reached them. The smell of machineries, ozone, and human perspiration attacked their nostrils.

"Wait here." The marine raised his hand and stepped out. They heard him speaking, but couldn't distinguish his words. In the docking bay, the conveyors activated and their metallic arms gripped a few of the containers, loaded them on their central tray, and drifted out in procession.

The marine peeked inside. "Come. Watch out, now."

Hesitating at first, the scholars waited for the last conveyor to leave the docking bay and got off the vehicle.

The conveyors lined up outside and unloaded their cargo on a floating platform. A worker, wearing the same kind of uniform the scholars had received, supervised the operation as he scanned the containers.

The marine winked at the scholars. "Better experience, arriving when you're expected, right?"

The scholars glanced around. The hangar hosted hundreds of drones at rest, aligned on both sides, still menacing, even if they appeared to be 'dormant.' Robotic transporters entered repair platforms with spare parts, mostly for drones, released them, and left for other deliveries. A few maintenance workers attended drones on the repair platforms, but that seemed to be the only human-led operation, as the rest worked unsupervised by humans, under the rules of an artificial intelligence coordination.

"The sentinels are probing…" said the Dean.

"They always do, even those over there," the marine nodded at the 'dormant' drones, "but your badges should cover you as long as you do not initiate hostile actions. Besides, you scholars have your ways, right?" He tilted his head knowingly.

"We do," said the Councilor.

The screeching sound of heavy blasters shots startled them. Toward the rear of the hangar, drones had initiated a testing of their gunnery under the watch of technical crews. The crews had interfaced the sentinels' 'brains' and monitored the results on a large set of floating panels showing a constant flow of data and diagrams related to threat prioritization, target acquisition, and selected offensive action. The targets, floating spherical blobs creating the simulacrum of different hostiles, exploded in a cloud of vapor each time the drones hit them.

"Sorry for the noise," yelled one of the technicians at the nearest platform. "With the ongoing fight against the Kritas terrorists, we're facing a surge in repair needs."

The marine spat on the ground. "Fucking terrorists."

Without hesitation, the Councilor nodded. "Yeah, fuck them!"

The Dean glanced at him, but the Councilor pretended not to have noticed.

The conveyors had finished unloading and moved slowly back into the loading bay. "We're done here!" shouted the worker attending the goods reception. The floating platform swiveled and drifted away, followed by the worker who raised his hand in a last goodbye gesture.

"Now, you're on your own," the marine said. "Behind me, you should be able to see a bulkhead marked MC2."

The scholars looked over his shoulder, and then nodded.

"Your journey starts from there. Your IDs will grant you access, at least until you get to the detention ward. Go now, and don't mind the smell on your way out. Good luck." He gave a nod, and headed back to the transporter. The bulkhead closed with a spiral and a huff.

"What do you suppose that remark was for?" asked the Councilor.

"I'm afraid we'll discover that in due time," said the Dean. "Time to move." Without hesitation, she started toward the MC2 bulkhead.

Chapter 13 - Through Closed Eyes

Dark Light

THE WALL OF THE DETENTION UNIT dilated. A marine inquisitor, severe in his dark uniform, entered followed by a scholar. The marine stopped in the middle of the cell, right in front of the gleaming cylinder that constrained Tancredi.

"Tancredi Gilmor," he called out. The prisoner raised his chin. Their eyes met.

Tancredi noticed his rank and snorted. "I would've expected at least a Colonel."

The marine grumbled. "Then you're less important than you think."

"Maybe, but more than what you pretend I am, since you're here, Captain."

The other scholar, who stood a few steps behind, grinned.

The captain pursed his lips. "The scholar here," he nodded toward his companion, "affirms we've gathered everything we could from you on your little expedition into the under levels."

Tancredi smiled. "He's lying," he said.

The scholar jolted and frowned. "I'm telling the truth!" He stepped forward to stare at the captain.

The marine's face turned red. He glared at Tancredi. "You think you're clever, do you? We have other methods to extort information from recalcitrant prisoners."

"I'm sure you do. I wondered when you would've started with your empty menaces." Tancredi shook his head. "The scholar's not really lying, but everything is a big word, and things can be hidden by those who know well how to search."

The marine reached forward, and his breath clouded the pristine transparency of Tancredi's cylindrical prison. "You're not being accused of treason, yet," he hissed, "but I'll rejoice when it happens. I'll show you how we deal with our enemies."

Tancredi sneered. "Enemies, you say? Like the Kritas female captured with me?"

That caused a flash in the captain's mind, just what Tancredi needed.

He sneaked through the mental images and their resonances, snippets of words and thoughts, and grabbed them all. Mekte was alive, and now he knew where they held her, but his fears had unfortunately received also a confirmation. He bent his head forward. His black eyes glimmered with such a rage that the captain's instincts made him retreat.

Tancredi's voice lowered to a menacing tone. "I won't talk to you, Captain, and the scholar here will confirm you that it's pointless to continue with the mental probings. So be a good lapdog and bring this news to your masters."

"How dare you..." the captain boasted a confidence that didn't match with the tension in his traits.

"Is this how you treat your enemies?" Tancredi pulled from the captain's memories the duress he had inflicted on Kritas' prisoners and their pain. Like a sharp boomerang veers back to where it comes from, he let those sensations slam against the surprised marine. The memories cut deep into the soldier's sensations, tearing and shredding through his emotional armour. He paled.

"Ugh," the marine gasped and stepped back. The scholar intervened at once and broke the mental grip, or at least so he thought; Tancredi let go without opposing what would have been an easy resistance.

"I'm sorry," the scholar said. "I wasn't expecting anything like that." He helped the marine regain his composure. He glanced at the prisoner and hesitated. "He won't be able to do it again anymore in my presence."

The captain's jaws clenched, but he nodded. The wall of the cell dilated. "You'll be sorry," he hissed between his lips as he reached the exit.

The scholar frowned. "How did you . . . That was cruel." He stared at the prisoner.

Tancredi stared back and breathed hard. "I'm not sure where cruelty lies anymore, scholar. Try to be safe in this new world."

The scholar's eyebrows puckered. He reached the exit, then pivoted to stare once more at the prisoner until the wall of the prison cell coalesced.

***

A plaque near the MC2 bulkhead read: "Maintenance Conduit 2 – Authorized Personnel Only."

"Well, let's see whether these IDs work." The Councilor stopped in front of the scanner visor in the bulkhead. The card in his chest pocket glowed, and a hologram showing his head formed in front of the visor.

"Wait for biometric identification," said the voice from the security system AI.

The blasters' screeching sounds and the explosions from the obliterated targets in the test area stopped suddenly. The drones were leaving the shooting range, and another group approached with a fast pace to take their place.

The two scholars turned to look at the new arrivals, and the hologram vanished, "Biometric identification interrupted."

A patrol of six drones passed in front of the MC2 as they headed for the gunnery test area. The last one slowed down and stopped, imitated by the other five.

"Stay calm and clear your thoughts," the Dean whispered. "We're maintenance workers and the manifest lists our tasks for MC2."

The drones reverted, their tail sections raised and pointed at the scholars, all at the same time, with a fluid, homogeneous movement. The blue light blades of their probing sensors brushed the bodies of the two scholars from top to bottom and back to then pause at their faces. "Identification," six emotionless voices exclaimed at once.

The ID cards in the scholars' workers uniforms lit up as the drones collected the data and verified them with the central security information system of the complex.

Seconds passed, and the Dean and the Councilor felt the drones' attempts to interpret their brain waves and assess the threat level they could possibly represent.

The scholars took long and slow breaths, closed their eyes to focus, and waited. A drop of sweat formed on the Councilor's right temple.

After interminable moments, the drones released the mental probing and the blue lights faded. As a choir that had reached the tipping point of a suspenseful symphony, they lined up again in formation and pronounced their verdict, "Identification confirmed, return to your duties."

The Councilor breathed out as the drones resumed their synchronised gait. "Six of them, probing at the same time . . . that wasn't easy."

"I know," the Dean sighed. "It was a real juggling to present them with coherent mental responses at the same time. I felt their probing compare the mental patterns from all sides."

"I don't think I could manage more than six of them."

The Dean gave him a worried look and nodded. "Let's hope we'll not have to prove your theory."

The Councilor faced the scanner visor again.

"Wait for biometric identification," the system repeated. Without further interruptions, the contour of the bulkhead pulsated, and its surface twirled open. The MC2 entrance alley revealed itself to their eyes, and they stepped in.

When the bulkhead closed behind them, the Councilor checked the itinerary on his tracker. "The first waypoint is on the second building. I hope these detours are worth the added risks of taking a longer route."

The Dean bent her head to the side. "We're supposed to be on a scheduled workflow, and we need to be checking a cryogenic unit there. It's actually a short ride on the transport network," she said. "Let's not waste time, then." She strode across the alley.

When they reached the platform of the MC2 hub station, shuttle shells in the inertial transit streams flashed through at high speed with their load of workers inside. At times, even faster container-only transports drifted across. Personnel left or entered those shells that had detached from the fastest middle stream to slow down and come to a halt at the boarding platform.

Floating virtual screens showed the travel information of each passenger, while they waited for their shuttle to arrive. A group of workers already waited on the platform and the scholars joined them; their ID cards communicated the tasks' manifesto with the expected destination. A virtual screen came into view, showing their faces and travel information. "Shuttle time of arrival . . .ten seconds," the screen announced.

The Dean leaned forward to glimpse at an empty shuttle shell that swerved through the various multi-speed streams. It merged with the slowest one and came to a stop in front of them. Its side dilated and the Dean boarded, followed by the Councilor.

With their backs glued to the rear wall, the surface adjusted to the contour of their bodies to provide support during the journey. The measure was redundant, though, and more to obey to security protocols than because of a real need as each shell generated its own inertial reference system. Passengers barely felt the accelerations, and perceived their journey as if they were at still while the rest of the world rushed toward them, trapped into the spires around a maddening hurricane's eye, even if the visual experience would have made more than one stumble without the wall support.

The shell's entry coalesced. The onboard virtual screen, similar to the ones on the platform, blossomed in front of them and confirmed their planned route, "Time to destination, thirty-two seconds." The shell detached, accelerated, and slalomed until it reached the central, fastest stream.

The two scholars glanced at each other and nodded. The mission had started with no surprises.

The shell left the central flow, entered a less congested one on their right and veered off toward the planned destination.

They followed the elapsing time on the floating screen, then their eyes rose toward a glow that was getting brighter in the distance; their point of arrival. The shell slowed down, then stopped at the platform. They left the vehicle.

On the floor, a bright orange strip lit up, tracing a path starting from their feet, and guided them, using the details of their workers

ID. The scholars exchanged a glance, then followed the glimmering strip to a short gallery that opened at the back of the platform and led them toward a conduit interchange.

Right before the end of the gallery, a warm breeze carried a faint scent of ozone. At the exit, they stopped for a moment. The gallery extended into a catwalk perched into the void. Around them, in all directions, white floating flat carriers transported cargo containers, others carried workers, and all followed intricate paths in the air and seemed bound to cross into a collision at every moment, but avoided a nightmarish pile up with a swerve at the last, most frantic possible instant.

The scholars hadn't exchanged a word so far. The Councilor checked the tracker and broke the silence. "We are within the second ring of the complex now." He took a deep breath. "Difficult to realize the actual dimensions of this place unless you see it with your own eyes . . . " He let his gaze wander around, in an effort to grasp the full extent of the conduit's size.

In the central section, at regular intervals, relucent columns of interlaced bluish bolts shone bright, and their humming conferred to the place the mystical feeling of the nave of an immense, esoteric cathedral.

In the distance, the interchange structure bent slightly to the left, even though the curvature was so slight that they had the impression of hanging on the right wall of an interminable canyon.

Their ID cards activated one more time, and again a floating panel showed up to form the label 'MC2675' in big letters and numbers. From the distance, an empty white carrier came drifting toward them.

"It's the largest military base in the planet," said the Dean. "Even I don't have the clearing's credentials to know all that takes place here. I'm afraid of what we might find today."

The Councilor nodded and checked his tracker one more time. "We'll know that soon."

The carrier joined to their catwalk, and they stepped on its smooth surface that lit up under their weight. Once detached, the carrier rose toward higher levels.

During the short flight, they had a better sense of the size of the whole structure, and the silence fell again between them.

In the navigational panel of the carrier, a spot pulsated slowly, then faster with the decreasing distance and time to destination. Soon their flight path became a straight line toward another landing platform.

The floating square came to a stop with a little thump when its edge fused with the ledge of a dark metal hatchway. On the wall, large blue letters with red borders confirmed they had arrived: 'MC2675'.

The Councilor touched the metallic barrier that blocked their path. He pressed with his hand, but it slipped over the surface, which offered no friction. He turned his head toward the Dean with a muted question on his face, but she just shook her head.

A scanner's light blade pointed at the ID cards that glowed in their chest pockets, while a second one brushed their faces and probed their brainwaves. They stood still.

The rim of the hatchway lit up, and the entry decomposed into four massive slabs that retreated with synchronized hisses into each of the sides of a square entrance. They entered the short gallery in front and reached a balcony overlooking a long hangar whose walls shimmered with a tremulous light.

A myriad of hexagonal cells composed the hangar's walls, and black drones, smaller but similar to the sentinels, crept along the walls on their eight pods, like arachnoids eager to feast on their prey. In their crawling, they stopped to operate on those cells that protruded briefly off the wall before returning into their sockets after the drones' manipulations.

"Where are we?" exclaimed the Councilor, in awe at the scene in front of them, but the Dean had already started down a flight of stairs that reached the ground level from the backside of the balcony. He looked around for her for a moment, when a flood of emotions reached him with a sense of stress and urgency. In fear, he bent forward over the balustrade. "Marla!" he called out, but regretted his lapse of self-control; he never had used her name, unless explicitly encouraged to do so and only in private quarters. His eyes finally found the Dean near a row of four protruded cells. Busy spider drones operated on their content, tapping hastily with their probes.

She turned. Pale. Her mouth agape.

The Councilor rushed to her side. "Marla..." he touched her arm, then his eyes focused on the scene behind her, and the words died in his throat.

***

There had been no more mental probing attempts. In his cell, Tancredi waited. He knew the military would be coming soon. They had erected a probing void around his cell; a mental desert now surrounded him. He had stretched his mind and had reached its borders. He felt he was stronger than the barrier, but forcing it would have revealed too much about him.

At the Law School, back on Earth, he had limited himself to be among the best, rarely at the top, and when that happened he made sure that he was only just about the very best one.

At the beginning, he wondered whether other scholars might have been doing the same, hiding their true skills, but with time he realized he exceeded their limits, even those of the mentors who taught them, and understood the reasons for the secrecy.

Meanwhile, in his cell, he was ready, and waited.

A disturbance sent ripples through and reached his mind. He closed his eyes and 'saw' the approaching essences, like faint shadows cast by a dying flame. He recognized those from the last visit plus two more: hardened and stiff minds that enjoyed no flexibility; two military guards.

The wall dilated and he opened his eyes wide, pretending to be surprised. The captain smiled, the scholar showed no emotions, but his squinted eyes revealed a tension, or a worry. The two guards stopped at the entrance, their traits fixed like statues of old warriors.

"Cuff him up," said the captain over his shoulder. His face harbored a grin, and he exuded satisfaction.

The guards moved forward. One of them aimed his blaster at Tancredi, while the other activated the crystal cylinder's control panel. His fingers flew on the virtual pad, and an oval slot opened in the crystal.

Tancredi extended his arms through the opening, the palms joined as if he was praying.

The cuffs closed around his wrists and extended up his forearms to his elbows, then they enveloped his hands as well. Tancredi frowned when the cuffs tightened.

The guard released the cylinder that spun and retreated into the floor. With a sigh, Tancredi bent his arms to ease up the tension in his muscles and joints.

"I like cuffed prisoners," beamed the captain, "they all seem devotees begging for a pardon," he chuckled, "that won't come."

Tancredi looked at him. "I see you yapped my message to your masters." He stepped forward.

Both guards blocked him with their blasters pointed at his chest. He bent his head and smiled at them. "Shall we go?"

The captain leaned forward and breathed on Tancredi's face. "You'll lose your arrogance soon. I'll rejoice when you make the ranks of our mindless Kritas militia. You won't even recognize your friend."

Tancredi stared at him.

"What was her name, again? Ah, yes, Mekte," the captain sneered. "I wonder whether she'll remember it, or you, for what it matters."

Tancredi jolted forward, but the guards restrained him.

"Don't worry, you'll see her shortly, joined by the same destiny, at our service for the rest of your hopefully brief life." He tilted his head to the guards, who pushed Tancredi out of the cell with the mouth of their blasters.

The captain smiled at the scholar, who had watched the scene in silence and had shielded all of his emotions. "This is the beginning of a new era, scholar." He left.

The scholar frowned and followed him.

In the corridor, Tancredi stopped after a few steps, all of a sudden, as if he had hit a hard wall.

One of the guards yelled, "Hey, what do you think you're doing?" With anger, a blaster's muzzle hit Tancredi on his flank. A harsh and sharp pain made him full aware of one of his ribs, but his mind focused on a sensation that not even the throbbing ache on his back could have eclipsed.

"What the..." the captain exclaimed the instant he saw Tancredi collapsing to the ground.

Chapter 14 - Hostages

Growing Up

THE EXIT WALL of the laboratory coalesced behind them, silencing the clicking noise from the busy, black arachnoid drones. The Councilor grabbed her right arm and made her face him. "Marla, talk to me."

She blinked and took a deep breath. "We need to go." She attempted a smile as she hunched past him, "Please, not here, don't draw attention to us." - "Never mix sex and work," she muttered passing a technician who had stopped to watch the scene. He gave her a half-smile and lifted his eyebrows.

With a light mental touch, she sensed amusement with no trace of suspicion or warning.

The Dean and the Councilor paced the corridor, staring straight ahead, until they reached a maintenance conduit and stopped to identify themselves with the security system. The floating virtual screen showed their adjourned manifesto. On the Dean's profile, a pulsating "FYEO" announced a private, encrypted message.

She exchanged a glance with the Councilor, then acknowledged the message. The scanner compared her retina's profile with the one from the fabricated maintenance worker's identity and confirmed the match. The beam excited her retina and the message appeared vivid in her visual space, invisible to everyone else: "Reach TG at once. We'll provide assistance as needed." The letters started to fade right after, just the time required to read them. She turned toward the Councilor. "Something's up. We need to hurry."

The bulkhead twirled open. The Councilor had just managed to utter her name with a pleading tone as the Dean rushed down the maintenance conduit. He shook his head and ran behind her.

*
**

The entrance to Grubeck's laboratory displayed the words *'Restricted Clearance – Authorized Personnel Only'* with no other detail, enough to prevent unsolicited interruptions to the ongoing operations that took place behind its walls.

Inside, in the center of the dimly lit hall, two med-units occupied a square elevated platform. The one on the left had its crystal canopy lowered on the silhouette of a body lying inside and hummed softly. Floating above its left side, a virtual screen detailed the subject's vitals. The rendering of a brain, a Kritas brain, spun slowly over the top of the med-unit.

A technician worked at the projected operations' central panel. His hands flew over the floating controls, manipulating diagrams and adjusting the levels of colored bars for the volume of drugs to be inoculated into the subject. He checked the impact of the procedure on the Kritas' vitals. From time to time, he nodded and muttered to himself.

At the back of the room, two other lab personnel in tight, dark green uniforms stood at a long semi-circular dashboard. Their attention was devoted to the virtual screens that showed flashes of broken scenes, some neat and clear, others blurred and veiled as if coming from a dream that was fading away despite all their efforts to relive those moments.

The sound from the images was barely audible in the lab, but it correlated in real time with the level of stress and its impact on the vitals of the subject in the med-unit. Blurred scenes, especially those containing verbal interactions, showed areas in the Under levels and repeated themselves in a never-ending loop, acquiring new details at every pass, becoming more clear in the process. Other scenes showed guerrilla actions, attacks to sentinel drones, and fights against marine patrols in the city.

On the floating brain above the med-unit, different areas highlighted, and the unit recorded the pattern of the firing neurons. At the base of the brain model, a darker area indicated where the implant central node reacted to the induced stimuli, and the summary from the analysis of its signals showed a growing percentage, closing in to reach completion of a full reverse-engineering.

The technician attending the med-unit panels nodded one more time. "If it proceeds without interruptions, we'll be ready soon," he spoke over his shoulder.

"Is the other prisoner being transferred yet?" a voice from the back of the lab asked.

"Transfer's taking place now, Doctor Grubeck," the technician raised his gaze at him. "They'll be here shortly."

Grubeck didn't bother to reply and, from his dashboard, initiated the synchronization with the second med-unit. He glanced at the second implant, ready to be applied.

He breathed heavily. He had explained to the Governor over and over that he couldn't promise anything yet, that the procedure might well work from a technical point of view, but leave them with a brain-dead subject nonetheless. To his surprise, he received no pressures about preventing that particular outcome, and was told instead to learn from the procedure, whatever the end result.

He shook his head at those thoughts. When he was asked to lead the connectome project, he considered it a recognition of his achievements in exoneural biology and physiology, but the idea of working on human subjects had caused him disturbing ethical problems he hadn't realized he actually had.

He joined the technician who was finalizing the configuration of the med units. "Run the implant procedure simulation."

A moment of silence followed his request. The technician turned his head. "We've conducted the simulation nine times already, Doctor Grubeck…"

"I like even numbers. Go for a tenth."

The second med-unit hummed while a projection of a second brain, a human brain this time, grew to full size. Grubeck grabbed the brain's rendering with his hands and examined the cerebellum and the stem area. He expanded the view. "Run the worst-case scenario with all preventive measures in place."

The rendering of a fully integrated implant formed on the back of the brain; filaments extended from the main body of the device until they reached their designated areas and penetrated the gray matter at the cortex, the cerebellum, and the brainstem. They lit up active. When the first filaments reached the ganglia and the hypothalamus, the crisis stormed once more; neurons started to fire without control, fed by a surging positive feedback from the implant itself. More areas of the brain fired up, until synapses started to collapse and the virtual brain died.

"Damn it." Grubeck sighed.

A stern voice from behind the curved main dashboard confirmed for the tenth time the verdict that sounded to his ears like a death sentence, "Rejection rate at fifty-seven percent again, Doctor Grubeck."

He nodded, and then got lost in his thoughts. It was too early to attempt any implanting of the Kritas device on humans, but his concerns went beyond a mere clinical problem. He didn't like the implications, nor the vaguely reassuring words from the Governor that had mitigated the issue a bit: *'We need to cover all possibilities, and it's a great learning opportunity for any scientist, right Doctor?'*

He had understood the veiled threat behind that 'any.'

The Governor had neither revealed his reasons for accelerating the project, nor explained the plans that depended on the results of the experience. He kept stressing that the project was of the utmost importance and that he would have them work on a human subject soon so they'd better be ready in time.

That moment had come, too early for the doctor's liking.

"Doctor Grubeck . . . Doctor Grubeck?"

The voice made him snap out of his speculations, and found himself facing his female assistant. He hadn't noticed her approaching; she always moved silently like a feline. "Yes?"

"The prisoner, Doctor Grubeck. They're waiting in the buffer zone." She gestured to make a security visor appear. Two guards accompanied a cuffed inmate.

Grubeck studied the group for a few instants, then retrieved the prisoner's transfer record, but it contained no details of charges or of any sentence. He squinted his eyes on the *'Classified - No Access'* words.

The visor showed one of the guards facing the prisoner and pointing a blaster at him, while the other stood in front of the lab entrance, waiting. To Grubeck, it seemed the guard was staring straight at him.

The prisoner looked young, barely an adult; maybe that could be a factor for a better chance of survival, Grubeck hoped. What could he have done to end up here? "Where's the captain in charge of the transfer?" he asked. "And, supposedly, the intervention was to be supervised by an inquisitor scholar . . . Where is he?"

On the screen, the guard at the lab entrance glanced back, then bent his head. "That information is above our security clearance." He raised his shoulders. "No worries, we'll take the prisoner back to his cell if you don't want him." He nodded to the other guard who, with his blaster, made the young man pivot on his feet, and pushed him toward the exit wall of the buffer zone.

Grubeck's eyes dilated. "Wait! We're running things on a tight schedule, here."

The guards stopped, and the one who had spoken before dropped his head and huffed. With a deliberate slow motion, he glared back. "As you please," his voice betrayed annoyance, "but make up your mind. We have other duties to attend to."

Grubeck shook his head. The lab entry wall dilated; the guards nodded and pushed the prisoner in front of them. They stepped inside the lab.

Grubeck addressed his assistant. "Get the prisoner ready. Surely, Captain Friedman and the scholar will be here shortly."

She nodded. "Yes, Doctor Grubeck."

He watched her walk toward the lab entry as if she floated over the pavement. *How could she move like that?* he thought.

The guards escorted the prisoner in, and Grubeck focused his attention back to the control panel, changed the standard deviation for the age factor in the implant simulation, and launched the procedure again. As the statistics started to converge, a timid smile rose to his lips.

An agitated chatter grabbed his attention. "What's going on over there?"

At the entrance, the lab assistant opened her arms. "I told them to leave but they insist that now that the prisoner is unrestrained, they can't leave before the arrival of Captain Friedman."

The talkative guard smiled, and voiced out, "Protocol, sir."

Grubeck rolled his eyes. "Fine. As long as they don't touch anything and don't interfere." He pointed with his head. "Go to the back of the lab. We will take over with the prisoner now."

His eyes followed one of the guards taking his place behind the dashboard and exchanging words with the technicians, while the talkative one escorted the prisoner over and onto the platform. Doctor Grubeck's assistant followed them.

As he approached, he studied the young man. The assistant scanned the prisoner's health parameters and collected the data on the bio-scanner. "Strong and healthy." She smiled.

Grubeck stepped forward and looked intently into the prisoner's eyes. "What have you done to end up here?" The prisoner stared back at him as if he hadn't heard the question. The scientist felt as if he'd been sucked into those eyes and into a primeval darkness.

"I'm sorry," Grubeck glanced toward the assistant, "what did you say?"

"That he's strong and healthy." She frowned. "Are you all right?"

"Right. I'm fine." He waved at the med-unit. "Take your place," he told the prisoner as he shook his head. He was sure he'd just asked him a question, but he had forgotten what it was.

Staring at the glowing panels of the med-unit, his last thought was that time seemed to be slowing down, then it stopped.

*
**

The smell of ozone filled the lab, and the screeching noise of the blasters' jolts brought back unpleasant memories for Tancredi. "Seal the room!"

The Councilor rushed to the wall and locked it, then applied the charges. "Just in case." He winked. "These'll fuse the wall if someone forces the entrance."

The Dean had already taken her place at a duty station of the lab main dashboard, pushing aside the dazzled scientist, unaware of anything, lost in the mental loop state the blaster jolt had sent him to. "How is she?" she hollered as her hands scrambled with the controls to interrupt the memory extraction procedure.

Tancredi opened the canopy. His hand trembled when he caressed her hair; soft and ethereal, it waved between his fingers. He waited for the med-unit to shut down before probing her mind. "She's still here!" He sighed with relief.

Mekte's breathing slowed down, and her face relaxed, then she jolted upright, gasping aloud. Her eyes widened, and she clutched the edges of the med-unit. Her mouth, agape, froze in a muted cry.

"Mekte..." Tancredi grabbed her shoulders, but her eyes didn't see him. He probed her mind again. With a gentle touch, he hugged her and rested her head against his shoulder, his mind reaching deeper. The looping images, provoked by the med-unit procedure, persisted and twisted as if they were captured in a wild maelstrom. He followed the flow, embraced her fear and her confusion, and made them his. The vortex slowed down, and he led Mekte to the memory of the Kritas' memorial, in the Under levels, where her father and mother rested.

Tancredi... You're here! her mind finally replied.

Tancredi breathed hard. *Come with me, now. Don't be afraid.* In their common vision, he reached for Mekte's hand and led her onto the catwalk, onto a passage into reality. For a moment, he clearly felt another presence there with them, but as he could sense that it wasn't a threat, he didn't chase it nor reacted to the intrusion.

Mekte sighed and her eyes found his. "You came for me . . ." she whispered and relaxed in his arms.

"Always," he said.

The Dean reached them and stood next to the med-unit. "So it has happened. And in my lifetime, even."

Tancredi turned his head and his eyes met hers. "What do you mean?"

"You have the same heightened gifts as the original Selected."

He didn't reply. Instead, he helped Mekte out of the med-unit. She stumbled with a sway of her hips, but he held her. "Lean on me."

She rested her head on his chest. "I feared I'd never see you again."

Tancredi raised her chin and looked into her eyes. "Nobody will ever take you away from me again. I promise."

The Dean looked at the couple. "And this, too, has happened..." They looked at her. Tancredi shook his head. "Tell me, when did your dreams of changing the world die?"

The Dean lowered her eyes.

"You saw things . . ." Tancredi continued, "Sensed it was wrong and, still, I don't sense outrage in you, yet."

"How do you know?"

Tancredi ignored the question. "Somehow, you knew about it, or at least you had your suspicions, but you did nothing."

She took a deep breath. "You're young. When you'll grow up you'll see things differently."

"So, is this what happened to you? You lost your vision? Your faith? You renounced the fight and accepted compromises, instead? It's just politics now?"

He murmured at Mekte, "I'll never fail you and what you saw in me." Holding the girl tight in his arms, he turned his sight back to the Dean. "I'll never betray *us*. *We* are the future." He stared back at the Dean. "Why did you both come?"

"You were . . .you *are* a singularity," said the Dean. "I couldn't just watch what was happening to you and do nothing for—"

"We need to go!" the Councilor shouted from behind the dashboard. "They found the little mess of bodies we left in Tancredi's cell." He rushed toward the exit wall.

The Dean grabbed Tancredi's arm. "They'll be here soon."

"Fuse the entrance!" Tancredi shouted at the Councilor. Then he read the muted question in the Dean's wide-open eyes. "They're here already," he added.

The Dean let his arm go and shouted in turn at the Councilor, "Do it!"

The Councilor reacted at once. The wall sizzled as the charges burned with a glaring, blinding intensity and sealed the entry.

Still supporting Mekte, too weak to walk by herself, Tancredi reached the dashboard and led her to a seat at the first duty station, then leaned forward as his hands dashed over the floating lab security panel.

"Doctor Grubeck?" a voice resonated in the lab.

They all looked toward the doctor, unconscious on the floor.

"Doctor Grubeck!" the voice repeated.

"What do we do now?" Mekte touched Tancredi's hand.

"They can't reach us in here, for the time being, and I sealed off all of the lab's external links." He caressed her hand as he spoke. "They don't know what happened here yet. Soon they'll bring the scholars."

Mekte's hand clutched his.

He smiled. "I'll stop them."

Under his touch, the virtual screens showed an empty buffer zone and the gallery beyond it. A sentinel drone was pointing its weaponry at the entrance. Marines in heavy assault gear took position behind the drone and at each side of the gallery; they drew out their blasters and got ready to fire.

With his back to the wall, a soldier side-stepped to the entrance and tried its security panel. "Locked!" He shouted, and retreated into position.

Tancredi sighed. "Tie them up." He pointed at the lab personnel on the floor.

"With what?" said the Councilor.

"We're in a lab. Find something before they wake up."

The Councilor exchanged a look with the Dean, who nodded.

"So," Tancredi nodded at her, "what was your plan in coming here?"

She shook her head. "We weren't supposed to get trapped."

"I see."

On a virtual screen, the sentinel drone scanned the buffer zone.

"They'll force their way in," said the Councilor.

Tancredi asked him, "Is everyone tied up?"

The Councilor directed his reply to the Dean. "Marla, maybe we should call for help?"

Mekte pointed at the screen the farthest to their right. "Look!"

In the gallery, military engineer squads had brought a molecule-breaking heavy drill and pointed it toward the lab's perimeter.

Tancredi nodded. "That's actually good news. It means they do care for the fate of whoever's here." He activated the comm link and said in a monotonic voice. "Doctor Grubeck is not available at the moment." He paused. "Might not ever be, if you make any attempt to break in."

Silence.

The Councilor pulled him away from the dashboard. "What are you doing?"

"What do you think I'm doing? Buying us time. Besides, the situation's not yet critical."

"What?" He sneered at him. "Not yet critical?" He waved at the screens behind him. "Marla, the boy's lost his mind."

The Dean's eyes focused on the young scholar.

Tancredi smiled. "Ma'am, your probing might be subtle with many, but it won't work with me." Without an effort, he repulsed the Dean's attempt to pore over his mind.

Puzzled, the Dean squinted her eyes to look at him.

Tancredi smiled. "I've no reason now to hide what I can do. Not anymore."

He stepped away from the Councilor and reached the dashboard again to activate an external link. "Who's in command out there?"

On the floating screen, a marine officer advanced. "I'm Captain Degas. Who am I talking to?"

"I've already asked another captain to let me talk to the commanding officer of this base. He refused. I'm afraid *captain* is not enough of a rank to start a meaningful conversation."

On the screen, the marine's jaws tightened.

"What do you want?"

"I believe Doctor Grubeck's and his collaborators' fates are a matter that needs to be discussed at the top. I'll share my desires with the base commander." Tancredi closed audio link.

On the screen, the officer reached the back of the gallery and got behind the sentinel drone, out of view.

"They'll come back with a counter-offer and we'll gain even more time." Tancredi faced his companions. "Now it's time to discuss, Ma'am, Dean of the Tribunal of Utthana, Protector of the Law." He paused for effect. "What will you do now that you know?"

Mekte approached him. "Now that she knows *what*, Tancredi?"

He looked at her, and his lips contracted.

She placed her hand over his heart. "Tell me."

He sighed. "Do you remember what I mentioned to you about the connectome and its relation to the Kritas' implant?"

"Yes."

"Good. We, I mean the humans, apparently have reverse-engineered the implant."

She stared at him.

"We... They... can rewire Kritas' brains." He glanced at both the Dean and the Councilor. "Isn't that exactly what you saw in that lab?"

The Councilor paled. "Marla." He bent his head toward the Dean. "How does he know this?"

She gave him a blank stare, then looked back at Tancredi and bent her head. "I believe Tancredi Gilmor knows much more than we can imagine."

Tancredi lowered his head in acknowledgement.

Chapter 15 – Pariah

The Watershed

THE BRIEFING ROOM LIT UP from the ethereal glowing of the virtual screen activated by the incoming communication.

Alone in his office, the base commander sat at his large desk with the main dashboard rising right in front of him, a subconscious attempt to place a shield between him and the reaction he expected would come soon from his superiors and the Governor. Not even one hour before he had sent an encrypted, private dispatch sharing the bad news and their most direct consequences. The summoning notification came right after, carrying a not-quite-veiled threat.

And yet, he reasoned, how could anyone foresee the unforeseeable? Despite the many obstacles he had faced in the military, that was something he had managed to do better than anybody, and he had propelled his career to increasingly demanding commanding roles, which he had played with determination and efficiency. Until now.

The virtual screen grew to the full width of the briefing room and blended into the walls. The commander stood up. "General." He saluted.

The general stared at him. His imposing presence froze those words that been lined up inside the commander's throat. He had rehearsed in his mind the defensive speech he'd hoped would have saved his job and grade, but now . . . now he hesitated, and the first drops of sweat formed at his temples. The silence of those first moments carried all the menaces the base commander had feared.

THE LAW

The general stood grave, his lips tightened to a thin cut through his face. The tone of his voice raised with each word. "How did you manage to screw up? You know what's at stake!" His eyes darted around the room, and he clenched his fists.

The base commander took a step back and stumbled against the chair. He felt the general might have struck him if he had been present physically in the briefing room.

"Who's helping that scholar, that Gilmor?" the general grunted.

"We don't know. All records seem to have vanished. There's no trace of any intrusion."

"You. Don't. Know!" He shook his head and took a deep breath. "Your job is to always know about these things."

The commander joined his hands behind his back and straightened his shoulders. He hastened a reply, lashing out all he knew. "We found the captain and the security guards unconscious in Gilmor's cell, together with a scholar sent from the inquisition corps. They were supposed to escort the prisoner to Doctor Grubeck's lab. They are receiving medical attention as we speak."

"Stop repeating the same nonsense from your dispatch." The general squinted. "Is there anything new? Have you achieved anything since?"

The base commander lowered his eyes for a second. "They want to talk to me, or they won't guarantee Doctor Grubeck's safety, nor that of his team members."

"Who's *they*?"

"Actually, the request comes from that scholar. We've heard only from him, from Gilmor. We have no access to the lab's local network, and probing is countered by what appears to be an unknown technology."

"There are too many things you don't know." The general caressed his chin. "Gilmor's only a young scholar, a recruit even. He can't be alone in this, can he?"

"We suspect a breach of our internal security. The vanished records seem to indicate—"

"*Seem?* You wrote you had everything under control." The general stepped forward. "Listen very carefully now. On the record, I know nothing of what you're perpetrating in your base, in the labs under your watch, or how you plan to rescue the scientists." He leaned forward and his voice changed into a hissing. "I won't even recognize your voice if I have to go along that route." He paused. "*Off* the record, you will fix this quickly or you're done. All evidence will die with you, Commander."

The marine breathed hard. "I assure you and the Governor that it won't be necessary. I'll meet with Gilmor, and I will put an end to this madness."

"Madness...." The general bent his head and talked to himself. "That might well explain the reason of your demise in case you fail." The link closed.

The screen froze and coalesced into a singularity of brightness before it disappeared. The base commander collapsed into his chair.

***

Grubeck and the lab personnel sat on the floor against the fused entrance wall, their hands tied together behind their backs. They hadn't talked much among them, nor asked questions since they had regained consciousness. The only female in the group rested her head against the wall, her eyes closed. She controlled the rhythm of her breathing, and Tancredi probed her when he noticed that; she kept her mind busy with meditation exercises. He let her pursue her tricks.

Grubeck stared at the floor between his legs. From time to time, he glanced up, but his sight never remained on anyone for more than a split second.

At first, the three lab technicians had looked up at Grubeck for instructions, but they had desisted since he had silenced their pleas, stating in no uncertain terms that he had neither instructions nor solutions to share with them.

From behind the curved long dashboard and the floating screens, the Councilor glared at them. "What do we do with those guys?" he asked, though to no one in particular.

The Dean glanced at Tancredi, who checked security and the movements of the marines gathering outside the lab. His head made tiny lateral movements, intent as if he was a hound sensing the trace of scent left by a prey.

"For the time being," she replied, "they're our exchange merchandise."

"For now," said the Councilor.

Tancredi interrupted the conversation. "They're erecting a sensorial veil, and they've brought in scholars."

The Dean and the Councilor exchanged a glance. The Dean's facial traits stiffened, then relaxed again. "I can't detect anything."

"No, you can't, yet." Tancredi looked at her. "You will when they'll raise it and start probing in here."

The Councilor humphed. "If you are so powerful, how come you're stuck with us in here?" He raised his eyebrows.

Tancredi smiled. "Now there are too many, but I've found the captain's mind quite malleable . . ."

"Is he for real?" The Councilor shook his head. "Marla, we should ask for help."

The Dean walked up and faced Tancredi. She looked straight into his eyes, almost pleading. "We have friends at the base, but I don't know what and if they could do anything in these circumstances."

Tancredi nodded. "If you attempt to get in touch with them from here, chances are the message will be intercepted and their identity compromised. Willing to risk that?"

"Not yet . . ."

"Good, a sensible decision. Let's see how things proceed then." He winked at her. "Now . . . now you should feel it."

The Dean's eyes widened. "You're right!" She gave the Councilor a nod.

"I can feel it, too. Right beyond the entrance." He frowned.

"Not exactly." Tancredi bent his head. "It covers the whole lab already, and they've attempted to scan everyone already, but I allowed them to see only our prisoners, so they know now they're fine."

The Councilor stared at him.

The warning of an incoming message appeared on all screens. Tancredi activated the comm link, leaving only the audio open from the lab's side of the connection. The marine captain's face appeared in the central section of the dashboard.

"Doctor Grubeck? What's the situation there?"

Tancredi sighed when Mekte's hand rested on his neck. He turned to smile at her.

"Nothing has changed, Captain. Doctor Grubeck can't answer you directly, but we both know he's fine, right?"

On the screen, the captain glanced to his right, to someone not in view. "We indeed wanted to make sure everything's fine."

"Has my request been received?"

"Affirmative."

"Good. Knock back when the Base Commander arrives." Tancredi closed the link and the image on the virtual screen froze before the screen vanished. "The Commander's out there already," he told the Dean. "They're puzzled and unsure of their next moves. At the moment, I think we have still more time."

"For what?"

"For your friends to come to your rescue, of course." He smiled. "But first, one thing." He stood up.

All eyes followed him as he approached the scientists. He knelt down and spoke with a soft voice so that neither Mekte nor the two scholars at the back of the lab could hear his words.

Grubeck kept staring at the floor as Tancredi talked to him. After a while, he raised his head and nodded. Tancredi helped him stand up.

"What's going on, Marla?" The Councilor approached the Dean.

"I don't know, but I think we're about to find out."

Followed by Tancredi, Grubeck stepped toward them.

"Please, untie him," Tancredi told the Councilor, who puckered his eyebrows. The Dean nodded at him, and the Councilor sighed and complied.

"Thank you," said Grubeck. He looked down and massaged his wrists. "There are other rewiring facilities like the one you've seen." He raised his eyes and fixed them on the Dean. She frowned and glanced at Tancredi.

"I told him exactly what you've seen," he said.

Her eyes widened. "So you've indeed probed my mind?"

He didn't reply. Instead, he nudged the doctor. "Talk."

The scientist took a deep breath and described the new brain rewiring facilities conceived to create armies of mindless, brutal assassins out of Kritas prisoners, rebels and civilians alike. "The recent tests prove the process is ready and the facilities can be operational soon."

He went on and revealed how the brains of the physically unfit Kritas equipped a new kind of floating targets, which were being used as training devices for an improved generation of drones. "The Governor is eager to dispel any doubts and demonstrate he can quash the insurgency and make an example from it for all other races under human's dominion."

Grubeck recounted how the Governor wanted to impress the Deans in Ahthaza and all factions in the Authority to win a wide support. "He ordered a staged demonstration of the violent reaction a rewired Kritas would be subject to when confronted by another Kritas having the original implant. A 'declared terrorist,' he said. He thought this last stunt would have silenced any possible internal opposition." Grubeck's eyes widened as he stared at the Dean. "And you were there! I recognize you, now. You must have guessed what his real aim was."

"Mekte . . . " Tancredi searched for her hand and pulled the girl into his arms. "I'm sorry." He paused. "Khulel's dead."

"No!" She paled and pushed him away. "It can't be." Her eyelids trembled.

Tancredi sighed and lowered his head. "The Governor had him killed in an atrocious way." He stared at Grubeck. "Tell 'em," he said in a firm voice.

The scientist cleared his throat. "After the delegations had left, the Governor approached me. He told me to be proud of what I had done for my race. Then he left." He paused. "I was alone and about to leave myself when the raucous screams of the female Kritas resonated loudly in the hall. Someone had activated the audio link. I watched the protection that separated the two Kritas as it lowered." He clenched his fist, and his voice broke. "That Kritas woman . . . She hit the other prisoner with a metal bar, and kept hitting, over and over again. I can still hear that horrible sound the skull made when it cracked."

A soft moaning behind them interrupted his revelations. Mekte had retreated into a corner and had crouched down. She hugged her legs and sagged her face between her knees. Her hair trembled in her sobbing, a shiver shook her tightened arms.

"Mekte!" Tancredi rushed to her side.

She retreated at his touch. "*You* . . . You are a race of demons. How could I've . . ."

"Mekte . . . "

Among the others, the barriers of incomprehension, apathy, and indifference trembled, cracked, and began to crumble.

There are moments in life, events that alter all our perspectives. They force us to either retreat, or change and move on, but time and memories, from that point forward, will always be remembered as 'before' and 'after' that moment.

Chapter 16 – Trapped

Deceptions

"SENSORIAL CURTAIN AT MAXIMUM POWER, SIR!" The engineers' squad leader snapped to attention when the Base Commander approached, escorted by four security guards.

"Very well, Lieutenant." He then addressed the nearby group of scholars, ready to deploy. "Are you confident they can't probe us and know what we plan on doing here?"

The elder one, a minute woman, advanced with a paced gait. Her purple collar insignia reflected her seniority among the scholars. "The curtain is strong, Commander. Any attempts will be lost in waves of vagueness and emptiness."

The Commander shook his head. "Whatever that means, scholar. For as long as it does what I expect it to do."

She lowered her head.

"Deploy your people and keep me updated on any new development. And discover who's helping Gilmor in there."

"We'll do." She bent her head to one side. The conflicting sensations of doubts, anger, and alarm she received from the Commander contrasted with the image of a veteran soldier used to battlefield hardship.

With her eyes, the elder scholar followed him as he paced toward the marines' assault squad, getting ready near the lab entrance. She turned to stare at the lab's walls, herself assailed by the same contrasting sensations.

The assault team members were intent to prepare their weapons. In pairs, they checked each other's gear. Their eyes sparkled in the eagerness to swarm into the lab through the breach that the molecular drill would have created for them. At times, the marines glanced at the lab wall in expectation and rehearsed in their minds the plan and their assignments.

The Base Commander paused to look at their meticulous gestures. Reassured, he continued his path beyond the sentry drones that now formed a barrier of metal, fire, and scanning powers to prevent any sortie or surprises from those besieged in the lab.

The marines had readied a mobile Command-and-Control room. "Wait outside," he ordered his guards who followed him at every step. He placed his hands on the entrance, which dilated and coalesced behind him as he entered.

Inside, officers were reviewing the assault plan on a 3D rendering of the lab interior. They rose their gaze at the Commander and snapped to attention.

He replied to the salute, then waved with his hand. "At ease."

Along the wall, each duty station relayed images and the voice from each assault squad team member, together with their vitals. Before the action, the support military personnel would have linked to the sensorial parameters of their assigned squad member and 'participated,' in remote, to the action, hearing and feeling everything the assigned marine experienced in the field.

The highest ranked officer in the CC room, a Major, approached. "Sir, I reiterate my advice. It's risky, there's no need for you to be physically here. We don't yet know what their real intentions are."

The Base Commander ignored his remark. "Request a comm link to the lab. Let that Gilmor know that I'm here."

The Major raised his chin. "Aye, aye, sir."

The Commander waited for the connection to be authorized from inside the lab. A floating screen blossomed in front of him, and he stared at a serious-looking young man. The young man looked straight into his eyes and—to the Commander—he did not seem that young anymore.

*
**

"I want to know!" Mekte pulled away from Tancredi and his feeble attempt to stop her. She faced Grubeck. "Tell me what happened."

Tancredi probed her mind before Grubeck could talk. With a firm voice, talking over her shoulder, Mekte warned him. "Stop it. My implant has not been rewired, yet."

Tancredi lowered his eyes and retreated his mind. The Dean stared at him and saw him tightening his lips.

Grubeck sighed. "She stopped smashing his skull only when her synapses disintegrated and she collapsed brain dead to the floor." He brought one hand to his mouth to repress a retch. "I'm sorry . . . Later that same day, the Governor ordered me to start testing the rewiring on humans, too." He gave Tancredi a shy glance. "You would have been my first subject."

"How long did it last?" Mekte asked.

Grubeck looked at her, perplexed. "The rewiring? It's supposed to be permanent."

"No. The rage, the killing fury before she died."

He looked at the others and frowned, as if he wanted to receive their pardon. "You have to understand, I had no choice."

"Everyone has a choice," said the Dean, sternly. "Answer her."

Mekte bent her head and slowly squinted her eyes in the Dean's direction—a Kritas 'thank-you' gesture. The Dean nodded in return.

Grubeck blinked a few times. "The procedure is not finalized, yet. It depends heavily on the subject." He glanced at the Dean. "It can go from a bunch of seconds, as with our first subjects, to a few minutes, thus just enough to carry out one attack." His voice regained some composure. "If the perceived threat is terminated quickly, the strongest subjects are able to sustain one more, maybe two more neuronic excitations and perform multiple attacks."

Mekte turned toward Tancredi and her eyes glared cold at him. "We need to find a way to warn Kaulm and the others."

"Who's Kaulm?" Grubeck asked Tancredi.

"Someone who could help us avoid a genocide." He glanced back. Then he looked at the two scholars. "We will need your help, too."

The Dean exchanged a look with the Councilor when a bright, pulsating sphere rose over the dashboard. Tancredi touched it to open the comm link. "I was expecting your call, Commander."

A marine colonel sustained his gaze through the virtual screen. "I wanted to look at the man who betrayed his kin."

"Did I, Colonel? I think you are here, instead, to make sure that what happens in this base will be covered up at all costs."

On the floating screen, the Colonel stiffened and his pupils narrowed for a second. "I don't know what you're talking about, scholar."

"Scholar, you say . . . I'm glad you understand who I am is not a grade, nor a temporary assignment." Tancredi raised his chin. "How much do the scholars know, Colonel? And what do you think it will happen when everything is revealed?"

The Colonel stepped forward, and his face covered the whole surface of the virtual screen. "You're making my decision easier to take, Gilmor. I always thought scholars were shrewd, but you show a serious lack of judgment."

"So you're ready to sacrifice the lives of Doctor Grubeck and his team . . ."

"This is not a negotiation. You all will be captured, or worse. They'll be remembered as heroes, unlike you and whoever's sharing your fate."

Tancredi felt the growing disarray in the scientists' minds when those words were pronounced. Again, he repelled with ease the mind-probing attempts that kept coming under the cover of the sensorial curtain.

"Indeed, this is no negotiation. Everyone here now knows what we face. Thanks for your help, Colonel. I'm sure we will meet again." Tancredi closed the link and the virtual screen coalesced. He turned around. "Doctor Grubeck, we don't have much time. Talk to your team, if you think that's useful. We're not forcing any of you to share our fate," he sneered, "as the Colonel said. But your decision might be the difference between life and death."

Grubeck paled.

Tancredi watched Grubeck as he joined his companions, their minds in turmoil. The rest of the group, Mekte included, stared at him with a puzzled frown.

"I know you have many questions," he said without turning, "but I can't answer them now, not yet, at least." He paused and closed his eyes for a moment. "Hurry!" he shouted. "To the rear wall!"

***

"Major!" The base commander erupted as soon as the virtual screen reabsorbed in the dashboard. He took the Major aside and lowered his voice. "Listen carefully!" He looked at the marine right in the eyes. "You will provide me with an encrypted briefing of the operation right away. The saboteurs' cell has been neutralized. Unfortunately, during the assault, the terrorists had time to kill all hostages in cold blood."

"Sir?" The Major's eyes widened.

"This is a matter of the highest security, Major. Moreover, all records of this operation have been corrupted and cannot be recovered by any means."

The Major hesitated.

"Do you understand what is at stake here? Do you really believe I came here in person just to talk to a traitor? We are at war, Major. Human security in Ahthaza is at risk." He stared at him. "After this operation, there will be heroes, or there will be more traitors..."

The officer gasped and stiffened. "Yes, sir!"

"I'll be glad to sign your promotion soon, Major." The Commander' voice took up a mellow tone. "Now, get ready to launch the assault."

The Major snapped to attention. "Aye, aye, sir."

The base commander supervised the moments before the 'rescue operation' with his eyes riveted to the countdown before the molecular drill would start vaporizing the lab's wall.

The marines charged their blasters to maximum explosive power, and the anti-personnel drone mines quivered as if they were living pests, waiting to dash on their prey.

Soon, the crisis would be resolved, the lab purified by the heat of micro-suns bursting all over, and the marines would obliterate any trace of what had just happened. The General, and especially the Governor, would be pleased at his resolve.

With a grin surging to his lips, he repeated in his mind the numerals that appeared over the dashboard, decreasing inexorably to zero. Soon, he would be able to message the General that the problem was no more.

***

The fumes from the disintegrating wall filled the lab. Its surface trembled. A glowing gas lingered and created an opaque veil, hiding from sight the nuclear death the wall was suffering.

On the outside, the marines lowered and locked their visor shields, protecting their faces, and activated the personnel mines that sprung on their articulated pods and dashed through the opening the molecular drill was creating. Muffled blasts and blinding flashes of white light gushed out the growing breach in the wall, triggering the reactions of the soldiers, who ran into the lab, their blasters drawn out, spreading death through the lab.

The visors in their helmets accurately reproduced the lab's settings through the thick vapor the mines had generated and highlighted the motionless bodies on the floor. The air filters prevented the acrid smell of burnt bodies from impairing the soldiers' focus.

In the command and control room, the Base Commander had followed the assault on the floating screens of the support team members. An unrestrained satisfaction had stamped a smile on his face. His lungs puffed his chest out with pride from a crisis managed with a swift and resolute hand. *"Idiot,"* he thought.

On the screens, while the rest of the team continued their swipe, two marines checked the lifeless bodies. A blade of light scanned their faces and a genetic probe penetrated their tissues for the DNA print. "Casualties' IDs in progress."

The rest of the squad surrounded an area further inside the lab. "Control? More bodies found, but we have a problem."

Chapter 17 - An Announced Death

IN HIS OFFICE, the Base Commander examined the detailed brief of the operation conducted at Doctor Grubeck's lab. The major who had planned the assault was waiting, standing behind the translucent virtual screens that showed the many details he knew by heart, which were enhanced and amended by quick brushes of the commander's hands. When something captured his attention, the Commander briefly raised his sight to glance at the major and nodded, then he continued to further manipulate the report.

"This is good, Major," he said after a while, "this is really good."

"Yes, sir," the subordinate replied without changing his at-ease stance. "Thank you, sir."

The Commander moved one of the screens aside to have a clear view of his subordinate. "When will you get confirmation of the DNA samples? And how could a mess like that have happened?" he asked while he expanded the 3D-view capture of the lab. His hand hovered on the secure erasing procedure.

"Very soon, sir. We suspect Gilmor detonated a DNA-scrambling anti-personnel mine prior to the assault." He paused and his lips tightened for a second. "I believe he must have guessed we didn't have the intention to take prisoners."

"A DNA-scrumbler, huh? Delivered by whomever tried to help him, no doubt." The Commander frowned. "This breach in security is highly concerning, but the preliminary results are excellent. They corroborate the thesis that Kritas terrorists helped the traitor." He recited the 'official' thesis to himself, "Together they tried to sabotage the whole programme and committed suicide when they realized we didn't flinch and had instead thwarted their plans." The Commander stood up. "Tonight," he raised his chin, bent his arms, and put his hands on his waistline, "the Authority's bulletin will be a great advocacy piece of propaganda and will shatter the determination of radicals all over the planet."

"I concur, sir."

"What impact will the loss of Doctor Grubeck have on the rewiring research?"

"Minimal, sir. The R&D team will recover shortly, and the scientist you appointed to take the lead will meet with the rest of the personnel today, both military and civilian."

"Very well, Major," he smiled, "and for that promotion...I need an aide," he paused, "a trustful aide. I'm sure you understand?" He bent his head.

The Major raised his chin with a sudden jerk. "Yes, sir. Thank you, sir."

"Very well, then. Dismissed," he said, taking his place again in his armchair.

The Major saluted, then left through the dilating wall.

The Commander sealed the office. A grin grew on his face. His eyes caressed the briefing final assessment: 'Two casualties confirmed: staff scientist Alderan Miller and first class technician Eliza Brook. Kritas DNA compatible with four more casualties. Two additional human DNA samples under mapping for identification. One DNA sample confirmed compatible with Tancredi Gilmor; 67% confidence level.'

"There goes Tancredi Gilmor." He sighed with satisfaction and he took his time to add a few more comments to the briefing he would send to the General shortly. For sure, the General would remember this as a good day, and maybe remember him as well, he mulled with satisfaction.

*
**

Aboard the flag ship, in a space sector far away from Ahthaza, the Governor slammed his hand on the main dashboard of his office. The virtual comm screen flickered.

"Inconceivable! I'm demanding to confer with the Dean immediately."

Imperturbable, the council member scholar's face didn't change expression on the floating screen, nor did his voice change tone. "I'm afraid the Dean is not available, Governor. I'm not—"

"Let me talk to the Councilor, then," the Governor interrupted.

"I'm afraid the Councilor is also unavailable, Governor."

The Governor listened to those last words as if they had been spoken in a foreign language. "Both unreachable and at the same time?" He squinted his eyes. "What are you scholars up to?"

"Governor?" The eyebrows of the scholar raised, and a smile rose to his lips.

The Governor's lips contracted. "The Dean will have a lot to explain the next time I meet with her. Inform the Council that I'll be in Ahthaza soon, and I want to see all of you."

The scholar lowered his head. "We'll be delighted to have you in Ahthaza, Governor."

With a snort, the Governor interrupted the comm link and raised a virtual security panel from the main dashboard. The ship's captain appeared. "Sir?"

"Captain. Cancel the last two destinations. After the next planned stop, divert our itinerary. Our next jump will be Ahthaza."

"Aye, aye, sir." The panel was reabsorbed into the dashboard.

He stared at the holo-rendering of the General, who had waited for the conversation with the scholar to end.

"What's your take, General?"

"Unusual, to say the least, but I don't have authority on the Dean and her Council. She's not required to communicate her itineraries in advance."

The Governor frowned. "Certainly, and she's never been a supporter of adopting a strong-hand policy against the Kritas."

"True." The General nodded. "She must be angry because of the news. Also, she seemed to have had a . . .a penchant for that Gilmor." He raised his eyebrows.

"Hmm, maybe you're right, but even if it all amounts to just her hormones, she'll regret her attitude. Anyway," his voice changed tone, "congratulations for the success of the operation. Now we can launch the second phase without fearing further interferences."

The General smiled. "*I enlightened* the Base Commander about his options, and," he paused and his smile grew broader, "even in the improbable case of an inquiry, all actions and decisions bear his name."

"Perfect. I'll see you soon in person, General."

The General saluted, and the Governor watched the hologram freeze and fade away.

With a quick gesture, he ordered the room to filter out all incoming communications until the arrival to their next destination, just before Ahthaza. The wall to his private quarters dilated. He stood up and strode into his inviolable private space. The wall coalesced behind him. He sighed. With his right hand, he massaged the stiffness he felt in his neck.

He dimmed the lights. On the central space of the main room, which he had used to entertain dignitaries from all planets—and his own, unconfessed private indulgences—the 3D rendering of the space sector under his ruling, with its 63 planetary systems of the old and defeated Kritas Alliance, glittered, turning slowly in the semi-obscurity.

"Ahthaza!" he voiced out. The star around which the Kritas' home planet orbited pulsed among the other systems, and the rendering expanded. He waited for the planet to come into full sight.

He looked at it for a few moments, then reached for the planet with his hand and clenched his fist around it. He pulled it in front of his eyes. The rendering shrank and followed the movement. He grunted.

"Fuck!" he exclaimed and 'threw' Ahthaza away as if he had just crushed an annoying insect and wished to get rid of it.

The galactic rendering obeyed his gesture, the star system flew back away from him until it became invisible. Other stars appeared as quickly as the others vanished at the opposite side of the space sectors now fluttering away from him.

His eyes kept fixing on a point in the direction where Ahthaza had just disappeared. He shook his head. If those scholars intended to create another problem in that Kritas' lair, he breathed hard, he would squash it with the same determination, and with no regrets.

Chapter 18 - The Fifth Circle

Revelations

THE INNARDS OF THE SECURITY complex were permanently filled with an acrid stench that caused throats to contract in revulsion. The feeble luminosity from the floating map, which detailed the intricacies of the infrastructure's network of tunnels and galleries, cast long, tremulous shadows on the elliptical walls.

The group advanced through the gallery in silence, in single file. The rhythmic sound of their steps on the metal grid that covered the floor rolled up the curved walls of the gallery and echoed from the roof. In the darkness, there was an eerie sensation that ghosts marched with them, hiding and lurking when the group reached a wide crossing, haunting their hearts. The higher vaults converged into the mouth of a service pipe above their heads. Under the grid, a conduit was gurgling with refluxes of haphazard chemical reactions that took place hidden in the depths of the base.

At each crossing, the group leader stopped to check in the security scanner—with paranoid nervousness—for each area, and examined the results on the floating screen before signaling that it was safe for them to proceed. His finger hovered on the trigger of his blaster each time he glanced at the dark throat of a new pipe above their heads.

From the back of the column, a young voice resonated in the gallery, "Nobody's following us, and it's clear in front." The voice had a reassuring tone, but the group leader breathed hard and continued his checks undeterred. "You have your methods, scholar, I have mine. Let's go," he said without turning. "It's safe."

"We might as well profit then for a pause. Everyone's tired," the voice insisted.

"I am as well. We will continue."

"Major," a female voice made him stop and turn.

"Ma'am?"

"I think Tancredi's right." The Dean walked up to the soldier. "We should stop. It's been hours now. Your setup at the lab must have worked, or they would be in pursuit by now."

He stared at her and puckered his eyebrows. Her face was barely visible in the dimly lit tunnel, but the Dean withstood his gaze.

"And it's true; I'm tired." She glanced at Mekte, who kept her distance from Tancredi.

The marine nodded. "Okay. As you wish." He raised his arm and rallied the other soldiers at the back of the line. "We stop here!" he raised his voice. "Set the security perimeter."

"Thank you," said the Dean softly, touching his arm.

He lowered his head, then looked one more time at the security scanner. On the screen, six blinking green areas formed down the tunnels where the patrol had deployed passive sensors.

They naturally split into three separate groups: the marines, the scholars, and the group of scientists. The marines sent oblique looks toward Mekte, 'the Kritas,' and shook their heads—whispering brief remarks among them.

Since they had left the laboratory at the base, each time Tancredi approached her with those little gestures lovers exchange in all times and planets, she stiffened and retreated. She turned her back on him and curled up on the floor, away from the others. Exhausted, she soon fell asleep.

He would have liked to have Mekte rest her head on his lap so he could caress her hair, appeasing her body and her mind, but the girl's heart was in great turmoil after the revelations about Khulel's death. He decided to sit next to her anyway.

Grubeck, his assistant, and one of the lab technicians moved instead closer to the marines.

Followed by the Councilor, the Dean approached Tancredi. "May we sit here with you?"

He raised his chin and waved his right hand to welcome her.

"Thank you," she said and took a moment to choose a spot in front of him.

"Your touch." She sat down. "Your mental touch, I mean, is soft. Light, almost impalpable. I've never experienced anything like that . . . delicate, ephemeral, even."

Tancredi looked at her without changing expression.

"You didn't learn this at the Law School."

"No. I didn't learn much at the school that I didn't know already. I learned, instead, of the many aspects and principles of the Law, and of the singular ability of our race to bend and twist them, even with all that has happened in our past."

Mekte moaned in her sleep and stretched her back slowly, then she curled up again against the wall. Tancredi bent over her. He raised his hand over the girl, hesitating.

"You're in love with her." The Dean tilted her head.

He turned and fixed his eyes on the Dean's. "I sense surprise in your words . . .and in your thoughts." Tancredi heaved a sigh. "And, yet, you're a scholar. After what you've seen and learned, do you find it so strange that I see through our differences and could love a Kritas girl?"

"Who are you, exactly?" asked the Councilor, who sat a bit further down the tunnel and who—so far—had pretended not to follow their conversation.

Tancredi glanced at him. "That's not important, for now." He then addressed the Dean. "Didn't you know what was happening under your watch?"

The Dean stared at the floor. "Maybe we didn't want to know." She raised her sight and looked at him straight in the eyes. "Our wounds from the war still hurt."

He stared back. "I look young to you, but I've felt the pain of billions. The greatest suffering came from us humans, from our oldest ancestors." His eyes focused beyond her, on images that emerged from his memory, vivid and excruciating as they had been on the first day he had received the revelation.

The Councilor startled. "You can't be talking about the experience of the first ones, the Selected . . .can you?" he said.

The Dean looked at Tancredi for a long moment, then smiled at the Councilor. "I think he is, dear, and that would explain many things." She faced Tancredi again. "So what are your orders? I suppose you're not here by chance, Tancredi Gilmor." She squinted her eyes. "If that's your real name."

Tancredi lowered his head. "It is. Don't look at me as if I were a weird phenomenon, or a unique twist in our evolution. I'm not the first. I'm not the last."

The Councilor slapped his thigh. "I knew there was something wrong with him!" he exclaimed. Then he stuttered, "I mean . . . different. I didn't mean . . ." He threw his hands up. "Oh well, you know what I mean."

Tancredi laughed. "No worries, Councilor. I can read into you and I know you mean no offense."

"Can you? I didn't feel anything. Are you probing me right now?"

"I never stop." He closed his eyes for a moment. "I *can't* stop. It takes years to learn how to cope with the constant exposure to the flux, the flood of emotions we wade through at every instant of our life."

The Dean nodded toward Mekte, still asleep. "Does she know that about you?"

"She knows me, but she doesn't know about me in this role."

"I understand. Will you tell her?"

"Of course. In due time. I love her, and I respect what she represents for me."

The treading of military boots down the tunnels made them turn. The silhouette of the Major and two soldiers emerged from the darkness.

"We should go," the Major said when he reached them. "The path is clear. Our cover still holds, but that's no reason to stay here any longer." He sneered. "You're going to like this: there has been a global broadcast with the coverage of a successful operation against Kritas terrorists. Tancredi Gilmor, a young scholar recruit, is depicted as a traitor and a double-crosser who's been working with the Kritas' most extremist fringes to sabotage the Authority's efforts for a peaceful integration of our two races on Ahthaza."

"What?" the Dean stood up. "How do they dare?"

"Oh, they've dared worse than that," said Tancredi. This time, with no hesitation, he caressed the sleeping Kritas girl's hair, which curled and bent as if it played a tag game with his fingers. "Mekte, wake up. It's time to go."

She blinked a couple of times before her nictitating membrane retired fully. She turned over and her eyes opened into his. "I was dreaming about us." She smiled, but then her lips contracted and she sighed. For a moment, Tancredi forgot all about their struggles, the new galaxy order, his mission, the Selected, and the tasks ahead.

The patrol the Major had previously sent forward emerged from the tunnel to their right. "All's clear, Major," said the leader of the squad of four.

The Major nodded, and then hurried Grubeck and his people to stand up before signaling the departure. "Let's move."

The group resumed their advance underground, the marines at the front, Tancredi and Mekte at the back.

The floating screen of the security device the Major kept checking with compulsive regularity sent ripples of light that ripped the darkness in front of them and cast long shadows on the curved walls.

The Councilor whispered his words, but Tancredi heard them clearer than if they had been shouted. "Why didn't they trust us, Marla? Why didn't they trust you, back on Earth? Why send him here?"

Silence.

"And how can we be sure he's not lying?" he added.

Mekte would have liked to reach for Tancredi's hand and interlace their fingers, but she restrained herself. To her, there and in that moment, Ahthaza, the Governor and the scholars, everything seemed like insurmountable obstacles and threats. She glanced at him. Before their capture, the only future that mattered, she shivered, was the one they were destined to build together. Now, she wasn't so sure.

Mekte and Tancredi kept walking a few steps behind the others, distracted by their own thoughts and trailing along a path their destiny was busy tracing.

"Mekte . . . " Tancredi whispered, but the girl pretended she didn't hear him and kept walking, her eyes fixed at the head of the column, from where faint bursts of light made their own darkness even more profound.

*
**

Perched on the top of Utthana's Tribunal, the Council Room hosted the deans who had convened in urgency from all over the planet. Their assigned chairs were arranged in two rows and formed what was known as the Circle. The deans had arrived in the council since the early hours of the morning. Their faces were gravely serious. Two seats stood out for being empty, the one of the Protector of the Law, and the second, in the lower row, assigned to the Councilor. They closed the Circle rows together like the clasps of a necklace of power, an end and a beginning at the same time.

The recent arrival of the Governor on the planet, and his request for a hearing later in the day, had prompted the urgent gathering in the capital city. Some of the oldest deans stared at the stony center in the middle of the assembly as if they were waiting for the scholars' emblem carved in the ancient slabs to animate and answer their remaining doubts.

The early morning had witnessed a flurry of questions addressed to the Council's Secretary, a role covered by the most senior dean among them. His deep and bright indigo tunic exalted his rank among the others, and he stood resolute near the raised chair of the Protector of the Law, the Utthana's Dean, on the outermost ring. The Secretary was answering the last enquiry, which came from one of the younger members who, with a broken voice, had urged the council to do all in its power to contact and seek out advice from their leader before exploring any further options.

"I've already shared with you all we know. We've lost all communications since their last message from the marine security complex." The Secretary's lips contracted. "We don't have any more news. We tried, but we've not heard back from the Protector, nor from her Councilor." Mute mental waves of worry and tensions reached him, and he paused. "We know they are alive." He raised his hands to invite everyone to regain composure. "They have received unexpected help at the base, and what the Dean has shared with us changes all parameters, as well as all we had assumed so far on this crisis."

A murmur rose in the Circle as the deans glanced at each other. In their mind, the same question kept burning from the first moments of the meeting.

The Secretary sensed trouble again and addressed the crucial point, the main reason for their gathering that day. "I know what troubles you. What should be our official position? The situation is serious. How shall we deal with it in the light of the recent news, and how can we satisfy the Governor's requests without raising suspicions?"

The dean from the northern territories stood up. "We have gained time. Ably, I concede that. The Governor and the military seemed focused on a different agenda, for now," she said, "but we can't maintain the old version any longer. We need to know more of this secret wing within the military and find proof for all the allegations."

A mental rumble of approval saluted her words.

"Order, please!" the Secretary exclaimed. "We know time is against us, but we need to agree first on a common stand and present a steady and compact Council when we meet with the Governor. If we are divided, he will exploit our weakness."

In the Circle, the deans looked at each other and nodded.

"The Protector's life is in danger." The Secretary's eyes went to the scholar's emblem at the center of the Circle. "*We all* are in grave danger. At the Protector's own request, we cannot rush to her rescue, nor put at risk the independence of the council with a public intervention, which will put the Protector—and all of us—in an even more perilous ordeal."

He paused to turn his sight around, resting his gaze on each member to ask for and receive a mental nod. "Us as well," he stressed. "For now, we need to rely on these internal dissidents in the military, the ones who call themselves the Fifth Circle." He took a deep breath. "And hope they're wrong—"

A mute alarm, that only by trained scholars could perceive, interrupted his words. From the paved stone center of the Circle, virtual floating screens appeared and showed the areas around the Tribunal's tower. The gardens crowded with the landing of multiple marine vehicles, and troops emerged from the opened bellies of the spaceships like vermin from a decaying body.

The deans goggled at the marines' deployment in front of all the entries to the tower and set to guard all accesses. Further troops secured the landing pads at the upper levels. In disbelief, the deans stared at the multitude of security screens that kept blossoming in front of them, all confirming an impossible scenario.

"What's going on?" the booming voice of the Secretary echoed in the Council. The deans startled at the words and stood up all at once. The whole council seemed to wave as if their members had been invested by a powerful windstorm when the entrance wall dilated and, from the main gallery, marine troopers swarmed in, blasters charged and drawn.

The soldiers marched in unison and surrounded the deans, who voiced their outrage in mounting anger and indignation. A heavy silence fell when the troops formed two lines that encircled the council. The soldiers stopped, tightly positioned shoulder to shoulder, and pointed their blasters at the deans.

The virtual screens in the center froze. The council members watched as the images that showed the marines' takeover of the Tribunal faded and, with an arrogant show of power, the Governor's shield replaced them.

From the gallery, the regular thumping cadence of military boots broke the silence and signaled the approach of another group, another intrusion. The measured pace of their gait contrasted with the fast deployment of the troops through the council room moments before; it was the marching of those used to dictating the timing of their appearance in all circumstances.

The deans' probing attempts slammed against the wall of a mental protective field that forced them to retreat and wait, assailed by doubts. Never before had the sacred enclave of the Council Room been violated in such a brutal manner. In the main Tribunal of the planet, the deans were trapped in their homes, and felt the stinging sensation of mortal danger.

An armed platoon, dressed with the silver uniform bearing the black and gold insignia of the Governor's special guards, entered and aligned to form two columns that extended from the entrance into the center of the Circle.

"Thank you, thank you, thank you," said a voice everyone recognized. The Governor entered the Council Room. "I'm glad to see you are all present." He glanced at the two empty seats and grinned. "Almost."

"Governor!" The Secretary started to walk down from the main central stall, but the nearest troopers blocked him. With a cold stare, they crossed their blasters in front of him.

The Secretary's eyes darted at the Governor. "What's the meaning of all this?"

"The meaning, you ask?" The Governor nodded to himself. "Indeed, what's the meaning of all this? And where is our beloved, trustworthy Protector of the Law? And her Councilor?"

The Governor stepped toward the edge of the Circle and stopped right behind the first line of marines who kept their blasters aimed at the deans. He stared at the Secretary, then, with a measured pace, ambled along the ring formed by the marines. He held his hands together, behind his back, and stared at each dean for a second before moving on to the next one. The deans glared back at him in silence.

The cadenced sound of his heavy boots on the ancient stone sounded like a metronome, heel and toe, heel and toe, heel and toe.

"No one knows?" he said, stopping halfway through the Circle's perimeter and turning his gaze around. All eyes were fixed on him as he resumed his march. Heel and toe, heel and toe, heel and toe.

A few of the deans glanced at the Secretary, who kept his eyes on the Governor's gait. The Secretary showed no sign of distress when the Governor finally walked the whole circle and stopped back in front of him. His eyes withstood the Governor's stare.

Pushing them apart with his hands, the Governor caused the troopers to step aside and created a clear path to the Secretary. "No one?" the Governor repeated.

The Secretary didn't flinch.

The Governor sneered. "It won't surprise you all, I hope," he took a few steps back toward the center of the Circle, "that I happen to know, instead?" He opened wide his arms and looked around.

Murmurs and mutters erupted at those words. The Governor let the commotion rise to a confused ferment. "Enough!"

"What have you done to her?" the Secretary asked with a stern voice.

"Done? Who? Me?" The Governor sighed. "I'm so disappointed. Such is the trust the deans have in me?" He waved his hands to encircle the whole assembly and raised his voice. "What the Protector has done to all of you! That's the question you should ask!" He raised his hand to stop the rising voices of the deans. "Quiet. Quiet!" he said and grinned.

The Secretary breathed hard and hissed his words between tight lips. "Are we under arrest?"

"That's an interesting question, Secretary. Should you be? As scholars, you have such a degree of perspicacity. You have the ability to get to the core of the motives driving the behavior of anyone." He nodded and looked around at the other deans, who followed the exchange, unable to guess what the Governor, still protected by a sensorial veil, truly had in mind.

He smiled wide. "I admire you for this. Believe me. Your capabilities are exceptional, and you have rendered many services to all planetary systems under the Terrestrial Union, but here . . . *here* something went wrong, and it is my duty to make it right before the plague spreads."

"What plague?" a dean voiced out.

He sneered without turning. "Corruption, divergence, confusion . . . I'm not that good with words. Betrayal, maybe?"

"What?" the Secretary exclaimed, giving voice to the outrage all of the present deans felt. "This is unacceptable, especially from you!"

The Governor snapped his fingers. Around him, visible to everyone in the Circle, virtual screens blossomed and showed images that startled the deans. There was no need to be a trained scholar to feel the tension rising among the ranks in the Council.

"Be the judge for what's unacceptable, now." A wicked half smile rose to the Governor's lips. He raised the tone of his voice, which resonated in the Council Room. "I hereby declare Martial Law in Ahthaza, and you all are now under my direct orders."

Chapter 19 - Damnation Or Salvation?

The Bitter Taste of Freedom

A LOW HUMMING BOUNCED OFF the walls of a deep gorge in the plains south of the marine security complex. A stealth vehicle rolled between the steep walls. The pilot kept the hull only a span from the sharp edges of the rocky bed, lulling the ship with skilled, precise steering. At times, a puff of dust rose when the ship flirted too close to the earthen obstacles. Its stealth cloak protected the passengers from the search probes launched after them, and the stoney walls of the rift hid its journey from inquisitive, prying eyes.

Inside the cabin, the Major and the marines who had survived the escape ordeal sat in silence, glancing from time to time at the pilots and toward the navigational instrumentation; their minds set on those friends who lost their lives. A price they knew they'd pay one day, too.

The onboard field emergency med-units took care of the wounded; the blunt tip of their thin pods mended visible scars and eased physical pain.

The Dean stayed away from the others. The tears and harsh lacerations that afflicted her weren't the result of physical injury. She hadn't spoken a word from the moment they had made it to safety and into the vehicle that took them away and saved them from a sure death. From her seat, the soft purring of the cabin muffled all other sounds.

She gave a deep, broken sigh. "I can't believe he's gone. Why? Why did he have to do that?" She raised her eyes, red and swollen, and searched for Tancredi's. He stood next to Mekte, who rested at his feet with her chin down, apparently asleep, and with her nictitating membranes closed to keep her secret tears from rolling.

"I didn't know the Councilor well," Tancredi said, "but in his last moments, he was happy. He felt he was doing the right thing. He had been the unpredictable factor that gave us our only chance."

The Dean looked at him, her eyes charged with a muted question.

"His last thought was for you . . . He did this for you." Tancredi added.

She brought one hand to her mouth and clutched her lips to crush a cry that rose from within and brought its load of pain.

"You know he loved you, right?" Tancredi bent his head.

Her shoulders sank, and she gave in to his inquiry. "I met him during my first year at the Law School." She paused and a brief smile lit up her face. "We would have had a different life together if we hadn't been scholars." She glanced at Mekte and lowered her voice. "Don't make my same mistake." She closed her mind like a shell and curled it up around her pain.

Tancredi nodded. "I wasn't in want of Mekte, or of anyone before I met her, but I need her now that I have her."

The Dean looked at him, she smiled but her lips trembled. "I need him more than ever now that he's gone." Her eyes begged him. "What's going to happen now?"

Tancredi turned his head and his eyes followed the contour of Mekte's profile. "I don't know if she needs me at all . . . " he sighed.

The Dean bit her lips. "I meant to us, and the scholars . . . "

He raised his sight. "What was supposed to happen from the beginning." He paused. "If all that happens is what must happen, we can do no wrong."

***

The view from the heights of his quarters in the Tribunal's tower made the Secretary's guts twist. Marines vehicles patrolled the streets of the Zero level. On the higher levels, up to the third one, traffic had been reduced to the strict minimum. The gardens of the Tribunal and its landing docks resembled the tarmacs of a military base, littered with fighters, sentinel drones, and personnel in uniform, never at rest.

The drones . . . The Secretary couldn't remember whether he'd ever seen that many squeezed in such a confined area.

He couldn't be sure, but he had the impression the drones acted now under different directives. During the day, the drone units behaved as he could expect, performing regular identity checks—though those had now become mandatory on all Kritas, rather than the usual, sporadic ones. Kritas were being stopped regardless of their business or whether they had the proper authorization to be on the streets. At night, the drones packed together like wolves hunting prey. At night, the screeching blasters hissed with anger. When that happened, the Secretary knew then that the wolves had scored one more kill.

He turned his back to the city scene below. "Is it too much to ask for some privacy?" he addressed the Military Police duo who were now stationed in his office at all times. He couldn't stand their presence anymore. They didn't reply, nor did they glance at him.

"I said, I'd like . . . "

"We have our orders, sir," the stern voice of the oldest of the two marines interrupted him.

The secretary stepped forward and faced the soldier. "I want to review the entire footage of the Protector of the Law's break-out before the Authority releases it to the public. It is stressful enough for me without your unnecessary presence." He raised his glance at the ceiling, talking to those who he knew were watching. "And I'm sure you have means to know exactly what I'll be doing on my dashboard, regardless."

The soldiers gazed at each other without showing any reaction. The one who had replied to him previously bent his head toward his right shoulder and muttered. "Aye aye, sir. We'll wait for further instructions at the exit wall."

At those words, the Secretary pivoted on his feet. "So? New orders?"

The marine raised his chin. "We have received the authorization, sir." Without further comments, the soldiers marched to the wall that dilated and coalesced behind their backs as soon as they stepped through the exit.

The Secretary nodded, raised his sight back at the ceiling, and uttered, "Thank you."

He reached his desk and activated the dashboard. It rose in front of him and shone bright, floating within comfortable reach of his hands. He hesitated, with his hands resting on his lap, then he took a long breath and gestured to access the records. The floating datasphere aligned in front of his eyes. He made them roll and let some expand when they passed in front of his eyes, bursting their content like flashes of memories, others contracted under his fingers. He browsed through them until he slowed down imperceptibly when he found the one he was searching for. His fingers contracted on a particular sphere when he verified that the encryption hadn't been violated since he had applied it the first time. *For the moment, at least,* he thought. He squeezed it.

He resumed the search as before until his fingers stopped at the footage the Governor had showed the council only three days before.

He grabbed the data-sphere and, pensive, turned it in his hands. He activated it and let the rendering float in front of his eyes. "I like to work with my hands," he commented aloud, "it makes things more real than just using voice commands." He sneered, hoping that his rant sounded silly enough to divert any suspicion on his little time-wasting manual search.

The footage in real 3D rendering started. The scene the Governor showed all deans in the Council Room blossomed in his office, expanding just beyond his desk.

The official bulletins had justified the enforcement of the Martial Law in Ahthaza as a measure dictated by the infiltration of a double agent—Tancredi Gilmor—among the Tribunal's assigned scholars, with a possible involvement of upper echelon scholars. The bulletins further mentioned a suspected possible involvement of the same Protector of the Law whose present whereabouts still remained unknown. This fact alone, the Authority had stated, justified the shutting down of all the Tribunal's facilities and their operations. A thorough conjunct inquisition had started, and was conducted by the military with the help of the embedded scholar units of which allegiance toward the Terrestrial Union and the Authority itself was not in doubt.

A few scenes from the classified footage had been released to the public, out of context, and to support the Authority stance: no scenario, no matter how improbable it seemed like full treason, would have been discarded during the investigation; every lead would have been pursued and all options examined in order to contain the crisis and bring to justice everyone involved. Terrorist actions would never undermine the resolve of the Authority.

The Secretary stood up and stepped onto the scene the rendering platform had created in front of his desk; the marines' military base hangar area became 'alive' around him with life-like details. On the platform, the Secretary made a quick turn on the balls of his feet while his gaze searched for familiar faces. This was the same scene that had sent a shock through the council members, a scene that determined when everything had changed.

Smoke from the moldering metal structures the blasters' shots had hit created contorted figures that twisted and sparkled, obstructing a clear view. He gestured to eliminate those details, and the clouds of smoke disappeared. The sizzling, floating traces from the blasters' bolts guided his eyes to a group of marines in heavy gear crouched behind a sentinel drone; he had frozen the rendering right at the moment the mouth of its guns spewed a violence of fire that would have annihilated any body armor if hit directly.

The Secretary walked in the direction of the fire, and the platform drifted under his feet, creating, for him, the illusion of movement. The hits from the drone pounded a net of etched metal pillars; a second, isolated sentinel drone, bent in a U shape, protected a human figure hunched over and behind it, partially hidden from view. The Secretary squinted, but then gazed further around. His eyes stopped at a corner where a group of people had found shelter. Blaster shots erupted from there, aimed at the base guards and at other drones in the distance that blocked that group's only possible way out.

He selected the inert elements for that portion of the scene and increased their transparency. The metal barriers faded away, together with the bulkheads and the walls.

He stepped closer and gasped. Behind a squad of eight soldiers, clearly in the act of protecting the group, he recognized the Protector of the Law, Tancredi Gilmor, and the others: that Kritas girl whose name escaped him in that moment, and the group of scientists who had worked at the military base. Their lead scientist, Dr. Grubeck, was among them, too.

He remembered how the Governor had accused the Protector, Gilmor, and the Kritas girl of conspiracy and of holding the scientists hostage. He had claimed they'd been aided by a group of rogue military, surely corrupted by who-knows-what promises of outlandish rewards—the Governor had alluded to that, too.

Whether the Governor had ignored the existence of the Fifth Circle, or just pretended he did, wasn't yet clear to the Secretary. Without a proper probing of the Governor's mind—not a possible and realistic plan now, he acknowledged to himself—he had no way to ascertain how much the Authority knew about the real nature of the enemy they faced, and the threat they represented.

In the rendering, the Secretary reached the group's position and examined the scene more in detail. *Grubeck and the others aren't hostages at all*, he thought. *They could easily back off and run away*. On the contrary, they stayed as closed as possible behind the marines and under no duress.

He moved toward the front of the group. The Protector was screaming and leaned forward as if she wanted to get away, but Gilmor held her firmly. Was she a prisoner? All others squatted down, seeking shield behind the structure he had just made transparent and which absorbed the brunt force of multiple blaster hits. Debris had flown around, scattered furiously by the violence of the energy discharge, frozen in mid-air each time the Secretary paused the viewing.

He let the scene advance a few more seconds. A voice full of hurt and anguish pierced the ears. "*Nooo!*" the Dean screamed as Gilmor succeeded in pushing her to the ground. "Get down!" he shouted.

The Dean's face contorted in despair and in the vain effort to snake out from under the weight of Gilmor, who had wrestled her down. She stretched one arm in front of her, in a gesture that carried all the hopelessness of the moment. Her fingers were fully extended when the Secretary paused the viewing again.

He knelt down next to the two scholars to look in the direction her arm pointed to. In the distance, the isolated sentinel drone he had noticed before had raised on its rear pods and all its forward blasters vomited fire. A man rode the drone as if it was a wild beast of the desert and attempted to tame it. This time, the Secretary reached the drone and his jaw dropped when he got close enough to recognize the figure. The Councilor! Gripped to the drone's back scales, his hands clutched around the neural transducers of the AI brain.

He stepped closer and raised his gaze to the Councilor's face. His eyes stared ahead, empty and void, his transfixed traits confirming what the secretary had guessed was happening: the Councilor had fused with the drone's AI, saw what its sensors saw, felt what the drone sensed; de facto, he *was* the drone.

The enemy fire had diverged from the area where the Dean and Gilmor hid, and was concentrated now on the Councilor and his drone. The Secretary's lips tightened; he understood the anguish in the Dean's face and the reason for the huge fireball he had seen in the footage the first time, the crucial pause it had created in the fight, and thus how the Protector of the Law, Gilmor, and the others had profited from that and managed to reach the exit.

He lowered his head, unable to look any longer at his old companion as he was making the ultimate sacrifice. He turned his gaze away and started toward the exit. There, he restored full visibility to all artifacts in the scene: the smoke, the flying debris, the sizzling fumes from the blasters' hits, all came alive. He let the scene resume.

The noise of the battle resounded among the bulkheads and the armored walls, as the other sentinel drones in the back of the hangar jumped ahead to face the newly achieved high-priority threat. The Councilor-drone raced forward, not caring to seek for coverage or safety, trying—on the contrary—to reach the enemy as fast as it could before it would have been too late for the others to escape. A high pitched "No!" had failed to distract him from the unfolding drama.

The Secretary recognized the voice; he knew who had screamed and now also why. The Councilor-drone accelerated, its armor hissing and melting under the fury of the enemy fire. A crack first opened in the outer protective layers, then the pods of the drone sped up even more, projecting its entire body into the attacking group of sentinels.

The intensity of the deflagration and the immense, blinding flash forced the Secretary to close his eyes for a moment right before a huge flower of flames bloomed and thickened. The heat and sound wave from the blast scattered everything that was not anchored firmly to the ground, and the air was then sucked back into the crater that the explosion had created.

A dense, thick smoke filled the hangar. The Secretary's eyes barely captured the Dean and the rest of the group as it pressed forward to the exit. The 'rogue' marines with them strafed the area until they all got out safe.

He waited for the scene to reach the last 3D frame. There was no trace of the Councilor in the empty, darkened crater. The Secretary joined his hands in front of his forehead, leaned forward, and honored the fallen.

Chapter 20 - Rebels

Enemy of My Enemy

SHARP-EDGED ROCKS LITTERED THE FOOT of a rugged cliff, scattered on the bare surface as if a giant hand had thrown them away in rage. In the twilight of the dying day, only a few sprouts of the sticky violet sponge-plant, common in the desert plains of Ahthaza, colored the otherwise lifeless, uniform gray of the plain. Far from the capital city, long shadows painted darker fingers across the lowlands.

"We are still too close . . . Are you sure we cannot be detected here?" the Major studied Mekte's face in search of any revealing sign of uncertainty, but the Kritas girl stared back, resolute, at the marine.

"You haven't found our underground cells in town for decades and you wonder about this place . . . Do you doubt my words?"

The Major didn't reply.

Utthana rose beyond the cliff edge; the higher levels shone engulfed in the last golden light of the Kritas' star. The gloaming half-light of the sunset would soon be replaced, though, by the darkness of the moonless Ahthaza sky, but the star Deneb was already greeting the sunset.

The transporter that had brought them there, to their appointment with the unknown, had left already. Invisible within its stealth cloak, the autopilot took the shuttle down into a furtive flight, ending in a ball of atomic fire when the countdown of an anti-matter torpedo would run its course; no traces left, but sure to drive attention far away from their location.

The sense of solitude grew stronger among the humans, but the rocks and the exposed ground, scorched from past battles, could not answer the many questions that infested their souls.

Tancredi searched once more for other sentient minds in the surrounding, but he found nothing; they were, apparently, alone. He nodded to himself. "It's only us here."

Mekte smirked at him. "Not exactly."

A cracking and scratching noise interrupted their exchange. Dust and smoke billowed from a sudden crack on the cliff's wall.

The marines jumped to their feet and drew their guns out.

Mekte opened her arms with her palms facing the ground. "Lower your blasters!"

The Major hesitated for a second, but he finally addressed his men with a firm voice. "Do as she says."

After exchanging glances with each other, with great reluctance, the marines fought their diffidence and obeyed the order.

Gathered behind the soldiers, Grubeck and his group took a step back as the rocks fissured further and revealed a regular pattern in the slit. A faint light came through and played with the twirls of dust. With a hissing noise, the slit widened, and the thin groove grew larger into an opening beneath the rocks, large enough to let two men through, shoulder to shoulder. Then, it stopped with a gruff noise.

The air filled with the smell of warm desert sand and metal. Mekte advanced, covering her nose and mouth with her hand. Her nictitating membranes had lowered to protect her eyes. From within the opening, the light cast silhouettes, which faded against the thin powder, cascading and settling in layers that swirled at Mekte's passage. Kritas' voices resonated from the inside and welcomed her.

Tancredi followed her steps; this time, he felt the well-known Kritas' veil but with a new, different reaction and a subtle change.

Since the early days of the humans invasion, decades ago, the Kritas cloak had protected the rebels' bases from being detected and stormed by the marines' forces.

Tancredi poked that new veil, and his mind felt it as if—this time—it welcomed him rather than pushing and repelling him back. It embraced him without putting up a fight.

He frowned and, befuddled, retired his touch. He squinted his eyes to look at the group of Kritas who were now standing at the entrance that had appeared among the rocks.

The one nearest stepped forward and presented a bundle of long bands to Mekte. She nodded back at Tancredi. "I believe you recognize these?"

His eyes twinkled.

"They won't object to them if it comes from you." Mekte bent her head toward the rest of the humans and handed him the bundle.

Tancredi stared at her as he took the bands. Then, with a flip of his hand, wrapped the sensorial deprivation straps around his arm. He squinted. "I'll see what I can do."

***

As soon as the last human had crossed the entrance, the fissure in the rocky wall trembled and puffed a thin dust that blurred its edges. Stones moved and shifted, finding a way to embrace each other again as if they'd been stuck together for millennia. Tancredi watched the scene with the same marvel he felt during his initial discovery of the Kritas hideout in the under levels. The fissure was no more, and the rocks concealed them from the rest of the world.

"You are in Kritas' territory now," a Kritas said with pride.

Tancredi gazed at him. Indeed they were. The gallery seemed built with the same slabs of ancient black stones that constituted the smooth pavement of the Alliance Square in Utthana.

"You're safe here," the Kritas continued. "Feel no harm, you're our guests, but we have to ensure our people's security first." He pointed at something behind Tancredi.

His eyes followed the gesture and found Mekte standing with a new resolve in her eyes, and something that looked like . . . hope ? She glanced at him in a furtive way before stepping forward to address the group of humans, each holding the strap that would turn them blind and deaf.

"Thank you for accepting this restriction. The bands you hold in your hands will adapt to your facial traits. It will be discomforting at first, but you should adapt quickly."

Tancredi gazed from Mekte to the rest of the group, probing them for any sign of trouble. They were nervous, but a couple of the marines showed more than just resentment.

He felt a spike of emotions. Grubeck cleared his throat and indicated Tancredi with a nod of his head. "Why don't you ask him to wear one?" he asked.

Tancredi shifted his mental probing from the marines to the scientist.

Mekte looked at the young scholar, and her eyes lingered on his traits for a couple of seconds. "Tancredi Gilmor has won our trust already."

Grubeck frowned. "So, you're not trusting *us*. Why take us here, then?"

The Dean's mind flickered and she voiced out. "They're not trusting *you*, yet."

Tancredi studied her for an instant before replying in turn to the scientist. "Dr. Grubeck, you were about to destroy my brain and my mind only days ago. I'd say you better wear your band now."

Grubeck tightened his lips, his eyes showing a mixture of shame and rage. "I was forced to." He shifted his weight. "I didn't like all they asked me to do. I wouldn't be here otherwise."

Mekte smiled. "You will have ways to prove yourself. You will show us the principles that guide your actions, Doctor Grubeck."

He nodded, and then lowered his head. Tancredi sensed gratitude coming from the scientist, so he relaxed a bit and stopped all further probings.

"All right, then," Mekte continued. "We are ready to go. Put on your bands now, and welcome to the land of the rebels."

The Kritas waited for everyone to comply, then lined up the humans and led them down the gallery.

Tancredi reached Mekte, stood at her side, and bent his head toward her. "Keep your eyes open. Anyone can betray at any moment. Sometimes humans feel they don't have any other choice."

Mekte blinked in wonder. "What do you mean?"

"Just a hunch, for now." He paused. "And thank you for what you said before."

His words made her stop; she gave him a blank stare.

"About the trust, I mean." Tancredi frowned, confused by her reaction.

Her eyes focused on his with a long, thoughtful look. "I lied," she said, finally. "You, too, have to prove yourself."

She turned and followed the others, leaving him behind–and wondering.

Chapter 21 - Winds Of War

Lies and Deceits

TRANSPORTERS LANDED AT THE MILITARY BASE, delivered their cargo, and took off again, repeatedly, without a pause in their tight, unchanging schedule.

Ground shuttles paced the short journey to and from the base hangars under the cold watch of hundreds of deployed sentinel drones.

Marine fighters patrolled an area of such a large extent that it flirted with the visible horizon. A corridor to the lowest orbit levels had been secured days before, when the first battleships had shown up in the sky above the base.

Watching the operations, the Governor nodded. He didn't want any more surprises after the recent major security breach. Heads had rolled, but that hadn't appeased his mind. He feared the search for military rogues—among all ranks—could cause delays in his plans, and he loathed delays. He breathed hard.

Time being of the essence, anything risking holding up his plans had to be squashed with adamant resolve and brutal swiftness. Too bad if innocents also had to pay a price in the process. If still alive, they'd be compensated and re-instated at the end of it all. He knew that making anyone forget any wrong was just a matter of matching the right price.

His quarters looked out over the ship port, and from his observatory deck he had a clear view up the hills to the north, undisturbed to the west and to the east, and over the protected military zone. Beyond the northern hills, the ground cracked and plunged into a complex canyon that extended for miles, a daedalus of chasms and wrinkles on the surface of the planet that continued up to the outskirts of the planet's capital.

He clenched his fists as his eyes followed the newest shipments reaching the base.

The newly appointed team of scientists proved even more capable than he had hoped and had been able to catch up with the project. Their new boss, whom he had personally chosen, knew well the price of a failure, as well as the rewards that would come with a success. It would've been better for her to know where Grubeck had gone, and join those pariahs if also *she* failed him. He wasn't keen on tolerating another disappointment.

The wall announced the visit of his aide. He let the wall dilate.

The aide caught his breath, short as if he had been running, and he probably had just done that.

The Governor raised his eyebrows and chin, and the aide snapped at attention. "Sir. We're ready. Doctor Rusitzky has finalized the procedure."

"Ah!" He filled his lungs. A smile rose to his lips. "Finally some good news," he exclaimed.

The groove in the aide's forehead relaxed. "Doctor Rusitzky said you'll be pleased to see the results first hand."

The Governor's smile widened. After all, it might have been just good fortune that Grubeck had left the stage. "Tell the Council Secretary that I request his presence at once in the main lab."

***

Rows and rows of med-units covered the entire surface of the lab, but for a brightly lit control area to the far right. In the area, technicians and scientific personnel monitored the synapses' rewiring process and the Kritas brain implants' functionality.

Their gestures showed confidence, and their interactions with the dashboards revealed the emotionlessness of a work routine, executing the various steps of the process with proven precision, like wheels of a mechanism that had as its only justification that of a brutal inevitability. The violence that had happened in Ahthaza were just a direct, ineluctable consequence of a long chain of past milestones.

Behind a large transparent wall and right above the control area, in grave silence, the Secretary observed the operations. A voice at the rear interrupted his thoughts.

"I believe we've never met in person before now."

He turned around and raised his chin at a young woman. "Indeed we haven't."

She wore the tight purple uniform of the Marine Science R&D Corps and had stepped into the room as if she owned the place. The wall coalesced behind her.

The two guards to the side of the entrance brought their blasters tight to their chests, at a slant. The guns were charged and ready to fire. Their stares didn't follow the woman's gait, though, nor did they seemed to care for the formality of the ongoing presentations.

She smiled. "Sheila Rusitzky." She lowered her head.

The secretary nodded. "Rutgen—"

"Oh, I know who you are, mister Secretary," she interrupted and smiled again. "Especially in light of the recent events."

His gaze examined her face. "Because you're here, I believe I should've made your acquaintance before as well...Doctor Rusitzky. I suppose the Governor has asked for your presence, too?"

"He might want to be the master of ceremony, though," she withstood his stare, "and formally introduce us himself. Let's allow him this pleasure, would you agree?"

The wall dilated and the guards snapped to attention, holding their blasters vertically by their extended arms. The Governor strode into the room.

"So glad you've accepted my invitation, Rutgen." He grinned, watching as the Secretary stiffened.

"Ah, I see you met Sheila already. She's the best thing that could've happened to us, and to Ahthaza. She has strengthened our efforts to quell the rebels' activities, you know?" He burst into a laugh. "What am I saying, quell. We'll crush them." He reached out to put his right hand on the scientist's left shoulder. "Thanks to our wonderful Doctor Rusitzky." The Governor's eyes sparkled, and he looked at her with pride, as if she was a direct product of his plans and mind.

Doctor Rusitzky lowered her head, feigning embarrassment, but the Secretary noticed and sensed she expected to be praised.

"Secretary," the Governor continued as his voice assumed a more serious tone. "I asked your presence here today because I count on your and the scholars' support in what can be, *will be*, rather, the decisive push to crush the Kritas' rebellion." His eyes fixed on the scholar's.

The Secretary withstood his gaze and tried, for an instant, to sense the Governor's mind. "The Governor knows he doesn't need to ask for our support in Ahthaza."

Not surprisingly, he encountered the same impenetrable wall of the mental protective field the deans had experienced in the Council Room. With a brief glance, he tried to localize a possible source for that field, but his eyes couldn't find anything revealing in the Governor's attire. He glanced at the guards; like human statues, they stood indifferent to what was happening in the room. They weren't shielded as the Governor, though. Their minds were keen and focused instead, aware of every detail and movements. He knew they would have shot him without hesitation if he had made any attempt to compromise the safety of the Governor.

"Of course, of course, Secretary. No need to ask, indeed, but this is a seminal moment, and I am delighted to share it with the leader of the scholars in Ahthaza."

The Secretary sneered. "Leader? I'm only a servant to the Council, Governor."

The Governor burst again into laughter and slammed his right hand against his thigh. The Secretary frowned.

"You're an intelligent man, Rutgen. Do you seriously believe the chair of the Protector of the Law to be still occupied today?" The Governor stepped closer. "The position's vacant." His eyes narrowed into a thin slit. "We share a future, Rutgen, and a brilliant one even." He paused, then his voice regained the lightness of a pleasant chat. "Thanks to our wonderful Doctor Sheila Rusitzky." He turned toward the woman, and a wide smile covered his face.

"I'm happy to contribute to *our* future success," she replied and bent her head toward the Governor. "But allow me, now, to show you a glimpse right into that future." She touched the transparent wall and revealed a control dashboard.

Under her commands, the floor shone from the wall and up to the middle of the room and flickered before it became transparent. With a little initial jerk, the room moved forward and drifted over the med-units below.

"This is our main lab," her gaze traveled across the area, "where the rewiring of the Kritas brains' connectome takes place." She spoke with a flat and monotone voice. "We perfected the procedure Doctor Grubeck left us with. A Kritas subject can now sustain multiple interactions with the induced stress in the presence of a rebel's implant, contrary to what happened with his old solution."

"Wait a second." The Secretary stared at the Governor. "I thought we weren't pursuing that plan anymore?"

"Rutgen, Rutgen." The Governor sustained his stare. "I never abandon plans, I refine them! Especially when we can profit from having the support of better minds to lead the operations." He nodded at the scientist. "Please, Doctor Rusitzky, continue."

She smiled. "We are proceeding with two kinds of rewiring, one aimed at infiltration, and a second geared toward seek-and-destroy missions."

The Secretary breathed hard. The room kept drifting forward until it came to a halt.

"As you can see," Rusitzky continued, "the rewiring of this subject is almost completed." Her hands waved over the dashboard with accomplished gestures, precise but gentle, as if she were caressing the commands. Below their feet, a Kritas brain rendering formed above one of the med-units. "When all the connections in this brain become stable, the subject will be ready for its training."

The Secretary gave her an oblique look. "*Its* training? That Kritas is an individual." He peered below at the med-unit. "And a very young female, even."

"It's a subject, Mister Secretary." Her voice had regained a cold impersonal tone. "Besides, young ones are best suited for infiltration."

The Secretary glanced at the Governor, whose eyes twinkled with satisfaction.

The Governor turned and his intense eyes fixed on the Secretary. "This time, we'll leave nothing to hazard," he said. "We'll have baits, and we'll strike with an efficient blow into the heart of the rebellion." He nodded to the scientist. "Please, go on, Doctor Rusitzky." The room resumed its drift, hovering above the lab.

"After the rewiring is completed, subjects are taken to the conditioning programme." The room reached the far end of the lab, and the wall dilated to let it through. "Here is where we prepare the subjects to become our weapons and deliver the final solution."

"I don't understand," said the Secretary. The second lab presented the same arrangements as the first, main one.

The Governor grinned. "And yet, the plan is brilliant in its simplicity."

Below the room, and still in their med-units, the young Kritas lay motionless, calm; some smiled, even. The bodies of the older ones, on the contrary, shook at times, assaulted by uncontrollable and sudden muscular spasms.

"Love and hatred, two of the most powerful forces in the Universe," the Governor continued, "and we will be using both to our advantage."

Two concave screens rose and floated before them. The Secretary's eyes widened. On the left one, he saw pleasant scenes of smiling Kritas couples, their hands stretched out, welcoming the youngsters; scenes of loving households, of caring families, of protective and prosperous communities. The right screen, instead, flared with bright and wavering flashes, burst of explosions, scenes of intense fights and of war, violence, and scores of Kritas against Kritas, killing each other, details of bodies ripped open by blaster shots. Scenes of rage and of blind fury.

Doctor Rusitzky's voice broke the curse. "We're preparing the baits and training the fighters."

The secretary watched her as she ended the phrase with a smile. He frowned.

"We're ready, Rutgen," said the Governor. "So you know, we've already started on the creation of the first assault units. We'll deploy them soon."

Chapter 22 - Reasons Of The Heart

Si Vis Pacem

AFTER A LONG WALK and in sensory deprivation, the Kritas had confined all humans in a large, vaulted crypt excavated off the naked bedrock. A set of polished stones worked as stools and constituted the only elements that broke the smooth surface of the floor. The humans had been kept without news for hours.

Mekte had remained with the other Kritas. When she had left, she sent a longing gaze at Tancredi.

He had respected her privacy until that moment and, later on, he couldn't get through an invisible veil that turned the whole area beyond the rocky walls of the crypt into the mental equivalent of a thick fog, like layers of organza skirts that blocked the view, the sensations, and all the emotions.

He could still manage, with an effort, to sense the presence of other Kritas through the veil, but that didn't help him assess their situation, and Mekte's last words had been a laconic 'wait here.'

"We've waited long enough!" The Major stood up.

"I agree," added Grubeck. "We shouldn't be treated like prisoners. We decided to follow them here, why the wait? Besides, we're hungry and thirsty."

Those words provoked the start of a small commotion. Tancredi exchanged a look with the Dean, who had remained seated and in silence.

After a long moment, she nodded. "Major Cargill!" the Dean voiced out.

Slowly, the agitation sedated. Tancredi repressed a smile as the Dean had used some of the proven scholars' mental skills to deal with tumults and uproars.

The Major dashed his gaze in her direction through the slits his eyelids had become.

The Dean didn't balk. "I told you I knew your name."

The Major puckered his eyebrows, then he remembered and raised his chin.

The Dean stood up. "You all know me, or at least you've heard of me. Hopefully, never while in the care of the Tribunal." She paused and all eyes turned toward her.

"You will face far more disturbing things than hunger and thirst, or an annoying and too long a wait, so stop fussing as if you didn't know what's going on on this planet." She looked at Tancredi. "The events of the last weeks and months, for how unsettling they are, can be the tipping point of those changes and transformations that will call us all to adapt and alter our judgment and perspectives." She strode up to the Major and looked at him straight in the eyes. She lowered her voice. "You must have known or suspected most of it, haven't you? Or you wouldn't be here either."

The Major stared back, and his traits revealed no emotions, but Tancredi could feel the Dean had marked a point.

"I've seen things that have alarmed me." The Dean turned to face all others. "I've lost a friend and a companion of a life time through what would have been senseless events only a few weeks before, and yet it has happened in front of my eyes." She took a deep breath. "And now we're here, in a place no one believed existed at all, in a reality no one thought to be possible." Her gaze moved toward the rest of the group. "I don't want my friend to have died in vain, and I will not allow any of you to become an obstacle for me to uncover the truth hidden down here and on the surface." She turned to look at the Major again. "You'd better now disclose what the Fifth Circle knows."

The Major filled his lungs and, standing, towered over the Dean. "Ok, Ma'am, we don't have much to lose now, but first," he nodded toward Tancredi, "who is he, really? Why is he so important for you to risk everything?"

"No. You first, Major," she said. "Then, I'll tell you everything about Tancredi Gilmor." She glanced at the young scholar.

Tancredi squinted. She knew very little about him still. He never had judged the Dean capable of lying with such a square face.

***

After a quick briefing, Mekte had been confined in a cell. She paced the room. No one had cared to answer her questions during the briefing, and then guards had escorted her into that cell.

"Kaulm!" she shouted once more at the ceiling. She knew someone watched and could hear her voice. Her head collapsed between her shoulders, and she knelt down. She grabbed her head with both her hands, her hair caressed her wrists. The cold from the stoney pavement sent a shiver crawling up her spine.

She jolted and jumped to her feet when a transparent panel rose from the floor and split the cell in two. The door of the cell, a solid, metallic slab, slid into the rock with a huff. A Kritas female entered and glanced in her direction for a moment before staring at the screen of the device she kept pointed at the girl.

Mekte didn't recognize the woman, but that didn't affect her much, and there was no time for formalities. "Why are you keeping me here?"

The Kritas didn't react, her fingers flirting with the symbols that appeared on the screen.

Mekte rushed to the transparent panel and the palm of her right hand slammed against it. "This is crazy! You don't know what you're doing. I need to talk to Kaulm right away!"

The Kritas rose her eyes. A cold stare made Mekte take one step back.

The Kritas checked her device once more and left. The dull metal slab sealed the cell again, and the transparent panel retreaded back into the floor. Mekte sighed and massaged her hand.

"Kaulm," she said in a soft voice. "I know you can hear me. I beg you. Don't waste time. We're all in danger."

Not far from Mekte's cell, in the control room, Kaulm stared at the two large floating screens showing Mekte's cell, on the left, and the humans' on the right one. Military personnel crowded the room; hovering panels and floating screens reported details from the guerrilla's operations that took place all over Ahthaza. The tension made everyone move with brisk gestures.

Bursts of excited, quick comments marked the rare good news, and rapid chatters interrupted hours of sedated silence. The eyes of many in the control room dared to check only briefly the number of units that were no more, or for which they had lost all contacts since their last reported activities.

"What have you learned from your tests?" Kaulm asked the Kritas woman who stood next to him, his eyes riveted to floating screen on the left.

She held her arms crossed behind her back and stared at Mekte, alone in her cell. The girl was sitting with her back against the wall and kept her face hidden behind her hands.

"The analysis of her implant's stimuli is complete and through." The woman paused. She took a long breath. "I honestly don't think she's a threat, or has been one." Her eyes fixed on Kaulm's with the same cold stare she had reserved for Mekte before. Without waiting for a reply, she turned her gaze back at the screen. "Believing her words, though, is a different dilemma, which I'm glad I can leave to you, Kaulm."

He nodded, more to himself than because of her comments. "Send the young scholar to interrogation," Kaulm instructed in a gruff voice talking over his shoulder, "and take the others to the rest area. Alert the labs. There, we'll question the human scientists."

Behind him, a Kritas in military uniform snapped to attention. "Yes, sir!"

The female Kritas frowned and squinted her eyes. "What are you planning to do?"

"Mekte has high hopes of this scholar, and she's no stupid girl. It's about time to see whether she has placed them well."

*
**

The interrogation cell. A smaller replica of the crypt, but for a transparent wall that split the space in two halves.

Tancredi knelt and gazed at the two sanded stones facing each other on the opposite sides of the transparent barrier. Polished, the stone on his half of the cell reflected a wraithlike image of his face. He closed his eyes and probed for the presence of others, humans or otherwise, but there too the Kritas field was strong and bent, embracing his mind, welcoming him again, but not giving in. Much stronger, and of a new kind, he reasoned.

He raised his chin and opened his eyes. He recognized the Kritas who had just appeared in the cell. "Kaulm."

The Kritas caressed the transparent wall and sat. "Tancredi Gilmor. We see each other again."

He followed the example of the Kritas and caressed the wall before taking a seat. "Where's Mekte? Is she fine?"

Kaulm bent his head and squinted his eyes for a moment. "You really do care about her . . . "

Tancredi had no need to answer that. "We face a great danger, Kaulm."

"*We?* Who's we, scholar?" Kaulm's lips tightened. "We faced danger because of humans for decades."

Tancredi frowned. "I could say the same, but this time we can stop that."

Kaulm bursted into a laugh, then stared at the young man and his eyebrows puckered. "You're serious. You do really believe that."

"There's the will."

Kaulm bent forward and got closer to the barrier that kept them apart. "Whose will, human?"

Tancredi straightened his back and stared at the Kritas.

"See?" Kaulm said and shook his head. "This is exactly it. You provoke me asking for trust, but are not ready to trust yourself."

"It's not that simple, Kaulm. Ahthaza is in a fragile situation."

Kaulm fixed his eyes on the scholar's. "Seriously? I haven't noticed." He snorted. "You need to talk, scholar. It is here and now. You will not have another chance."

Tancredi agreed.

"So that's why you spent time with Mekte . . ." Kaulm said when the scholar stopped his story and took a deep breath.

Tancredi stood up at once. "No! That's nothing to do with it. I—"

A loud, deep, penetrating noise resounded in the cell and cut his words short. Kaulm jumped up to his feet and brought two fingers to his ear.

"What's going on?" Tancredi's eyes widened as he attempted to probe the Kritas who was listening to words only he could hear.

Kaulm took a squint at him. "Your words will soon be tested, scholar."

With a hiss, the door slid up and two heavily armed guards entered and stood at attention, one at each side of the exit.

Kaulm turned on his feet. "Escort him," he ordered. The transparent barrier lowered.

Once he reached the exit, Kaulm stopped and turned; the guards had flanked Tancredi tightly.

"I'm curious to discover what will guide your steps now. Will it be your brain or your heart, scholar?" Kaulm looked askance at him, then strode into the corridor.

The guards gave a big push to the young man, with a not-so-much veiled satisfaction and rammed him out of the cell.

*
**

A group of armed Kritas took the humans out of the crypt and escorted them into a wide gallery. 'We have orders to take you to the resting areas,' their leader had told them.

One moment they all seemed part of a leisure visit to the place, with casual chatter among themselves and with the Kritas, the next it was all screaming, blasters shots fired, and a Kritas dead on the ground, part of his face and neck evaporated after a second direct hit shook his body. His left flank was still melting and fuming from the first shot.

With a jolt, the Dean had thrown herself to the floor and landed heavily on her right side. Her elbow sent spikes of pain so intense she thought she had broken it. She kept it close to her chest with her left hand, and her eyes had swollen with tears. With an effort, and muffling a cry, she managed to raise her head when more

Kritas arrived shouting, and more shooting resonated through the gallery.

Through the tears, she saw Grubeck and his assistant collapse to the ground, but she didn't feel that tearing sensation when a life is broken short. She breathed with relief. To her amazement, the Kritas had shot only to stun. Then, a dark curtain fell over her eyes, her head wobbled, and she lost consciousness.

Chapter 23 - Diktats Of The Brain

Para Bellum

A BRIGHT DOT APPEARED on the main tactical screen in the Command & Control room of the Intruder's class vessel.

"Commander!" the operation officer called out, but his superior hadn't let his eyes off the screen since the beginning of the operations and reacted at once. "Alert all units. Operation Hammer of Vengeance is a go." Then, he activated the encrypted comm link, and the Governor's face blossomed bright over the dashboard.

The officer raised his chin. "Sir, we've received the signal." A heavy silence fell in the CC room as all personnel paused their activities in expectation of the next phase.

The Governor grinned. "Finally. All our efforts will be rewarded." He took a deep breath. "We don't need prisoners, Commander, but I want the leaders. You know what to do, right?" He leaned forward and his eyes pierced across the distance and through the comm link to force the Commander to stand at attention.

"Yes, sir. Understood, sir."

"I want live reports to the flag ship. Do not fail me." The comm link interrupted.

The commander exhaled. "Launch the assault!" he ordered. With a jolt, all officers in the room reacted as one, enacting a plan that involved neither hesitation nor compromises.

Aboard the flag ship, the Governor turned his back to the floating dashboard in his office. He smiled at the algid Sheila

Rusitzky. Her eyes glistened, while an opaque veil dulled those of the Council Secretary, who stood in silence.

"You see, Rutgen, I was right in asking you to make the journey with me here. I hope you feel you're treated as your rank deserves." He stared at the Secretary, who puckered his eyebrows, but felt compelled to lower his head in silent acquiescence.

The Governor thrust his chest out. "It's a new day, the beginning of a new era for Ahthaza. Today, we bring death to Tartarus' realm, and we'll cut off his head."

The ships of the assault flotilla gathered on the higher orbital levels to initiate the descent toward their target, following a slow spiral course. The Governor watched the pattern develop on the tactical screen. He grinned as a vision of the coils of a powerful snake tightening around its prey crept into his mind.

"What do you mean?" the Secretary asked.

"You really have no idea, have you?" The Governor exchanged a mocking look with the scientist. "Seriously?" He stared at him. "Where do you think the Dean of Ahthaza is, and her *protégée*?" His hand touched the dashboard behind him. "Their capture is only a matter of hours away now, and I don't need any more proof of the scholars' betrayal."

The Secretary stiffened, but sustained the Governor's stare.

"What I really don't get," the Governor muttered to himself, "is how the scholars could side with the Kritas scum . . . "

The door dilated, and two military guards entered and stood at attention.

The Governor didn't take his eyes off the Secretary. "He's guilty of treason, like the others. Take him away."

The scholar didn't react. Without any resistance, he waited for the guards to flank him and put his arms in restraints behind his back. He groaned when the restraints tightened the elbows together.

"You're wrong." The Secretary glared defiance.

"Am I? Weren't you and the whole Council aware of the Protector's mission at the marine security ward? Didn't you try to keep that from me and the Authority?"

"You're a fool."

"Genius is always mistaken for madness by those who can't grasp it." The Governor gave a nod to the guards.

He waited for them to take the Secretary away and for the door to coalesce. "It's all thanks to you, Sheila." He stepped closer to the woman. "You'll be rewarded." He touched her arm.

Her smile grew wider.

***

Units of the Kritas militia had swarmed the hub at the crossing of galleries where a shooting had taken place. The armed personnel had cordoned off the area where the medics attended the wounded and the stunned humans.

Kaulm stared at a dead Kritas. The blaster shot had eaten up more than half his face and head. He sneered at Tancredi, still escorted by the two guards. "You bring death wherever you go, *human* . . ." The harshness in his voice twisted his last word. "Isn't that ironic? In your language, you pretend human means being compassionate and caring . . ."

"Why is Mekte not here?" Tancredi asked.

"You'll see her at the right time and place. Maybe."

Tancredi filled up his lungs. "You know the story of my race, Kaulm. But I wouldn't forget the role yours has had in the Third Loss. *We* know what death means." He glanced at the Dean, who had regained her consciousness under the care of a Kritas medic. "How are you? What happened?"

"Yes, Dean of Utthana," said Kaulm with an irony in his voice. "Share your story with us." His stare got colder. "But be quick, we don't have much time. Our location has been compromised."

The Dean was sweating, giving her face a transparent sheen. The pain was gone for the most part, and the Kritas doctor had just finished casting her arm. "It will be healed in one hour," he told her. "The plaster will open itself when the process completes. You may discard it then."

She lowered her head and forced herself to a smile. "I thank you for your help."

The medic nodded, then joined the rest of the emergency team.

"Marla," said Tancredi, "please . . ."

Her eyes widened and she sighed. "I thought no one would ever call me by my name again . . ." Her gaze drifted away as she searched for the shadows of those lost forever. She sighed and addressed Kaulm. "A Kritas patrol took us with them, they said they would have escorted us to a more comfortable area where we would have received food and water, rest, and be briefed. Especially the scientists."

"I know, I issued those orders," said Kaulm in a stern voice.

"Right." She blinked. "Along the route, people started asking questions. At first, the Kritas who escorted us didn't provide much information, but then they started to talk more freely. When we arrived here . . . it happened so quickly. Brutal, and abrupt. One of the marines attacked and disarmed a Kritas, took his blaster and opened fire. I don't remember much more than that. I lost consciousness and woke up attended by your doctors."

"That's nonsense. Enough, human!" Kaulm lashed out.

"I'm sorry . . .I should've . . .I didn't expect that at all."

The ground trembled, and a thin dust fell from the vault. Kaulm glanced at the ceiling and his eyes burned with rage. "We are wasting time we don't have, Gilmor." He turned his back to them and shouted, "Proceed with the evacuation!"

"Marla," Tancredi's voice softened. He took her hands in his. "I can help you remember, if you allow me."

She nodded.

"It will be different from anything you know and expect."

She looked at him, resolute. "Whatever it takes." She opened up her mind.

In the gallery, Tancredi stumbled but regained his balance at once. The world around him faded away as he thrusted forward into the Dean's mind.

The Dean shivered when she felt Tancredi's presence penetrate like a knife tearing a veil apart. She offered no resistance, though, and Tancredi found himself in darkness, floating above a shimmering vortex of sounds, images, and feelings, like tiny twisters that sparked when approaching each other. Voices, sounds, flashes of memories, the most recent ones twirling in the upper layers of a spiral, trapped in thick glue made of sadness and remorse.

The images and voices he searched for rushed through in the turbulence of the whirling mass of Marla's personality. They roared past and around with a growing intensity that hummed louder as he approached them. He entered the flow as he had been taught when he was a child, learning his way in practices and skills honed by the millennia. Then, without even trying, the resonance between their minds settled, and he embraced it all, and saw and heard everything.

***

The steep rock face broke the monotony of the vast flat, dry land south of Utthana, erupting like a wart on the planet's skin. Long after sunset, its shadows had vanished, married to the darkness that gave the sharp hills a false sense of smoothness. A plainness that would disappear at dawn, when each stone and each spike would have claimed their identity in the familiar embrace of the new light.

The sky above glistened with bright new stars that didn't belong. Spaceships entered the higher levels of the atmosphere. Like Vespers announcing a new dusk, the ships brought with them the grim message of a darker night. Then, those stars fell, one following the other, tracing the velvet vault of the night with a luminous dance orchestrated with the minutia of a script meant to awe the most discerning audience.

More ships followed, and more bright points appeared until the sparks arranged in two circles, one at a higher altitude one, formed by the larger vessels, and a tighter one with only the Intruder class ships. The circles descended closer and closer to the rock formation, like two crowns bestowed upon the head of the heir of a fabled realm.

The space between the Intruder ships in the inner circle glimmered and billowed in the night sky. The air became a fluid, thick ribbon. The ribbon shone brighter and expanded to engulf the ships until they disappeared from the view. Flashes sparkled within, and pursued each other until they fused into a vibrant halo that grew menacing, dazzling, and burned with the heat of an erupting volcano.

The air crackled, and the acrid smell of ozone filled the scorched planes. Lightning erupted from the halo and connected to the ground, which trembled under a vicious hammering. Jolts of clouds of dusts burst over the plain, and rocks scattered when the first thunder hit them angrily. A second later, a blinding, cascading inferno battered the slopes with fury and shattered the stones. The heat from the blasts fused the first layers of the ground, and the hill broke apart with a loud crack, shaking as from the pummeling of a violent quake.

As it came, the deluge of fire stopped, and all was silent. The violated ground and the offended stones, whose wounds glared of a dark, red light in the renewed darkness of the night, hissed their indignation with white plumes of vapor. Smoke and steam waved out of the fractures inflicted by the sheer power the marines' vessels had vomited to the ground.

The Intruder spaceships turned round as eager vultures do in their final spirals over a dying prey, then drifted apart to free the area for the vessels waiting in the outer hovering stations.

The large transporter ships murmured as they opened their bellies to release a shower of huge, threaded metallic cones that spiraled their way through the air toward their impact points on the martyrized land. At the altitude of one mile, the cones opened flaps that slowed them down and increased their spin rate to maximize, at impact, their penetration into the soil.

Within a few seconds, the cones hit the land and screwed firmly into the ground. When the downward momentum stopped, they twirled in the opposite direction to level up with the surface. With a huff, the bases opened like the petals of a composite flower. From their dark opening, sentinel drones swarmed around, searching for their targets as they approached the lamenting hill.

Behind them, the first armored marine vehicles crawled out and took position. In the lead unit, the commanding officer stared incredulously at the reports on the tactical screens.

"Amazing. This confirms it," he said to himself.

The standard probes showed an untouched hill formation, its slopes and angles, the cliffs and ridge structures undamaged as if the attack had never happened.

"All units in position," he transmitted into the encrypted channel. "Confirmed presence of a cloaking field of unknown origin. Neutrons scattering analysis reveals the presence of an underground infrastructure. Sentinel drone scouts operational. Over."

Aboard the flag ship, in a geostationary high orbit above the suspected Kritas base, the Governor frowned. He activated the direct comm link to the operation commander. Floating above the main dashboard, his head came into view.

"Commander, get the Kritas units ready. Deploy them at the first signs of resistance." the Governor said.

"Aye aye, Sir."

The Governor nodded. His glance wandered over each of the floating screens around him, his eyes and ears into the action field.

The first marine units were closing in on the hill. The sentinel drones had reached the cracked rock walls and penetrated into the fractures. Their descent had started, crawling on their front pods and keeping an arched back. In the darkness, the mouths of their blaster cannons pulsated with anger, eager to deliver death. The drones activated their scanners, and the Governor's eyes narrowed as he stared at the screens. The scene of a sloped gallery with no end came into view.

*
**

Rumbles rippled through the base, the humming sound rolled along the galleries' walls and trapped, lingered in the empty halls.

The Kritas command had had the upper level secluded and had deployed a first line of defense to meet and counter the invading forces.

The clearance of all equipment proceeded, and the Kritas had moved further underground where the base connected with and opened into both a natural and Kritas-extended labyrinth of tunnels; a web of cliffs, ledges, and galleries that had allowed the resistance to hide and to survive the human invasion in the past.

Grubeck and his team of scientists had been sent away with the first wave of the evacuation; the marines, closely guarded this time, had followed with the second group. Tancredi had stayed. "I won't leave without Mekte," he told Kaulm who acquiesced in his request. "It might be the last time you see each other," he replied.

In the main control room, Kaulm and his staff officers knew they would be the last to leave and would wait for as long as the forces deployed in the upper level held and resisted the assault. A unnatural calm pervaded their gestures and their voices.

Screens showed the advance of the bulk of sentinel drones toward the base entrance, now exposed and vulnerable. Other drones, in groups of two, dashed ahead, scanning the area, hunting for targets, low on their pods, and rushing from cover to cover.

The armored marine vehicles took position around the rocky hill.

Tancredi stared at the scene. "It's an all-out assault." He faced Kaulm. "How long do we have? And where's Mekte? She should be here by now," he asked.

Kaulm squinted and glared at him. "Maybe there's just enough time for you to see her, if I don't decide otherwise." He paused. "I've not made my mind yet, scholar."

Tancredi frowned but nodded at the scenes coming from the surface. "Can't you stop them?"

"This is not a high-security military base, Gilmor, it's a hideout. Once those drones get inside the pit, it will be only a matter of time until the enemy reaches this level, and we'll suffer the loss of many lives." Kaulm snorted. "Our most valuable defense was obscurity, being undetectable. A defensive asset we have lost. Your race is treacherous."

Tancredi filled his lungs with a deep breath, and exhaled slowly.

Kaulm stared at him. "I still see an enemy in you, even after everything you've told me. The safety of my people is my only concern now."

"It's not by chance that I'm here in Ahthaza," Tancredi said. "Peace cannot be built on blood, violence, and indiscriminate killing. Violence fuels violence, not peace. War happens, but we need to work hard to create peace."

"I heard you. Still, I believe you hold something from me, and that makes me wonder . . . We won't have a chance if *we* is just us, the rebel forces and this elusive Fifth Column." He sneered. "They've already proven to be as unreliable as every other human."

Tancredi glanced at the screens. "You're right. I did hold something from you." He faced Kaulm. "I told you I was sent by Dan Amenta. But not in his role as the leader of the Terrestrial Union, though. He sent me as the Brethren of the Keepers."

Kaulm eyes widened. "The Keepers? So the legend still lives?"

Tancredi's eyes burned with a renewed intensity. "It's more than a legend. I am a Keeper."

*
**

In Utthana, the green zone where the scholar's building rose had become a detention area. The military controlled its perimeter and turned it into an inviolable barrier, creating—de facto—a prison out of the premises. On direct orders of the Governor himself, all scholars' movements had been restricted, with no exceptions. The military monitored their communications too. No scholar could leave the quarters during the imposed curfew, from dusk to dawn.

In the green zone, many waited the outcome of a thorough investigation, not knowing what the next days would bring. The Tribunals, instead, maintained a minimum level of activity supported by those scholars who also served in the military.

That night, in the compound, the scholars received a new internal communication, one coming with the seal of the Authority itself. Furthermore, the military high command ordered all civilian scholars to view the transmission and acknowledge within the hour.

The Council Secretary, the communiqué continued, had been arrested, charged with treason and conspiracy to commit treason, together with the Protector of the Law. Both scholars had been immediately suspended from duty. The Authority also announced that overwhelming evidence existed against the two criminals, and— as proof to the accusations—released the unamended footage of the Protector of the Law's involvement with a rogue military organization, the self-proclaimed Fifth Column. The Authority assured that everyone involved would be tracked down, arraigned on those charges, and prosecuted to the fullest extent of the law.

That night, the scholars had to watch the unthinkable and witness the death of the Councilor, which had been only a disturbing rumor until then.

After the end of the footage, the Authority seal decomposed. A new message formed in a sort of virtual puzzle, assembling on the floating screens through a multitude of tiny image tiles. The trojan-horse record the Secretary succeeded to activate the last time he was in his office had reached its destined target, at last.

The familiar face of the Protector of the Law appeared. Tired, and solemn, she spoke. "Dear fellow scholars . . . ," the grave tone of her voice commanded immediate attention. She recounted the recent events; the unsettling discovery of the Authority and the Governor's plans, and how their purposes undermined the foundations of the Law and negated the unalienable rights and the principles the scholars fought for and had sworn their loyalty to; the sacrifice of the Councilor, the existence of the Fifth Column, and her hopes for what could come next. "Be ready. It is a necessary exercise of the power bestowed on me as Protector of the Law," she continued, "that I declare you hereby absolved from all allegiance to, or dependence upon, the Authority in Ahthaza, the Space Marines Command, and the Governor himself."

When the message ended, the records disintegrated and returned to an untraceable state before they finally erased. The Authority seal reappeared on the floating screens, and the transmission officially ended, without any sign the military had detected the highjacked communication.
In their rooms, bemused, the scholars, a few at first, then in increasing numbers, as if guided by a common will, made the external wall of their rooms transparent and stared with their eyes riveted beyond the pavement of the esplanade to the crevice that cut deep into the ground. A faint glow brushed its edges.
From the esplanade, the scholars' silhouettes appeared as dark ghosts against the translucency of the building. Ghosts that were ready to haunt the world.

***

After breaking through the Kritas base entry, the first sentinel drones reached the end of the gallery. A large, metallic bulkhead stood before them, blocking their advance. Their internal directives made them spread out to the walls and ceiling and contract their pods to reduce the chances of becoming targets.

The ones at the rear aimed their cannons to the barrier and prepared to concentrate their fire against any possible hostile action.

One of the drones dashed forward and stuck to the bulkhead. Then, it crawled slowly, moving in a circle from the edges, spiraling toward the center, leaving a translucent trail behind it. Once the drone reached the center, it stopped and flattened its body. The drone's entire structure sizzled. Fumes billowed from its joints and intersections. The other sentinel drones retreated.

The translucent trail ignited, and the drone shone from the heat it generated. The bulkhead itself glowed, and metal started to drip to the floor.

"All units ready, drones are penetrating," announced the commanding officer on the tactical channel. The screens whitened for a second when the drone blasted itself off and vaporized the metal barrier. A breeze came from a large pit that opened in front of them and blew away the lingering vapors.

At once, like a horde of ravenous predators, the drones jumped forward and flooded downward, firing their cannons.

From the bottom, the Kritas responded. The first massive drone carcasses fell down the pit, exploding as they fell. Debris slammed against the walls and turned the pit into a furnace, flames roaring upward while the rubble rained down, forcing the Kritas defenses to scramble for shelter.

Tancredi focused on the tactical screen. His pupils dilated, and his mind absorbed the events that followed, cascading as if trapped in an inexorable avalanche.

On the surface, two transporters had landed in front of the entrance to the base. Heavily geared infantry units disembarked and entered the gallery with a coordinated and perfectly synchronized expedited march. Their boots hit the ground in unison, and the soldiers covered the distance to the pit's edges without missing one single beat.

He frowned and startled when one hand grabbed his right arm. His eyes met those he longed for. "Mekte!" he exclaimed.

She smiled. "I'm sorry I've doubted you."

His eyebrows puckered with a muted question.

"I've heard what you told Kaulm . . . the record of your conversation, I mean. I believe you," she added before Tancredi could open his mouth. "So, there's hope, right?"

He hugged her and held her tight to his chest. "Oh, Mekte."

Kaulm's lips contracted as he watched the scene. "Our people will not be able to resist much longer." He pointed at the floating screens. "Especially with those new forces joining the fight."

Tancredi raised his eyes, let Mekte go, and stood with his hands on her arms.

She looked up at him, in search of a miracle. She imagined he would have the answers to all her fears, that he would turn the impossible into reality, and that his future would also be hers. Her heart stumbled when he spoke.

"There's nothing I can do, Kaulm."

Kaulm stared at him. "I thought you said . . ."

"Your sensorial veil . . ." he bent his head, "and I can't reach anyone from down here. None of those who would matter, that is."

"Kaulm!" Mekte exclaimed. "We need to lower it."

"Are you crazy?" Kaulm took a step back. "And allow the humans to discover everything?" He shook his head. "No, the charges will seal the upper levels, and rubble will be all the humans will be able to see and detect." He smirked. " They can claim their victory and think everyone perished in the explosions. There's no—"

"Commander!" a frantic voice interrupted their exchanges.

On the main tactical display, surfing down the magnetic field waves created by the drones arranged along the pit walls, the first elements of the assaulting infantry had reached the level defended by the Kritas. From the foothold, at the expense of a great number of their units, the infantry had launched the attack.

The Kritas' first defensive line had absorbed the first impact. A wounded officer stared at them on the display. "Commander!" the officer repeated with a broken voice. "These are not marines. They're Kritas!"

Setting his jaw, Kaulm turned and slid Tancredi a look across his shoulder. "What have you humans done?"

"What we feared the most . . . What we feared the most." Tancredi lips tightened.

Kaulm reacted at once. "Withdraw!" he shouted at the screen. "Blow everything up!"

The officer replied with a limp, blank gaze, as if the life was sucked out of him. "We're pinned down, sir, but they won't pass. Safe return. Out." The image froze and faded out.

"No!" Mekte paled.

The walls trembled.

CHAPTER 24 - QUANTUM OF HOPE

A NEW END. A NEW BEGINNING.

THE AUTHORITY CALLED THEM 'rebels and terrorists.' They are all dead, by official declaration, that is. The planet Ahthaza is isolated; an iron curtain is imposed by order of the Governor. The last events, the recovery operation, and the virtual reconstruction of the last hideout of the rebellion's leadership, had become the recurrent theme of all bulletins from the military and from the Authority.

The guerrilla acts across the planet died out, and that alone gave the Authority and the Governor credibility to their cover ups. Because nothing contradicted them then, they must have been telling the truth.

The truth. How elusive a word, how mutable a concept, how farther from the truth can this word be when the vanquished cannot state anything to the contrary and the conqueror alone professes his own gospel?

The Governor stood in front of the still-fuming rubble of the scholars' building in the green zone. He was delivering a speech for the Authority's official statement. A 3D camera unit floated in front of him. "The Kritas rebellion has committed the ultimate crime," his gaze wandered for a long moment on the ruined building, "perpetrated against the very people who looked after them, who worked toward the full integration of all Kritas into the Terrestrial Union." He paused. Two sentinel drones advanced, stomping heavily on the ground, causing puffs of dust and crushing the smallest debris under their weight.

"But the war is not over yet." His voice became solemn. "We might have won a great battle and undermined their resolve. We might have chopped off the heads of the Hydra, and their leaders have burnt, buried under their own hubris and their misguided minds. It is not over yet." The two drones closed in, pounding the ground with their pods, and took place to each side of the Governor. With a whirl, the floating camera zoomed in.

"A new course of action is now established. Humans will not risk their lives anymore; our soldiers will not face the rebels' violence and their blind savagery. We will turn their own brutality against the remaining ones . . . "

Deep under ground. Deeper than the Third Under level itself, in a communication center hall, the floating screen faded away and the sudden obscurity gave the room the features of a primeval cavern.

"I cannot stand watching him any longer," said Tancredi. "He's ready to kill every Kritas and cover up his wrongdoings with a straight face." He clenched his fist.

After the battle at the rebels' hideout under the rocky hill, the survivors and the wounded had made it back through ancient underground tunnels to Utthana. The net of the oldest underground tunnels and emergency shelters, built decades before in advance of the invasion, had kept Kritas' flame of hope alive, although a faint one.

"I'm afraid their cover-up might work. Everything now only happens underground, unseen." The Dean sighed. "And those Kritas 'death squads' patrols make the situation even more complicated than before." She looked at him, trying to detect any sign of second thoughts. "How long can we hide and survive?"

Tancredi glanced at her. "I know what you're thinking, and no, I don't need to probe your mind." His lips contracted. "We didn't have any other solution available. We needed to make all Kritas' implants inactive. This is how they could be tracked down."

"I'm surprised you convinced Kaulm."

"We need to thank Mekte for that miracle. She understands who I am."

"I see. It has been shocking for all of us. I mean, all us scholars." He looked at her with flinty eyes. "The scholars have failed their mission in Ahthaza. You've been part of the problem, while you should have prevented it instead."

"We didn't know everything we know now."

"It was under your eyes. You ignored what was strikingly evident." He turned his eyes away. "I need to go now. Mekte and the others are waiting for me."

The Dean watched him leave, then she lowered her head. Her eyes burned. She had lost the one she cared for the most. The guilt crawled into her heart and strangled it. Tancredi had made her look into herself as if she was a stranger. Everything she had renounced and the lies she told to herself for years. Yes, she had failed, and she made the scholars in Ahthaza fail too.

She took a deep breath and sank to her knees, feeling the sting of regrets for all the things she had not accomplished, and for her failure at love. She had spurned love when it had been offered. Mocked even, in the secret of her mind. That regret was the one most burning. She felt empty, alone, and barren, with nothing any more to look forward to.

From the corridor, Tancredi heard her sobbing and gasping for air.

Indirectly, the blockade of information to and from the planet would have actually favored a covert Keepers' intervention, but Tancredi hadn't been able to contact his brethren yet, although this fact alone would've raised suspicions and questions among the Keepers in the months ahead. At least he hoped so. Sometimes, no news is bad news, he reasoned as he walked toward the central hall.

Mekte greeted him with a smile that widened his heart. He stopped in front of her and took her hands. "How I found you is short of a miracle, but a bigger one has yet to happen."

She squeezed his hand. "You'll make it happen. For us." She touched her abdomen.

"I'd love to have your faith. I don't know if I can pull it off."

Kaulm overheard them and approached, leaving his staff officers waiting for the ceremony to start. "It is time, but I first wanted to congratulate you two personally. It is a real miracle. And it gives me hope, too."

Tancredi lowered his head.

Mekte smiled and stepped aside. "They're waiting, and they do have faith."

Tancredi nodded. "Yes, it is time."

Together, they walked to the balustrade of the main, top-level central balcony overlooking the assembly gathered below in the entrails of Ahthaza.

He looked down. A warm, dense air, charged with the breath of thousands, filled his nostrils with the pungent odor of sweat. In the vault and along the walls, a multitude of new light blobs shuddered like flames in a sweet breeze. The semi-obscurity they had lived for months now, hiding from the fury of the rewired Kritas death squads, seemed bright to their eyes accustomed to the darkness.

The floor of the vast cavern resembled a crop field waving from the gusts of a rebellious breeze, so many people had flooded in and filled the space. He nodded to himself when he saw the scholars mingled freely among the Kritas. These last, dressed with their black uniforms, tall and slender among the humans, shifted their gaze around, nervous for the presence of so many scholars but the tension of the first days had gone.

The humans still wore their tunics, the same they had when they escaped through the chasm in the green zone. Their tattered, torn, and ripped tunics would soon be replaced. Seen from above, their patches of colors created the illusion of waterlilies floating over the ripples of a dark pond.

Also along the walls, and along the carved spiraling ramps, Kritas and humans crowded the ramparts, waiting for the message, and expecting a change. Then, a murmur rose, and reflected off the ceiling of the cavern. All eyes shifted from Kaulm and the other leaders to the couple, which held hands next to each other.

It grew louder into a deafening roar when men and women, Kritas and scholars, recognized Tancredi and Mekte, the Link joining their races.

Tancredi raised his arm. The crowd fell silent. "Find each other!" He waited for those words to break all barriers. The crowd hesitated, but his voice had resonated across the many hearts and minds. The echoes made his words reach Kritas and humans from everywhere.

"Look at each other!" Their eyes dashed around, carrying still too much diffidence.

"Indifference is the death of history." His voice resumed, stronger. "Indifference is your death. It creeps in your souls, like a brute, scorching lava.

"What happens in this planet . . .the evil that befell everyone thrives because of all hearts abdicating to its will. Indifference weaves a cobweb that tangles the mind, and those who should care, do not."

He looked at their tired expressions, depressed, disillusioned, afraid to believe again. "This shall not be your fate!" A shiver gripped the crowd. Mekte's hand tightened around his.

"We are all victims," Tancredi resumed. "Those who hoped and those who couldn't, those who knew and those who chose not to. When you stand silent, you are worthless. Do you realize now what you have done?" He spoke to ears who could not miss what he meant. The words sent ripples through the crowd, and Tancredi saw many scholars lower their heads. His voice bounced back from the thick, rough-hewn stone walls as glimpses of light in the half darkness of the broad hall.

"No one is going to answer that. We who have been active and we who have been indifferent, it is now time to break these chains. Rise up, instead, and stand next to each other like limbs of one body. Things developed so swiftly that few realised how truly dramatic those events and their consequences would be. *There is no legitimate authority anymore on Ahthaza!"*

A low rumble, as if it came from the belly of a predator, welcomed his words. It echoed off the rock walls. The crowd billowed and eyes sparked with excitement. Tancredi saw the scholars' auras glitter, and their emotions flowed this time, free from shame and fear. He raised his arm. The cries faded, a deep murmur reached the higher levels, making each stone vibrate in tense expectation.

"Today, everything here speaks of our shared history and pride. Despite all the dramatic changes, I have a firm conviction, which is based on truth and justice, that here is your newly found courage, here is your ultimate stronghold, here is where we sow, and why we will prevail!" The murmur grew louder. "From now on, you will do things that you think you cannot do. I've not come to destroy, but to fulfill the Law to the fullest. And I stand here, before you, assured of your support."

His gaze touched all faces, his mind explored all hearts, and he found them the same.

A hand grabbed his. He turned his head. Mekte's eyes glittered.

Further down the hall, a sound resonated with increasing strength. "Tank, Tank, Tank, Tank . . ." every voice chanted, and he felt like a thousand thunders were snared between the ancient, uneven slabs.

He vowed to himself to deliver the tempest, and a new deluge.

THE END

Note to the Reader

There's one more thing I'd like to add after this journey together in "The Law"

Sales are great, press releases, interviews, live radio guest appearances are exciting, climbing the ranks and entering the Top 100 Authors for my genre is exhilarating, but nothing beats the support of all readers and friends and fellow writers who share the thrill with me. You're the best readers any writer could ever have. Without you giving my stories a chance, nothing would ever be possible.

"'Tis the good reader that makes the good book; in every book he finds passages which seem to be confidences or sides hidden from all else and unmistakably meant for his ear; the profit of books is according to the sensibility of the reader; the profound thought or passion sleeps as in a mine, until it is discovered by an equal mind and heart."

~Ralph Waldo Emerson

Humbly yours.

"The Law" is about the reasons of the heart versus the diktats of the brain. The struggle between what you *feel* you must do, and what you *must* do because of how you feel.

"The Law" covers the themes of "Law and Order", racial tensions, repression for security, and love between two young members of different races who believe they can change the world.

It is my fourth novel as I've Author-published a science fiction trilogy with the first volume released late 2012 and the third and last volume in May 2014. The trilogy had been picked up for republication by "Booktrope Publishing, LCC".

Thank you and, please, share your impression with other readers online with a review on Amazon at https://www.amazon.com/Law-Tribunal-Trilogy-Massimo-Marino-ebook/dp/B01KCOWUB0/

With best regards,
Massimo Marino

APPENDIX – THE PAX HUMANA

FROM THE HUMANS CHRONICLES

THE HUMAN RACE HAD destroyed its original home planet, Tiamat. Refugees took the third planet from the Sun, called it Earth, and fell into millennia of dark years, marred with violence, technology regression, and oblivion. The human ancestors warred again at a planetary level once they regained the old power and knowledge. Earth risked following the same destiny of Tiamat.

The Môirai, a once-leading alien race, describe these events as Losses; the First and the Second happened under their watch. As the leaders of the now-dismantled Môirai Confederation, they justified and obtained the agreement for a decisive intervention to prevent a final Loss. That event, which is aptly called the Third Loss in all Humans Chronicles, is Year Zero TL of the new era.

After the culling of the human race, perpetrated by the Môirai, the new transgenic mankind, the Selected, were born. People thrived with the aliens' support, and peace and security reigned on Eridu, as the planet Earth was known by the Môirai and in the galaxy.

A cosmic conspiracy—involving other races—pushed the world close to the brink of self-destruction and saw the first confrontations against the Kritas.

The new race of man leadership—the Selected and their progeny—prepared for revenge once the betrayal became evident. The first Selected, Dan Amenta, became the leader of the transgenic humans and the first human Keeper, member of a fabled millennia-old organization that held the Moîrai empire together, until the events that lead to the empire collapsing.

A new neurological drug, Fusion, heavily produced on Eridu/Earth, had created the path for a rapid evolution of the new humans capabilities and brought richness and good fortune. The new humans had played a crucial role in the galaxy organization and became aware of their strength.

Dan Amenta of Earth established a new order and set a new course that ripped apart the foundations of the galaxy, with the help of the Keepers (read The Daimones Trilogy).

After the year 161 TL (from the Third Loss), the institution of the Law, built on the empathic capabilities developed after the genetic mutations from the Moîrai and the development of the Fusion nootropic drug, kept friend and foe at a distance, and the human leadership stood revered, feared, dreaded, and hated, all in equal proportions.

The Empath Scholars, the benevolent enforcers of the Law, worked to guarantee peace and security in all planets, and all planets were subject to the laws of their Tribunals.

The Scholars are masters of inquisition of the mind, question those who cross their path, find the most secluded answers, and undermine even the strongest of the wills. The ones under trial, those under the full weight of the Law, cannot oppose the inquisition, and their minds are opened to the probing Scholars.

This is the fundamental rule of the Law. These were the foundations of the 'Pax Humana.'

Made in the USA
Coppell, TX
12 April 2022